GW00890440

BED OF ROSES
AND OTHER STORIES

To Sally

with best wishes

Helina Sreenivat

Bed of Roses
and
Other Stories

Halina Szeremeta

The Book Guild Ltd
Sussex, England

This book is a work of fiction. The characters and situations in this story are imaginary. No resemblance is intended between these characters and any real persons, either living or dead.

This book is sold subject to the condition that it shall not, by way of trade or otherwise, be lent, re-sold, hired out, photocopied or held in any retrieval system or otherwise circulated without the publisher's prior consent in any form of binding or cover other than that in which this is published and without a similar condition including this condition being imposed on the subsequent purchaser.

The Book Guild Ltd
25 High Street,
Lewes, Sussex

First published 1997
© Halina Szeremeta, 1997
Set in Baskerville
Typesetting by Southern Reproductions (Sussex)
Crowborough, Sussex
Printed in Great Britain by
Bookcraft (Bath) Ltd, Avon

A catalogue record for this book is
available from the British Library

ISBN 1 85776 220 7

CONTENTS

v

ACKNOWLEDGEMENTS

Many thanks to my sister-in-law C.E.C. for her most generous help and encouragement.

Also thanks to Ewa K. for the assiduous proof-reading and above all for lifelong friendship.

Halina Szeremeta
London, 1996

BED OF ROSES

I

The stairs at Number 7 Rosetta Way gave the impression of being wide and comfortable. There were 14 steps in all between the ground floor and the first-floor landing. At the bottom, one encountered four steps, then at a small square plateau the stairs changed direction, turning a full 90 degrees left and so continued straight up to the first-floor landing. A long window ran parallel to the ten steps of the second segment of the stairs

Anne was so used to mounting these stairs that she often said she could run up them with her eyes closed. She used to joke like that in the past; nowadays, with her sight nearly gone, she sometimes did shut her eyes when climbing upstairs, relying on counting every single step as she took it and moving her hand along the bannister in time with her feet. Counting diverted her attention from the breathlessness she felt halfway up the ten-step stretch. It also gave her an excuse to walk slowly, to pace herself so that she would arrive upstairs in not too bad a shape. Clutching the bannister, taking deep breaths and at the same time knowing how many more steps she must conquer made the effort of moving around half-blind more acceptable. Once on the first-floor landing, Anne would sit down in an old armchair, deposited there for this precise purpose, and marvel at her achievement. Another day behind her. Without any help from outside. Good.

After a few minutes' rest she would get up and resume her walk towards the bathroom and thence, having attended to the evening washing rites, thankfully to her bedroom. The important thing nowadays was to leave all the objects necessary to her evening and morning toilet in their proper place, so that there would not be the frustrating hunt for important, if commonplace, items such as mug and toothbrush, face towel and the cold cream without which Anne could not get herself settled for the night. Sometimes on waking up she felt a bit confused – perhaps the effect of the sleeping pill had not yet worn off – and so it happened more and more often that she would fail in her efforts at keeping order during her morning toilet. Then in the evening, tired out and longing for bed, she would experience the disagreeable task of searching for the miscellaneous objects which seemed to elude her. This made her very cross, because any apparent inability to cope could imply – even bear out and underline the opinion generally held by her daughter and friends – that she should sell the house and retire on its proceeds to a nursing home or suchlike.

Anne knew that in some respects there was a grain of truth in what was being said; she was willing to consider the proposition objectively sometime – 'But not yet, not yet,' she murmured to herself.

On the subject of moving she was a divided person. The burden of living on her own, the impotence which she so often experienced during the daily routine of managing her affairs, overwhelmed her sometimes and started her on the trail of seriously thinking about moving. But it only took one successful day in which she managed to fulfil most of the required tasks and take the right decisions without any hitches for the thought of resigning herself to other people's mercies to recede.

Forty-odd years is a long time, thought Anne, at last relaxing in her old bed, experiencing immeasurable comfort in stretching her limbs, adjusting her posture to the well-known, well-worn shape of the familiar mattress. This bed had been Anne's refuge for the last 40 years – ever since she moved into the house in Rosetta Way as a young bride. This bed had been a panacea for all kinds of aches and pains, physical and mental. For nights of loneliness and ecstasy. So it didn't seem all that odd that Anne, in her attempts to pray, always thanked God for the bed, her bed, the 'Bed of Roses' as she sometimes called it in her thoughts. The name had occurred to Anne because of the splendid, if faded, counterpane patterned with large cabbage roses, pink and red. Anne used to count them quite often, arriving at a different total each time she counted. She could never remember whether she was including in the count the 'half-roses' – the ones cut off by the seams – or leaving them out. Now, with her eyesight in such poor shape, she could not entertain herself even with this old game any longer, but no matter – she knew they were there.

Anne thought that in the event of moving, with the giving up of all her possessions, the parting with the double bed, her marriage bed, would be the most difficult test. Somehow she equated it with giving up her independence, because, as she well knew, she would never be able to accommodate this large piece of furniture in sheltered housing or a nursing home. Her daughter, Stella, expressed a wish to take it off Anne's hands when the time came and in a way Anne was glad, but in another way she resented the idea. If she could have had her way she would have made a giant bonfire when the time came and, as if imitating some eastern tradition, would have burned it as a funeral rite, no matter the intrinsic value of its carved headboard and bottom end, its sturdy structure even after so many years.

Anne's bed had played an enormous role in her life. It was there that her child had been conceived. There that she had mourned her late husband and her only lover had rekindled the woman in her. The bed was her solitary companion during long, dreadful nights when sleep would not come to extinguish the crushing feeling of defeat she had experienced the only time in her life that she had tried to get her own way and failed. And the tears? And the laughter? And the sounds of passion? Surely these things were too intimate to pass to future occupants?

Not that it was going to be easy to take leave of any other

piece of her bedroom furniture. Anne sometimes wondered at the curious bond which she felt with these few inanimate objects that furnished her bedroom. The oval mirror in a gilded frame was now slightly dimmed with the moisture which must have penetrated between the frame and the backing. It was from that mirror that she had taken her confidence in her young days. It also reflected sad changes in her face and figure as time added years to her appearance. Yet sometimes, not really believing her tired eyes, she thought she could suddenly catch in it that old vision of herself, the way she had looked soon after moving into the house. Then, her hair, abundant and full of vigour, had encircled her handsome, oval face, gave a frame to the slim, long neck and the rounded breasts. It might sound unrealistic but Anne was still convinced that even now she looked least worn out and aged in her old oval mirror.

Then there was the chest of drawers she had shared with her husband. It was an old-fashioned piece of furniture, with deep drawers capable of accommodating a whole variety of clothes and odd items. The bottom drawer particularly was dear to Anne's heart. It used to be commonly called 'the treasure chest' because it was filled up to the top with small and large useless objects of no real value but too precious to part with. At one time it had contained her daughter Stella's baby clothes which, because of one simple outburst of anger, became just a heap of unrecognisable shreds of material. It also housed several pairs of gloves worn on special occasions, some trinkets, lace handkerchiefs hardly used (souvenirs of holidays spent abroad) and quite a lot of other things, the reason for keeping which had been long forgotten.

Under the window stood a small sofa covered in brocade which had once been golden but now was fading into grey. Anne and her husband, Sloane, had liked to sit there for a while before undressing for bed, particularly if during the day something had happened to upset their relationship. They called it 'the sofa of reconciliation', and if either of them sat on it, it was a signal to the other that all was forgiven, a truce was about to begin. So there was nothing else for the other to do but to sit down alongside, clasp the outstretched hand and simply exchange smiles. No need for apologies and no need for shows of repentance. Just a quiet moment while their relationship underwent a change of heart, so that the unpleasantness could be discarded like the crumpled clothes they had worn that day, now destined for the laundry basket. So they could go to bed feeling their union strengthened by the obstacle they had overcome.

But all this was in the past. Some of it might appear to an outsider like a lot of sentimental nonsense . . . Anne pulled herself together. She took a sleeping tablet, turned on the radio, listened for a while, then switched it off, as well as the bedside lamp. Having settled herself comfortably on her left side, she waited for sleep to come, to blot out the reality of her old age, her fears, her half-forgotten moments of happiness and despair. Anne waited for dreams.

II

The town where Anne spent her childhood and adolescence had no claims to distinction. It had no archaeological remains, no historical connotations, neither could it boast of significant beauty spots or tourist attractions. Its inhabitants, mainly solid, ordinary citizens, kept their feet firmly on the ground, lived and died in the most natural manner. Some moved away, a few came to live in it for various reasons, none of them extraordinary. The majority of the working population commuted to the county town in the vicinity, where they were employed in more or less mundane occupations. Others had local businesses or independent means.

A few were employed in, or had other connections with, a small but rather exclusive public school for girls, located barely a mile out of town. The school concentrated on boarding pupils, for the most part children of parents working overseas, but it accepted a few day-girls from the town in the shadow of which it had functioned for the last 50 years.

5

Lastly, one must not forget to mention the town's long-established connection with the army. For over two generations a famous regiment had maintained its depot, including the base of the regimental band, on the outskirts of the town.

It was in these distinctly ordinary circumstances that Anne's childhood was spent as the only child of a respected doctor known to most of the prominent people of the town. Her father was always busy, hardly ever at home, rather remote, barely aware of his daughter and wife, by nature preferring solitude and his own company.

Anne's early childhood was uncomplicated and simple. Living in the provinces she was allowed to retain her innocence and freedom much longer than children living in large, more sophisticated cities. Her pleasures were mostly homespun: the swing in the garden, picnics by the river, walks into the countryside. Those happy days of childhood were mostly remembered as long summer days, full of sun and flowers, or crisp, chilly mornings of early autumn and spring. Winter really meant Christmas, first in anticipation and later as a memory which lasted well into the New Year.

One could not decribe Anne's childhood without mentioning at some length Anne's mother, her personality and the importance of the influence she exerted over her daughter's future. Presentable rather than pretty, perhaps more intelligent than might be suspected, she found herself with a lot of time on her hands. Her only child, Anne, was very receptive and attentive yet at the same time inclined to flights of fanciful ideas which she could not execute on her own and for which she needed a partner. That partner she found in her mother, who with her quick mind and well-developed imagination, could easily tranform even the most ordinary happenings into exciting adventures and dramas. And so, what started as a well-meant attempt at entertaining a rather solitary child, soon provided an impetus which became an alternative way of life for the daughter. For her, the slim line dividing the real and the imaginary started to blur, so that when a game was over Anne felt disappointed and let down

6

and would in an inexplicable way put the blame on her mother. Was this because of the indisputable fact that in all these departures into the world of fantasy it was the mother who led, the daughter who followed? The trouble was that while Anne's mother considered these diversions into the realm of imagination as delightful sorties into a common land of childhood nostalgia to be indulged in at leisure, Anne felt deeply hurt and dismayed when forced to abandon her dreamy existence. So more and more she came to rely on her mother to bridge the gap, to ease her out from the happy land of stories, adventures, images. She found it increasingly difficult to disengage herself from these exciting, unreal yet how satisfying experiences where there was always a happy ending and a lot of drama . . .

On entering the mist of other relationships, as time went by, Anne found herself appealing to her mother to disentangle the problems she encountered, running back to her and the dream world at the first sign of trouble, disenchantment or pure cruelty experienced in the company of other children. She could not understand that her mother was now no longer able to manipulate the course of events for her or simply sit her on her lap and utter those comfortable, reassuring words: 'Let's pretend . . .'

In fact Anne's mother never realised the agonising dilemma Anne had been forced into by the utter contrast between the climate of her home, with its security and enchantment, where one way or another things were ordered to her liking, and the so different, ordinary, sometimes unfair, always competitive ways of the world outside.

And so on the other hand, Anne started to feel inadequate, and on the other, began to blame her mother for not influencing, one could almost say ordering, the reality outside to fall in with her wishes. Her mother became a necessary interpreter, a dispenser of consolation prizes for the disappointments, slights and failures which Anne was not able to withstand on her own. Mother became an essential fixture in Anne's life, for whose love and attention Anne was to compete in later years, never quite satisfied, expecting perhaps too much from somebody who was after all only an indulgent, well-meaning person. How much it could have been avoided it is difficult to say. It might be said that we bring into this world our own destinies, but the truth of the matter is that not until her mother's death was Anne able to call her soul her own.

III

When Anne finished junior school, which was close to her home, she was enrolled in the adjacent girls' public school as a day-girl. She was equipped with a smart uniform, slightly on the large side to allow for growth, practical satchel, a felt hat with the crown beribboned with the school colours, and two pairs of white gloves to be worn in all circumstances. Then she was taken by her mother to the meeting place where a school bus collected and delivered all the day-pupils. There she was left to herself.

Straight away, on the first day, Anne struck up an acquaintance with another girl, finding that they were both new pupils and so could not join in the noisy reunion of the other girls returning to school after the summer holidays. Ignorance of the prevailing ways of behaviour drew them apart from the rest of the crowd and at the same time facilitated their contact. Soon they were exchanging information about their families and pets and when on arriving at school they were told to pair off before entering the large assembly hall, they decided on the spot to stick together. They were lucky enough to secure adjoining desks and from these simple beginnings a friendship grew between the girls.

Anne liked and admired Christine mainly for those facets of character which she herself found difficult to emulate. The self-confidence and quick wit, coupled with great enthusiasm, boldness and ease with which Christine manipulated all situations – mainly to get away with things – suited Anne admirably. She possessed an equal if not superior brain and was the authoress of quite a few school pranks, but when it came to the execution of her wild schemes, it was Christine who took over. Anne simply lacked the nerve, a commodity Christine was well equipped with – one could almost say overgenerously.

Their families knew of one another, though they were not actually acquainted. That was soon remedied, since Anne and Christine became inseparable, in school and out of school, sharing their homework, their recreation, even spending the odd night in each other's home. Anne's parents thoroughly approved of this relationship, hoping that Anne, with Christine as an example, would lose some of her inborn shyness, become more confident, learn how to stand up for herself and so leave behind the fanciful, imaginary world she still inhabited for much of her time.

Christine's parents were not all that much interested in her inner personality. She was their fourth daughter, the youngest, for the moment happily settled at school. She did not burden her parents with any problems of her own and so their attention focused more on their other children. They were rather preoccupied with their older daughters, one of whom was approaching marriageable age with no offers in view. Then there was the question of further education or employment for all three of them; an extra pay packet in the near future would be most welcome in this household because, as everybody knows, growing daughters cost money.

So Anne and Christine were given general blessing by the grown-ups and their friendship grew in strength from year to year. They went together through the usual stages of girlhood: the sharing of sweets, the giggling stage, the clumsy, hidden experimenting with make-up pinched from Christine's eldest sister. They went for walks together, did each other's homework, on rare occasions visited the cinema (when the programme was judged to be suitable by their parents) and, of course, always paired off before assembly and on other occasions such as school outings and nature walks.

This close relationship didn't make them any too popular with the rest of their form, particularly as both girls, but

9

especially Christine, had a quick tongue and ready reply when challenged. As day-girls, they never became fully integrated in an institution which primarily catered for boarders, being in some way envied for their freedom to go home after lessons, having their families on the spot and so not fully appreciating the tensions and miseries of communal living. Also, being pretty, clever and obviously well-to-do made them predictable objects of envy to the girls who could not hope for similar advantages. Still, it did not seem to matter to Anne and Christine, secure in their background and successful in their ventures.

Years passed, punctuated by the constant need to let down the hems of Anne's dresses or to get new outfits. Each year an extra candle was lit on her birthday cake; the presents she received stopped including dolls and tended to take the form of books, or charming 'out-of-school' clothes, light in texture and design.

The half-dreaded, half-exciting 'curse' duly arrived, first for Christine and not so long afterwards for Anne. It brought about a slight change in their behaviour and precipitated a discussion which understandably occurred about this time.

'Now that we have "it",' suggested Christine, 'we are ready to make love and have babies.'

'What do you mean?' inquired Anne, only very scantily prepared on the subject by her mother.

'Well, of course, now we are women,' answered Christine. Taking a piece of paper, she clumsily drew a picture of the technical side of lovemaking. (She had purchased this information from an older sister for the sum of one shilling.) The drawing was far from accurate – obviously her sister, though informed, was not yet fully initiated into the mystery of sex, so that Christine's second-hand knowledge was even more inaccurate.

Anne was perplexed; she firmly believed that Christine was better informed and more knowledgeable in various aspects of grown-up affairs, but she couldn't take kindly to this startling disclosure. At home she didn't have the same sort of encouragement and challenge to grow up as Christine, living in proximity with older sisters who already had one eye on the opposite sex.

But soon both girls became aware of the impact they had on the boys and young men they met when doing errands for their mothers or waiting for the school bus. Christine was well equipped to deal with the looks which followed them and could outstare any male they happened to encounter. She was even not above sticking out her tongue if she did not like a particular remark made in passing by a cheeky youth.

When Anne was nearly 13 a significant change happened in her life. One summer day Christine, quite excited, informed Anne that her cousin, Sophie, was coming to live with her family in the autumn, and would be attending the same school, probably even the same class. This had come about owing to the untimely death of Sophie's father. Her mother, to cut expenses, would have to remove her from her present boarding school. Placing Sophie with Christine's family would go a long way to reducing bills. Anne was very excited at the news; she was quite prepared to admit the newcomer to her relationship with Christine and form a trio. Sophie lived in the country and so promised to be an interesting example of rural upbringing whom Anne would mould to the sophisticated (in her opinion) ways of the town.

A few days before the beginning of the autumn term Sophie arrived and was soon brought over to Anne's house to be introduced. There was no awkwardness displayed; the girls liked the look of each other and soon Anne's room resounded with laughter and noisy exclamations. Confidences were being exchanged, pictures of favourite film stars were compared, the joys of breaking school rules in which Christine (with Anne's help) liked to indulge, anticipated. Yet on their second or third meeting Anne couldn't fail to notice the growth of a certain intimacy between the two other girls. Gradually she sensed a feeling of being shut out. In a way this was unavoidable; the two cousins not only shared the same house but also the same bedroom. Anne suddenly realised that she couldn't compete in retaining her rightful place.

On the last day before the beginning of the term Christine, as usual forward and direct, asked Anne outright with whom

11

was she going to pair off before assembly the next day, as she herself had now got a new partner and wouldn't be able to oblige. For all Anne's perspicacity, that thought had not occurred to her; she was for a moment literally speechless, looking helplessly at Christine. Then she spoke haltingly: 'What do you mean, Christine? We were always together – you can't just walk out on me!'

'Of course I'm not walking out on you,' Christine answered coolly. 'It is just that now I have Sophie with me and she has more rights to my friendship than you have. You must understand that, Anne.'

In a little while the cousins went off, leaving Anne absolutely prostrated. She simply could not face the next day at school, in the crowd of her contemporaries, each of them pairing off with a friend of long standing, and herself looking on and either joining the detestable Myra, whom no one wanted to know, or even worse, should Myra have found a victim, having to walk alone at the end of the class. There seemed little Anne could do, although she desperately looked for a solution.

Feeling utterly heartbroken, she spent the rest of the afternoon in her room devising plans of escape from her predicament. But, overwhelmed by the futile pain of rejection and fury at Sophie, who had robbed her of her friend and confidante, she could conceive of no clear plan of action. Finally Anne decided to feign sickness and stay away from school on the first day of term, to which she had been looking forward so much.

Next morning she was late for breakfast and when she appeared she claimed a headache and general queasiness. Her father touched her forehead, looked into her throat and pronounced her fit. 'Just first-day-of-term excitement,' he declared and urged her to hurry, otherwise she would miss the school bus. This was precisely what Anne had in mind as an alternative. To arrive late at school and slip cautiously into the asembly hall, too late for the pairing-off procedure.

She was partially successful in her plans, She was too late at the pick-up point for the school bus and so missed the meeting of the day-girls including Christine and Sophie. But when she arrived eventually at school, having caught a corporation bus which ran nearby, the bell had not yet gone and the first thing she noticed was the cluster of classmates surrounding Sophie, making her acquaintance, with Christine officiating. Soon the bell sounded, each form started walking towards the assembly hall and Anne had to follow on her own, eyed with great satisfaction by the less charitable of her fellow pupils.

For a long time Anne was to remember that lonely walk which seemed to last much longer than usual, her attempts at holding her head high, though tears filled her eyes, trying to smile and not succeeding, appearing calm while seething with a whole range of emotions: frustration, anger, self-pity and above all a sense of injustice. The first few days at school were pure hell. She was prey to all sorts of sarcastic remarks; she tried to make friends with one or two girls, only to be cold-shouldered. The cousins spoke to her in what she felt to be a rather condescending way, careful to underline the changed situation.

Anne's parents noticed her unusual quietness and at the same time a disturbing irritability. They also noticed the absence of Christine. Anne anxiously waited for the obvious queries and dreaded them. For the first time in her life she would have to admit a total yet undeserved defeat. But the questions never came. Her parents must have guessed what had happened and after a few weeks inquired whether Anne would like to cycle to school. They were prepared to anticipate her Christmas present by a couple of months and buy her a bicycle. And so by this generous action they salvaged a bit of Anne's self-esteem. She became the proud owner of a shiny bicycle and so was spared meeting the perpetrators of her torment at the bus stop.

IV

In a peculiar way, it was the acquisition of the bicycle that

13

pushed Anne on to the road of being a solitary person, a trait that increased with the years and affected her future relations. Speeding along on her bike she felt free, exhilarated and independent. It did not matter so much that she was alone. She nursed her past wounds yet began to discard the need to have friends or to share her feelings and experiences with others. The abrupt ending to her relationship with Christine and the taste of her new independence somehow, and to a large extent subconsciously, left a lasting mark on Anne and made it much more difficult for her to form deep and spontaneous relationships with people she was to meet in later years. She would not allow herself to be hurt again to the same extent and consequently, by way of insurance, always kept a part of herself ready to fly from lasting entanglements. Without knowing it, she was shaping within herself a quality which later became very evident and which neither marriage nor motherhood eradicated – that of keeping some small, not well defined part of herself strictly out of bounds. She became very much her own person.

Anne's school boasted a very good choir. The music mistress had a string of letters after her name and over the years had built a standard of excellence in the school's choral performances; they had a reputation both in the town and beyond. Anyone possessing a good voice had to join the choir, and the walls of the music room reverberated constantly with young, fresh, well-disciplined voices. Anne, endowed with a pleasant soprano voice, was a member of the choir practically from the beginning, unlike Christine, who was to all intents and purposes tone-deaf. After the break with her friend, Anne became even more involved in the choir's productions and on a few occasions was actually chosen to sing solo.

Music and a growing eagerness to beat Christine in marks increasingly filled Anne's life in the next few years. In her contest with Christine she was fairly successful for various reasons. To start with she now had more time to do her homework undisturbed by the presence of another person with whom it was fun to gossip and fool around. Also she now had more motivation to do well at school. This was the only

14

way open to her to settle her score with Christine – the only friend she had ever had, now her adversary – and so to restore at least in part her wounded pride. Lastly, by paying more attention to the excellent teaching she had been receiving, Anne became really interested in several subjects, the study of which came to her with reasonable ease. This in turn opened a whole host of possibilities, introduced her to the beauty of poetry and literature, and broadened the horizons of her rather childish outlook on life. In fact she became intellectually aware of the many exciting facets of knowledge.

Another positive aspect was that her music commitments provided her with a convenient opportunity to open up, to join with others in a communal endeavour and to enjoy the sharing. It satisfied in her the natural need, which exists in practically everybody at a certain level, to enter into some sort of contact with other human beings in an aesthetic and pleasurable activity, albeit without deeper personal involvement.

She was thus overjoyed when a novel idea was proposed by the music mistress – that the higher-grade pupils should attend the gala concert given yearly by the band of the regiment stationed in the town. It was a formal social occasion supported by all the local notables; tickets were sold out well in advance of the date of the performance. The proceeds were donated to various local charities. The girls were to attend the concert as a group, wearing their full, best uniforms, felt hats and white gloves. They were instructed at length about their behaviour and given an introductory talk about the works to be performed and their composers.

On the appointed evening, chaperoned by two mistresses, they made their way to the spacious church hall, the largest auditorium in town, and sat down in the allocated seats, well aware that the headmistress might be watching them. As soon as the music started, Anne found herself totally absorbed. Her senses seemed to tune in so well to the sounds and harmonies that her young body experienced an emotional thrill such as she had never known, never before experienced. She sat there, immersed in contemplation of the ever-changing

15

melodies, unaware of her surroundings, coming to only at the end of each piece to join in the blistering applause. One of the pieces contained a fascinating, evocative solo performed on the flute by a young, handsome soldier. Anne couldn't take her eyes away from the concentration on the young man's face. Really, she commented to herself, this was more than concentration, this was inspiration. She could have gone on listening for ever, taking in the haunting melody, the inspired, disembodied face of the musician, when the solo faded . . . and the whole orchestra took up the solo theme, developed it at length, let it escalate to a stupendous burst of sound, then finally brought the movement to a beautifully executed finale. There followed fantastic applause, acknowledged by the conductor with several bows. When he made the soloist stand up and receive another rousing ovation, Anne suddenly realised that she had fallen in love with the unknown flautist.

Anne left the concert with her school companions but did not join in the excited chatter actuated to a higher pitch by the enforced formality of the last two hours. She hugged her secret to herself, already beginning to feel guilty. Had anybody noticed anything strange about her? Nobody must find out about this very important emotion that she was carrying within herself. How could she? A common soldier! What would her mother say? And the headmistress? In fact Anne herself was almost ashamed to have to admit that she had fallen under the spell of the haunting melody and its interpreter. I must pull myself together – she quickly resolved her problem – it is just too stupid for words.

In the period following the concert, Anne found it difficult to concentrate on her work, was prone to sit at her desk drawing all shapes of doodles while inwardly meditating: What is his name? How can I find out his name? It was as far as her conventional nature let her venture. It seemed to her that knowing his name would satisfy her curiosity and quench her romantic thirst, particularly if he had a common, ordinary name like John or Jack. But she saw no way in which she could acquire the information she was after, so she compromised and decided that if she could see him again in broad daylight, in ordinary circumstances, she would soon recognise the absurdity of her feelings.

She started to study the local paper avidly, seeking for any mention of the regimental band's appearances or of forthcoming parades. She had an idea that on some Sunday afternoons in summer the band performed in the local park and so, laden with ever-growing desperation, she waited for the programmes for the summer season to be announced in the evening paper. In due time she was rewarded with a short notice at the bottom of the second page: 'At the Memorial Bandstand, Central Park. Sundays 2.30 p.m. The seasonal Sunday Afternoon Concerts of the Regimental Band will commence on the first Sunday in July and continue for six weeks.' But would he be amongst the players? Anne knew that solo flute did not often feature in the repertoire suitable for the popular band concerts, prone to include jolly, high-spirited numbers. On top of this, how was she to induce her mother to come with her to the park? She could never go there on her own – it was just not feasible, even if she was not wearing her uniform. There was no one to confide in, to help with a suitable alibi – no, she must inveigle her mother to come. She hoped for the best.

That Sunday the weather was not very promising. It was rather chilly, not at all the kind of weather for sitting in the park listening to music. After church, on the way home, Anne's mother asked what Anne's plans were for the rest of the day. 'I don't know,' replied Anne, trying to look rather miserable. 'I have a bad headache and feel quite sick.' Her mother looked at her anxiously and of course reported to Father as soon as they reached home.

Father in his usual brusque way looked closely at Anne and pronounced, 'What I recommend is a long brisk walk in the afternoon – it's probably due to all this chocolate she gets through in the day. Why don't you both go out after lunch for an hour or so?' he added, as Anne knew he would.

It was relatively easy to manoeuvre the afternoon walk in the direction of the park. The sound of some lively tune drew

17

them towards the bandstand. There were some vacant places in the first few rows and before her mother could object, Anne settled in one of them, from which she had a clear view of all the musicians. Mother had little choice but to follow.

Anne searched the faces of the assembled bandsmen. They looked somehow different, more at ease than during the concert. She noticed after a while that there were no flute players and was about to give up the fruitless, desperate quest when her eyes fell on a familiar face. Yes, it was him, now playing a trumpet. The effort of playing slightly distorted the remembered features. Anne concentrated on that one face, readjusting herself, trying to monitor her feelings about it. The player looked younger, less inspired, but nevertheless aroused in Anne the same emotional response. She relaxed her posture somewhat, only now realising that she was sitting practically on the edge of her chair. Thoughts rushed through her excited mind. What should she do now? How should she behave? How could she learn his name? Attract his attention? As far as that wish was concerned, it seemed to fulfil itself on its own. The trumpet blower simply felt Anne's unwavering stare and, in a pause which occurred in the trumpet fanfare, searched the audience for this inquisitive gaze. Meeting Anne's eyes he averted his own but in a short while glanced again, once, twice, as if to make sure that he was not mistaken. In the end, having made sure that it was his face that was being so closely observed, he returned the gaze with more confidence, even smiled slightly. And so it continued till the end of the performance, a sort of visual encounter, absolutely oblivious of anything else on Anne's part, more surreptitious and controlled on the part of the soldier bandsman.

Anne's mother was ready to leave, in fact she gave Anne a slight push, but Anne sat as if transfixed, watching the band packing up and slowly edging towards the assembly point. It was then that somebody shouted: 'Look out, Peter, you're leaving half of your music behind,' and the object of Anne's admiration turned back to pick up some sheets of music. Evidently he, too, was a bit unnerved by this curious, innocent flirtation of the two pairs of eyes. Anne got up as if suddenly released from a spell. She had achieved her aim, she had learned his name. Peter sounded heavenly to her. That name branded itself into her brain with intensity. Now she could dream about the unknown flute player – call him by his name, imagine all sorts of romantic adventures.

Two months later the Second World War broke out. The regimental band left town. Anne never saw Peter again.

V

As the war progressed, its consequences became increasingly apparent to Anne, though her immediate family was not directly involved in a personal way. To Anne, war meant chiefly shortages and inconvenience; one had to make do with what one could get. As fears of invasion receded and the threat of bombing diminished, though still present, war became an exacting and frustrating time with coupons, rations and queues to contend with. There was the constant desperate longing for victory and peace.

But her family life was certainly affected. Father was ever more busy filling in for the doctors who were called up. Mother started part-time war work at the local hospital. The house was often empty and cold, particularly in winter, when Anne got home from school. Rations hardly stretched to provide what one might call an exciting meal, especially as her parents, being thoroughly patriotic, would not avail themselves of any black market opportunity. Anne too was roped in to make a contribution to the war effort; in her case this meant knitting socks and balaclavas. She abhorred knitting and sometimes wondered who would wear the slightly misshapen garments she managed to produce; most likely they would be rejected as unwearable in some final sorting.

The only recreation was the weekly visit to the cinema and this Anne enjoyed to the full. There were wonderful Hollywood creations to marvel at, so unlike her surrounding reality, which was so drab and depressing. As her stay at school neared its end, Anne wished for victory just as much for her own sake as for the country's. She wasn't at all keen to join the army or be sent to work on a farm or in a factory, but the alternative of continuing her studies at some college of higher education was not so easy to achieve. Her marks, though good, were not brilliant. In any case, Anne had no clear idea of what she wanted to do with her future. In the event, she did not have to make an immediate choice. VE Day occurred just days before she was due to finish her last term, and so Anne was liberated as it were at one stroke from both war and school.

Anne was becoming an adult person. In the autumn she joined a secretarial school in London, coming home for the weekends. She was starting to form some new relationships – on the whole unsuccessfully – knowing she could always go back home to her loving, if somewhat hard to understand, parents.

One reason Anne came home so regularly every weekend was her pet dog, Lucky. Lucky started his life as an exceptionally unlucky dog. Abandoned by his previous owners, he spent some time (Anne could never establish how long) living the life of a stray. Presumably he survived on scraps rescued from dustbins or other garbage, surviving the cold weather in some sheltered hideouts. When Anne happened to notice him, he looked very much the worse for wear, with mottled hair and runny eyes. She came across him one early winter evening on the way from the cinema where she had been to the early afternoon show. She was really not supposed to be out on her own after dark, particularly since American troops had moved into the barracks which had been vacated by the regimental depot early in the war. But as the years of war passed by, the supervision exercised over Anne slackened considerably.

So Anne, hurrying home, noticed some strange shape by the road, which on closer inspection proved to be a dog. She knelt down by its side, not knowing what to do. She could not abandon it and yet she was sure her parents would not take kindly to such an intruder at a time when food was so scarce. The pitiful appearance of the dog made it problematic whether it was going to survive even if taken in. Nonplussed, Anne decided to leave the dog and go home and plead her cause with her mother. But to her surprise, as she moved away the dog made an effort, managed to get to his feet and started to follow her. Encouraged by the dog's action she began to egg him on with promises of food and shelter. The dog walked very slowly, sitting down from time to time, so that when they arrived at the house it had got quite dark and Anne's mother could be seen watching out at the gate for her. In a way this facilitated the inevitable first encounter, because the first words her mother uttered were: 'What's that you have got with you?' So Anne put her arms round her mother's neck (in genuine affection) and explained her meeting with 'Lucky' – the name she had already given the stray.

Mother, visibly relieved at Anne's safe homecoming, was caught off guard and could not remain detached, watching the pitiful progress of the animal. Given half a chance, for example if the question of having a dog had arisen in conversation, she would never have agreed to taking on any extra responsibility at that particular juncture. All similar proposals on Anne's part were always answered in the same way: 'Wait, dear – perhaps after the war.' But here was reality, the dog standing by the gate, his head down but his tail trying to wag with as much strength as its owner possessed. 'What will your father say?' she asked.

But Anne had her answer ready: 'He will not say a word if you agree.' She went on, almost crying now: 'Please, Mother, we can't leave him to starve. How can we go into the house and leave him here out in the cold? He'd be dead in the morning and neither you nor I could bear that!'

There was some truth in what Anne had said. Her mother thought for a while, then took charge of the situation. 'Stay with him for a bit while I get him a bowl of soup. If he's had some food then we can put him in the garden shed for the night. Tomorrow we'll bath and de-flea him. And only then will I let him into the house.'

Lucky took a fortnight to regain his strength but much longer to acquire a shiny coat. Anne didn't mind waiting, the very idea that by a fluke she had become a pet-owner – a proposition which her parents had rejected whenever she had suggested it previously – carried her through. It was enough that Lucky, after a few days' rest, began to wait for her by the gate when she wheeled her bicycle down the road and on seeing her would rush to meet her. It was enough that he proudly accompanied her to the corner of the street when she started out for school in the morning and then, on being told to go home and wait, would obediently turn back, though his tail would be forlornly lowered. And so Lucky's looks did not matter so much (and even with a new coat at its best he would never be a ravishingly handsome dog). A mixture of two, maybe three, breeds, he looked somewhat like a large, strange type of terrier. But his eyes made up for his lack of definite ancestry. They were rather sad and inclined to get misty when he was forbidden something. Yet on happy occasions, such as the promise of a long walk, they shone with joy and seemed to acquire a special, particularly touching glint.

It was the walks on the common that were responsible for the first acquaintances other than new schoolmates that Anne made in her adolescence. One is inclined to believe that people who walk dogs fall into a special category and on the whole are friendly souls, always ready to exchange a few remarks, starting with the weather, then some compliment about their respective charges and, later, even some personal details which normally they would not confide to strangers.

Anne became friendly with two or three walkers who took their dogs on the common more or less at the same times – usually about mid-afternoon, as soon as Anne got back from school. At weekends, it would be in the morning. One middle-aged lady in particular became Anne's most frequent companion. She exercised two rough-haired terriers – mother and daughter, it transpired on closer acquaintance. It was Lucky who brought the owners together, being always interested in the ladies. The owner of the terriers was a retired teacher, a spinster who because of her profession was well versed in talking with young people. Anne found herself telling Miss Cooper all sorts of things. Sometimes she astonished herself by the ease with which she could hold her own side of an argument. She couldn't have done that either at home or at school. As well as Anne's confidante, Miss Cooper became a source of all sorts of information useful to Anne in her schoolwork. They made a curious pair: Anne tall and slim, Miss Cooper rather podgy and inclined to waddle. They soon became known to the other walkers and their animated discussions gave rise to many an inquisitive remark. Anne learned to express herself with surprising confidence, such as she could never have mustered or even attempted with any other grown-up.

On some occasions Miss Cooper would appear with only one dog, stating that the other was 'indisposed'. When Anne asked if she had taken the dog to the vet, Miss Cooper would answer that there was no need and it was only nature asserting itself. And Anne knew what she meant – Miss Cooper had serious reservations when it came to Lucky's credentials for the possible fathering of her 'darlings' ' offspring. It wasn't that she had never bred dogs, far from it, but that was before the war. The war had put a damper on so many activities – canine as well as human, so it seemed. Anne found the euphemistic way Miss Cooper spoke a little funny when, after all, it was only referring to her pets' natural cycle of fertility, but she respected this attitude as proper, almost endearing.

As soon as Anne had qualified in secretarial skills she started looking for employment. London just after the war offered scores of possibilities and Anne felt that taking a job locally would be a retrograde step. So she settled in a bed-sitter not far from Fulham Broadway station. She soon got quite used to some degree of independence and was not prepared to let the family close round her again. Her visits home became less regular and consequently her walks with Lucky and her relationship with Miss Cooper suffered. Not that Anne minded. She had begun to grow away from her friend and confidante, finding new interests, new ventures in which to express her personality. Sadly, she started to view Miss Cooper as a frumpy old lady, rather outmoded in outlook and pretty ridiculous in appearance.

So it was a surprise for her when on one of her weekend visits home her father gave her a message from Miss Cooper, who was one of his patients. She asked Anne to visit her as she was not at all well – and in this way she was also trying to explain to Anne why she no longer met her on the common. Anne in fact had been quite pleased about the absence of Miss Cooper whenever she happened to exercise Lucky. It gave her a way to distance herself from and eventually end their strange relationship.

She found she was not at all keen to go to see the old lady and kept putting it off from one weekend to the next. In fact she never made the visit. Some time passed, other activities occurred, on several weekends she missed going home. Obviously Anne was forsaking her old loyalties and acquiring new ones. Then one weekend she found a letter waiting for her at home. It was from a firm of solicitors informing her that a certain Miss Cooper had bequeathed her the entire contents of her library, numbering over a thousand titles. Anne felt very small and grieved at the news. She suddenly remembered this quiet but well-informed mind, so sympathetic to Anne's inquiries and searchings. In a way, she had been a sounding board on which Anne had tried her first original (or as nearly original as possible) thoughts and assumptions. Yet the only time this friend had asked something of her she had let her down. It simply illustrated that for all the high-sounding principles Anne expressed, deep down she was merely an egoistic, rather selfish adolescent, ready to take but not to give much in return.

Incidentally, after Anne's mother died, Lucky simply vanished. Perhaps instinct told him that there was now nobody left in Anne's household to take care of him and he must seek another sanctuary.

VI

Anne knew she was going to be too late. Call it premonition, call it intuition. She looked at her watch. The train would not

24

reach its destination for another half an hour. Then it would take a good half an hour to get a taxi and reach the house. Anne would not let her thoughts go beyond this point. She drew back from thinking about what she might find once she was in the house. *I will have enough opportunity to consider the matter once I am on the spot.* She kept repeating this vague proposition in order to calm her nerves.

Anne felt guilty. For the first time in her life she felt she had let her mother down. Her mother's letter had arrived two days ago and she should have been on the train immediately. It had a curious tone, a mood of reflection, of that tranquillity which fills a person after solving a problem, making a decision. But was there anything else between the lines? Anne chose not to notice it at the time, though she could not get her mother out of her thoughts. It was only this morning, when she was getting her breakfast, that a strange anxiety overwhelmed her. Suddenly Anne knew her mother's letter was a cry for help and, being so untypical of normal behaviour, might mean anything.

Several sentences in the letter sounded contrived, as if put there for a specific reason, and seemed to have little or nothing to do with the subject matter. Commenting on some gossipy news about neighbours who were divorcing, Anne's mother wrote: 'But then, my darling, parting is sometimes the best way, in fact the only way.' And again later, as she discussed the desolate look of the garden in late autumn, there was the sad reflection: 'Somehow I feel like the autumn myself, except that my winter will not give way to spring except in you. Be my spring for me and flower freely, released from the sadness and constraint that the earlier seasons put upon you.'

There was no mention in the letter of Anne's last visit, which had included a somewhat unfortunate confrontation. Some of the blame, perhaps all of it, could be attributed to Anne's vulnerability, which always lay in wait, cloaked by the acquired wisdom of experience which advised against delving too deeply into the past, into the unsolved, unresolved traumas of her relationship with her mother.

25

On the whole, one could say, a sort of truce held between them for many years; they learned how to avoid dangerous subjects in their conversations. Local gossip, the state of the garden, the availability or otherwise of home help, usually provided enough material to allow the visits to take place in a friendly and tension-free atmosphere. But these two people, who sincerely loved each other, at the same time suffered from complex claims, problems beyond their control to which neither could find a satisfactory resolution.

The last time Anne went home she found herself in breach of the truce. On what at the time sounded like a provocation, she accused her mother of saying things she didn't mean, mainly in connection with her daughter's achievements in life. Anne suggested there was a measure of condescension, contempt even, in what her mother said. Mother denied it vigorously, asking Anne the question she had asked her over and over again in the past in similar circumstances: 'What do you want of me? How can I prove to you that I am sincere, that I mean what I say, that I fully accept you as you are?'

But Anne would have none of this. Her reply suggested that her mother regarded her as a failure, a total disappointment of her motherly expectations. 'You only pretend you approve of me to keep me quiet,' was her answer. 'In fact, you have given up on me. Anything I have done or could do in the future will only strengthen your opinion. I don't really mind – but for once in your life admit it!' She raised her voice and continued: 'If anyone is to blame it is you – you and your impossible standards that only showed off my inability to cope with life! Yet I didn't ask to be born!'

'Yes, that at least is true. It does seem that the so-called "gift of life" you received from your parents has proved to be of doubtful value to you,' interjected her mother, somewhat sarcastically.

'Admit you never wanted me in the first place.'

'That is not true and you know it!'

'I know what I know! Ever since I can remember I had to earn my place between you two. I kept trying and hardly ever felt welcomed. That is the main reason for my present

26

problems. How can anyone love me if my parents found me unattractive?'

'You are talking pure nonsense, Anne. If you doubt our love after all the evidence at your disposal, nothing will make you change your mind. But then you always took your advantages for granted and looked for some quality of love which doesn't exist. If you persist in this irrational quest you really run the risk of not being able to make any emotional contact in the future. Beware, Anne, I am thinking only of you. Stick to what is possible, forget those fancy ideas which have not served you well up to now!' Her mother was speaking in a loud, pontifical tone – the very intonation Anne abhorred.

'You don't love me – you only preach at me!' screamed Anne and shot out of the room, slamming the door behind her.

The next day Anne took the 5.30 train back to London. There was no mention of the painful scene of the day before. Mother was her old self; Anne too had recovered her composure. What had happened was nothing more than a repetition of countless similar confrontations. I'll never learn, thought Anne. Why can't I keep away? I know Mother loves me, but not in the way I need. I must remember it, but oh! Will I never learn?

A myth existed for a long time in Anne's family, propounding a theory about her mother's independence of spirit and self-reliance. Everybody admired it and commented on it. Yet in a way Anne suspected something different. When her father died several years previously, she was confronted by a particular dilemma. She read an unspoken wish in her mother's eyes which seemed to say: 'Come back home to me!' It would have meant Anne scrapping a carefully built, precariously maintained, illusory – but at times believed – life of her own. It would have meant going back to her youth, perhaps even childhood and all that mixed, unsettling relationship, which didn't do anything for anybody and only brought hurt – deep, savage and immeasurable.

Hoping to be refused, Anne put forward another idea. Her

27

mother would be welcome to come and live with her. Somehow she knew Mother would never accept such an offer because it would have meant giving up the house, the happy memories (are memories really happy or do we pretend they are so as not to feel cheated by life?), the feeling of being of importance in her own right. Coming to live with Anne, she would become an appendage instead of being a dominant factor.

So, of course, she thanked Anne but refused. Ever since then the situation had not changed. Once a fortnight Anne came home for the weekend and enjoyed it on the whole, her mother being good company. Anne could air her views, could listen to her favourite records, while both of them did some needlework. Anne felt at peace and content in general, as well as happy in the knowledge that next day she would be on the 5.30 train to Victoria.

And yet Anne knew there was a part in her mother that she would never be allowed to discover, a place she would never be able to enter. And that made her angry and anxious to go away and never see her mother again, while at the same time she knew herself to be incapable of achieving her deep-felt desire to wound. She wanted her mother and hated wanting her. She knew she must break from her, yet at the same time she wanted to stay with her for ever. She was confused, irrational, contradictory and above all torn. She was torn between independence and peace of mind. Because that was what her mother had given her: peace, serenity, hope, sometimes refuge. Things were easier to bear with her in the vicinity; she understood the whimsical jokes Anne made, she absolved her from guilt, she cherished her.

But there was also the other feeling, of her mother holding something back, as if she was at a point of departure at any moment, as if she could disappear suddenly and finally, leaving Anne prostrate.

When Anne had a chance of leaving home, her mother did not object, which only strengthened Anne's insecurity; her attempts at making other relationships almost always failed because they never compared favourably with the qualities of her relationship with her mother, so that after some new false start Anne would return to the familiar, often maddening, quite often cruel love of her mother.

Now, sitting in the train, impatiently waiting for the journey to end, Anne suffered mixed emotions. She felt very guilty and was already half preparing in her mind a halting defence for not having come earlier to see her mother. Yet somehow she knew that this time there would be no absolution forthcoming. She would have to shoulder her guilt alone, absolve herself within her own resources as well as she could. As soon as the train stopped, she jumped down from it and, gathering what strength she had, pressed on to deal with what was in store for her.

It was not easy to get a taxi at this time of day. Anne had to wait quite a long time before one became available. The congested streets of midday meant that it was more like an hour before she alighted from the taxi and opened the gate leading to the house. As soon as she had done so, her legs felt as if made of lead. As much as she had hurried earlier, now, when only a few yards separated her from the front door, she could hardly move. She knew her mother was dead and she did not want to face it.

Slowly she walked to the front door, with grim determination searched in her handbag for the key and inserted it gently into the lock. Somehow it became very important not to make a noise. She shut the front door behind her, instinctively looking for Lucky, who normally would greet her exuberantly. But there was no sign of him. Anne walked straight into the sitting room, where she knew she would find her mother. And there she was. She was sitting in her armchair with the high back, half-facing the fireplace and the row of photographs on the mantelpiece. Her eyes were open, as if in the last moment of consciousness she had concentrated on the familiar faces of those dear to her. Death had been kind to her. She looked peaceful and somewhat surprised, as if the very dying had been easier than she had imagined. Her head rested against the back of the armchair, her hair, a bit disordered, spread around her face. Her body slumped slightly to one side.

There was no note. Just two empty bottles of pills, a tumbler with the remains of some liquid. Anne sat down on the armchair opposite. She looked and looked as if trying to engrave this picture on her memory. No multitude of feelings overwhelmed her. Just one question occurred to her over and over again: *'Why?'* In some extraordinary way, one thought struck her – it seemed all her life so far and the tangled relationship with her mother had been preparing her for this very moment, that things being as they were, there couldn't have been any other ending. And a new and in some way cruel thought illuminated her. 'I'm free!' said Anne aloud.

It was while attending to the business of the estate of her late mother at the solicitors' that Anne met her future husband.

VII

In later years Anne came to regret that she did not have a white wedding. At the time, however, it didn't seem to be important. Money was not all that abundant. It was scarcely nine months since her mother's death. A white wedding is somehow associated with a full church of well-wishers; it calls for bridesmaids, music and a display of flowers and to put it bluntly, neither Anne nor Sloane had enough relatives or friends to fill the church. These considerations dictated quiet, sensible nuptials, dignified and restrained. In the end Anne chose a cream two-piece and a floral display in her hair. The wedding photographs contain only eight people: the bridal pair, two aunts apiece, the best man and Anne's cousin, Sally, at whose house the wedding reception was held. The guests soon departed, leaving just the two of them quite ready to face the future. They felt fairly confident, since they had a basis on which to start.

Sloane's getting a new job had necessitated a move to London, so Anne had sold her mother's house and invested the money in a semi-detached Victorian residence at number 7 Rosetta Way. Their honeymoon was spent in the new house, which was not yet completely furnished though they had the furniture inherited from Anne's parents. These completely changed circumstances at the beginning of Anne's married life only underlined the mood she was in. This was to be a new beginning for her; the past was done with, best forgotten, the memories – some good and some painful – had been laid to rest. What counted now was the future, and that looked to hold quite a promise.

If Sloane's contribution to the marital set-up was not as imposing, he certainly made up for it in the excellence of his brain. It soon became apparent that his legal and financial experience, together with a rugged determination, would serve him well. All that was needed now was a little luck, and there was no reason not to be optimistic on that score.

So the newly-weds moved into the house in Rosetta Way and spent quite a lot of time and all available resources on making it a home. Soon curtains appeared, rugs covered the floors and furniture from the old house was deployed to its best advantage amongst the rooms. Sloane was cooperative; he liked things to look nice, enjoyed handiwork, was full of ideas.

And then, of course, Anne and Sloane were deeply in love. In retrospect it must have been a more romantic affair on Anne's part. Sloane was a man of few words, but deep down at the core of his being there existed a profound source of pure unequivocal devotion to Anne which never changed. Sloane was a one-woman man.

From the start they managed to establish a mutual trust and unity of purpose. They both believed in living within their means, having an inborn inclination to save rather than overspend. They were prepared to wait for the good things in life, preferring the certainty of solvency to the anxieties of unpaid bills. It might have made their life just a little bit pedestrian but both of them were disposed to find excitement in activities and outlets which did not necessarily carry a price tag.

There were many details to be attended to in the new house and, when satisfactorily resolved, to be admired. The garden too held an innumerable amount of large and small challenges. They were fully occupied. In consequence investing in the latest gadgets for the home or going on expensive outings did not figure high, if at all, on their list of priorities.

Then, on the unexpected death of one of his superiors, Sloane gained considerable promotion, to a real plum of a job. This quite dramatically changed their financial circumstances, but at the same time necessitated a substantial adjustment in their self-orientated way of life. Now the words 'the company' acquired a different meaning. They began to take precedence in the day-to-day life of the young couple. Gone were the days when Anne could expect Sloane to appear punctually at a quarter to seven, ready for the evening meal. Some evenings, even after a late homecoming, as soon as the table was cleared files and books of reference emerged from Sloane's smart briefcase and some more work was put in. 'The job has to be done' became a familiar expression and Anne would accept it. After all, Sloane was ambitious and it seemed as if the necessary opportunity was at hand.

She would turn the television on, but soon discovered that it interfered with Sloane's work, so a spare room was turned into a study, a large desk purchased, together with a whole assortment of shelves. In a little while the shelves were filled with necessary literature, mainly dealing with financial matters, some textbooks and tables on related subjects. Anne suddenly discovered that she must rely on herself for distractions. The honeymoon was quite definitely over.

The resultant situation, as well as the realisation that she was not getting any younger, turned Anne's thoughts to motherhood. There had been very little talk about children in the year since Anne got married. Being cautious by nature, the young people wanted first to establish a steady marital relationship – and to tell the truth, they were quite happy by themselves.

Now, however, the proposition looked much more realistic, since Anne had no need to go out to work to supplement their income. On the contrary, there was even some surplus cash which could be put away. The baby would fill the spare time Anne had acquired and prevent her from feeling shut out from Sloane's new involvement. It was becoming evident that Sloane would go far. He enjoyed being extended and his temperament plus brains made him a promising candidate for further promotion. Where babies were concerned, Sloane held no firm opinions. He liked children, as far as could be ascertained at the moment. He would love to have a son, most men would, but he did not explore the many and complicated aspects of parenthood. However, he was sure he could easily leave the practical side of baby-raising to his wife, whose capabilities in management he had come to appreciate.

Thus Anne embarked on motherhood with enthusiasm and gladly put up with the inconvenience of pregnancy. She would, perhaps, have liked Sloane to be more involved in the week-by-week development of their future offspring, but quite early in her marriage she had perceived that their union was a partnership with fairly clearly defined roles – he was the provider, she the manager.

Anne's little daughter, Stella, was born without fuss, and without Sloane present to hold Anne's hand, one day in spring. For one thing, Sloane was in a meeting when the pains came, but anyway Anne had quite enough gumption to 'go it alone'. She was well prepared, suitcase and all, and actually drove herself to the hospital, which was quite near. She left the car in the car park, announced to the surprised hospital staff, 'I have come to have my baby,' and then collapsed from the effort.

Some hours later the baby was born, perfect in every detail. Anne was relieved to have had a comparatively easy time. She proudly showed the baby to Sloane, who arrived in the afternoon, laden with flowers and apologies. But Anne did not mind at all. She felt confident that the first step towards their glorious future was taken. What was there to stop them?

VIII

Stella was conceived a year after Anne and Sloane were married, and Anne was already 29 when the baby was born. The child was delicate, often suffering from colics and earaches. She was skinny and rather plain-looking, which, of course, Anne didn't notice, being completely wrapped up in motherhood. So much so that Sloane at times felt shut out and neglected. Anne was unable to help him because her emotions became temporarily so immersed in childcare that all her other relationships didn't matter, were secondary. She came to regret this later, when the long years of bringing up a child started to become somewhat tedious, less absorbing than before. Sloane by that time was himself immersed in pursuing his career and was willing, in fact welcomed, their division of labour.

Stella was a difficult child to bring up. She had a will of her own, which very early on became a problem for Anne. Thwarted, Stella was inclined to become obstinate and seemed not to respond to any displeasure shown by her mother. She was a very self-contained child, relying on her own resources to sustain her composure. Guilt, if indeed she felt any, did not appear to bother her unduly. In fact, as long as she could get away with things, she showed little emotional dependence on either of her parents, yet being an intelligent child she compensated for that apparent deficiency by general conformity and adaptability. Except when she decided to differ – then she would become absolutely determined to have her own way, no matter the consequences. Anne would ponder on this particular side of her daughter's character and could not make up her mind whether it was a trait which would later in life land Stella in many head-on collisions or whether this occasional obstinacy denoted a future strength of character which, if correctly developed and channelled, could become a definite basis for adherence to moral codes and principles.

Stella's school reports seemed to echo Anne's observations and so it came as no great surprise to Anne that the difficult years of puberty exacerbated matters between her and her daughter. What complicated the situation and was probably responsible for a great deal of pain and anxiety for Anne was her own ambivalent approach to the problem confronting her. She remembered her relationship with her own mother and the difficulty she had experienced when she tried to rebel against her to assert herself, yet at the same time her helpless acquiescence to the stronger personality. She remembered the failure to break the too-close bond with her mother, which even when finally severed in superficially accepted terms never left Anne quite free from a feeling of dependency and even guilt.

So when dealing with her daughter she made allowances, taking for granted that Stella reacted in much the same ways as she herself had done. And here probably lay the fundamental mistake in Anne's thinking. Stella was very different from Anne, her personality did not resemble that of her mother. She was made of stronger, sterner and more durable material. She never needed Anne in the same way that Anne had needed her own mother. Stella in some obscure way enjoyed the tug-of-war as if subconsciously preparing herself for the battles she was to encounter in the future. She had an inborn confidence, she felt secure in the core of her being and was never – or hardly ever – swayed by emotional appeals from her mother. She looked to the future with that kind of confidence which is based on few if any explainable prerequisites, yet is the greatest gift one could be endowed with by nature: the conviction that life was created for one's enjoyment and therefore should be made use of, all the fun and all the thrill one comes across to be extracted in the fullest degree – and the bad, the painful, to be edited so as to be bearable, relegated to those regions of one's mind which are rarely if ever visited.

Anne, accustomed to a different climate in her childhood and youth, was inclined to lavish on her beloved and cherished child all the qualities she possessed. And there high on the list figured emotion, even sentimentality. In keeping with this feeling, she treasured all the little reminders of

Stella's babyhood: first shoes, first dress, a book of records which gave details of Stella's development in the most endearing terms. There was a scrapbook of first drawings, first written sentences, letters to Santa Claus – all sorts of things. Anne kept all these memorabilia in a special box and on occasions liked to sift through the different items, sometimes on her own, sometimes showing them to her daughter.

After a more than usually bitter encounter with her daughter, soon after Stella turned 13, when in that particular battle of wills Anne scored a victory, she found her special box destroyed, the contents thrown about, scattered all over the room, the baby's clothes cut to tatters, pictures thrown out and shredded to pieces. Anne wept as she gathered the remains of her fondest memories, putting them on her bed. She was at a loss what to do. She had no idea how to react. She was unable to confront Stella, because she couldn't trust herself. Those torn, useless reminders of some of the happiest times in Anne's life seemed to signify more than a childish desire for revenge. They suddenly acquired a deeper meaning, that of cutting herself off from an emotional bond on Stella's part and of an irretrievable loss on Anne's part. Anne felt betrayed. She was surprised at her own feelings. Why should she feel betrayed? Was it by Stella? By herself for not suspecting her own flesh and blood of being capable of such cruelty? By being forced to recognise the fact that her child was a stranger in a way she had never suspected?

There was a hollow feeling inside her which even anger could not fill, a sense of sadness and loss. She could not bear a confrontation with Stella. Some link which held them both (or so Anne thought) was broken and really it did not matter any longer that it was Stella who was the culprit. There was a more important factor confronting Anne, more valid and more immediate than punishing Stella. Anne had to admit that her perception of her daughter's relationship with her was an illusion. She shrank from the truth yet knew the illusion was gone for good.

Anne was always to remember that particular event. As time went on it became apparent that Stella was blessed with all encompassing self-sufficiency. She did not hesitate to leave home when an opportunity arose and very early let it be known that her future would impinge only marginally on Anne's life – and only when it could be to Stella's advantage. That did sadden Anne. Bearing in mind how long and painful her own leave-taking of her mother had been, she accepted this state of affairs regretfully yet at the same time with strange relief.

She still cherished the mutilated treasures of Stella's babyhood and childhood. In the first few months after Stella left home, Anne was often to be found holding these lacerated remains, hurt no more but, rather, surprised that even now she was unable to part with them. After Sloane died and the time came when the past first loosened and then lost altogether its hold on reality, things changed. Looking back only made Anne bitter and more lonely, so she decided to do something about it. One day she burnt the lot.

IX

The quietude of the summer afternoon enveloped the whole neighbourhood. It seemed that all the gardeners in the vicinity had finished attending to the cosmetics of their lawns and put away their mowers for another week. For a change no music could be heard from the nearby flats and no one was engaged in noisy games in the adjacent gardens. At times a solitary car passed by, but even this sound hardly impinged on the peace.

Anne and Sloane had enjoyed a lazy afternoon in the garden; teatime arrived and was duly observed, now they were both happily relaxing. Anne watched Stella, their daughter, who had just passed her third birthday, wheeling a doll's pram along the garden path, stopping from time to time to straighten her baby doll, which was inclined to slip down as the pram trundled over the uneven pebble surface of the path. Stella looks a treat, thought Anne, and suddenly it occurred to her that now was the time to broach a subject with her husband which had been occupying her thoughts, on and off, for the last few months. She looked inquiringly at Sloane, half-dozing in his garden chair; he seemed to be at peace with the world and entirely contented. It was as if this tranquil domestic scene banished from his mind the usual preoccupations connected with his job and all its responsibilities. Yes, Anne reassured herself, now is the time. And without further hesitation she asked Sloane the direct question: 'Listen dear, isn't it time we had another baby?'

There was a longish pause before Sloane opened his eyes and looked non-committally at Anne.

'Do you think so? Of course I want another baby, but is this the right time? Do you want another baby just now?'

'Yes, I do.'

'But Stella is only three. She still needs a lot of attention and care. Will you be able to cope? You know that my job takes most of my time and with the best will in the world I won't be able to give a great deal of practical help.'

'I can easily manage as long as I know that you think it is a good idea. I want you to tell me exactly where you stand on the subject. It can't be just my decision . . .'

'Of course I would like another baby and we can well afford it. It is just . . .' Sloane hesitated. 'At this stage in my career – I think I should warn you – I can't promise to be as much help to you as I should like when the baby comes. It seems rather unfair on you.'

'It's the moral support I want from you.' Anne smiled teasingly at her husband and got up to take the tea tray into the kitchen.

Sloane stayed behind, closed his eyes again and slowly turned over in his mind Anne's suggestion. I hope she's right, was his last thought before he dozed off.

It was therefore not surprising that Anne found herself pregnant a few months later. She was overjoyed and so was Sloane. When the doctor confirmed that a baby was on the way, things began to fall into a similar routine to that of Anne's first pregnancy. Yet the obvious anxiety of the first few months was not as apparent as in the first pregnancy and when the

38

halfway mark was reached Anne started to get down to the practical side of preparations for the baby's arrival. There was the room to be redecorated and the furniture to be assembled. Some thought should be given to Stella going to a day nursery. But all this was well within the scope of Anne's capabilities. She was at peace with herself; what's more she was sure it was going to be a boy. A son for Sloane! She enrolled Stella in a nursery, just for a few hours daily, so that she would not feel too much the intrusion of another human being into the intimate relationship with her mother which existed at present.

Anne's monthly visits to the clinic provided a welcome break. There she made several friends amongst the other expectant mothers, and a couple of months later that was where she actually met her neighbour from the adjoining house. Susan and her husband had moved in quite recently and before meeting her at the clinic Anne had hardly ever seen her. Susan had been in a teaching post and had only just resigned.

It was inevitable that these two expectant mothers, although differing in age, should find much in common and little by little they became quite close. In fact, to Anne's surprise she found herself drawn to Susan. Taking into account Anne's lack of ability to relate to others, this might be regarded as remarkable progress. On the other hand, the presence of Stella was an encouraging example to Susan, a joyful demonstration of what was lying in store for her in a few years' time. Anne was able to introduce Susan to the more complex aspects of pregnancy, pass on some tips, discuss the best way of dealing with approaching problems and generally share the waiting period.

When the half term of Anne's pregnancy was past and it was becoming quite obvious to everyone that the baby was well on the way, Anne experienced probably the happiest time of her life. She dearly wanted to have a son and her instinct continued to tell her that her dreams were to be fulfilled. She boldly decorated the spare room in blue, and blue was the dominant colour of the outfit she bought for the baby. Not for her the cautious yellow!

A spring baby affords a special thrill for everybody concerned; it seems to be so much in harmony with awakening nature, longer days, milder weather. And so the happy anticipation of the event was even further heightened for Anne and her husband. Stella was told to expect a wonderful surprise, meanwhile she attended the nursery and grew more and more confident in her encounters with people outside the family circle. Then, when only a few weeks separated Anne from her eagerly awaited confinement, things began to go wrong. First Stella had a bad bout of influenza. She needed extra nursing care and there were several broken nights. A couple of days later Anne woke up with a sore throat and wicked headache. Nevertheless she had to take care of Stella because Sloane was away and not due home for two more days. So she carried on with her duties as well as she was able, hardly having time to take the rest she was recommended.

Stella recovered but Anne's illness seemed to drag on. A regular check at the clinic revealed high blood pressure; she was advised to rest and given some corrective tablets. A week passed, then on the next visit to the clinic the staff looked somewhat concerned – Anne must come into hospital for the remainder of her pregnancy as there were certain signs that the baby was not in the right position for birth.

Hurriedly arranged help in the form of an agency nanny did little to allay Anne's anxiety. Sloane tried to take over some of the care of Stella, but his involvement with his career, as he had predicted and warned Anne about, took precedence over a domestic crisis. Anne, aware of this, fully accepted it but of course she had never before been in a situation where she had to depend so heavily on his time and help. So far his financial support had allowed her to solve most problems arising from the unpredictability of life.

But this time it was different. She lingered in hospital; she was advised complete rest and gently told by the doctor that he was doing everything possible to bring about a satisfactory outcome. She didn't like the sound of this, but the doctor seemed to be reasonably optimistic. Except that then Anne noticed some change in the movement of the baby, there was a definite slowing down in the activity of the foetus. Anne started to panic and called the nurse, who in turn called the doctor. A consultant appeared and the position of the baby was thoroughly examined, apparatus to monitor the baby's heartbeat installed and then, quite suddenly, a desperate fight to save the baby's life began. Anne was dazed; she felt like a detached onlooker when faced with the responsibility of decision; Sloane couldn't be located: the emergency certificate had to be signed by Anne. Before she knew what was happening she was anaesthetised and wheeled into the operating theatre.

Some time later she came round in the ward, dopey and exhausted. Suddenly an urgent and penetrating thought made her sit up. 'Where is the baby?' she asked, and repeated more loudly: 'Where is he?'

The nurse answered soothingly: 'It's a boy, he is very tired and is in the Intensive Care Unit.'

Then Sloane appeared, looking in a strange way diminished, as if the news he carried made him shrink physically. He took Anne's hand and said quietly: 'It is no good, Anne. He is dead.'

X

It didn't take long for Anne to realise, after she had been discharged from hospital, that Susan was avoiding her. In a way, Anne understood. Her neighbour was a month away from her own confinement; she needed a secure and cheerful atmosphere. And there was Anne, the very personification of what can happen, of what potentially may lie in wait for everybody – misfortune. Anne herself was not really keen to talk to Susan – what could she say? 'Never mind, you will be luckier'? Or, 'Lightning never strikes twice in the same place'? Her own distress needed healing; she was not even quite sure that on meeting Susan she would find the necessary tact and composure. And so days passed, weeks even.

41

But as chance would have it, she met Susan one day right in front of the gate and it was too late for either of them to seek cover, so trying to look reasonably cheerful Anne smiled and said: 'Dear Susan, how well you look! Pregnancy suits you!' Susan started to cry and suddenly it was all right. There was no need for explanations and apologies. Just two women sharing in grief, a woman's grief with all its depth and sensitivity to each other's pain. Anne, by that time crying herself, tried to reassure Susan that her anguish held no envy, no ill-wishing. Susan couldn't get beyond saying, 'I am so sorry, so sorry.' And somehow that sufficed. They communicated on a level which could not be expressed in words but which was comprehended by both, a purely spiritual level.

Not long afterwards Susan gave birth to a bouncing baby, a boy, both mother and son doing well. Anne didn't go to see the baby – that would have been too much for her – but as the weeks passed she found herself more and more often at the back room window waiting for Susan to bring the baby out and leave it in its pram for a daily nap. So far Anne had felt absolutely frozen. Her baby's room had become taboo, her relationship with Stella very efficient but scarcely emotional. Sloane was very supportive but could do little to help. It was up to Anne herself to put together the pieces into which the death of her son had disintegrated her being, but for her this was still impossible even to consider.

And so she watched over somebody else's baby's sleep and in a strange way this brought about a change. She began to function emotionally, but not necessarily rationally. Her vigils at the window grew more prolonged and if the baby started to cry she had to exercise all her will-power not to rush out of the door and pick it up. Anne knew that would be wrong and felt guilty about the impulse. She tried to stop herself from such obsessive behaviour, sometimes going out as soon as she had delivered Stella to the day nursery. She would visit art galleries, go shopping, go to the cinema and then hurry home to her window post to catch a glimpse of the baby. She felt very disappointed if the pram was no longer in its usual place.

She tried to talk to Sloane about it. He sympathised and

suggested she should go away for a while or try to get pregnant again, but unfortunately he didn't seem to realise how urgent and overwhelming Anne's problem was.

Then a 'For Sale' board appeared at Anne's neighbour's gate and Anne realised that soon the baby, 'her baby', would be gone. Sloane was very relieved; the problem seemed to be solving itself; soon some other people would buy the house and the the unfortunate situation would stop preying on Anne's mind and emotions. But for Anne it was another matter; she was to lose a baby for a second time. She could hardly contain herself. She stopped sleeping and prowled around the house all night, greatly annoying Sloane. She found it difficult to perform any household duties. She simply couldn't bear the thought of 'her baby' disappearing.

Anne never could recall what finally prompted her to take that particular course of action. It might have been that something of the sort had been evolving in her subconscious from the very beginning. It might also have been true that the idea of never seeing the baby again, the baby whose daily routine she so diligently observed from behind the curtain, suddenly caused her to give way to what was unaccountable, verging on crazy, behaviour. She simply opened the side gate of her neighbour's garden, walked boldly, as of right, into the garden without so much as a look round, approached the pram, picked up the baby, which was sleeping soundly – and slowly, so as not to waken it, returned to her house, put it in the crib in the unused nursery, covered the baby in a most delicate manner with the still pristine duvet and stood silently at the bottom of the crib, watching.

The baby woke up, slowly, probably in response to being put down, but it did not cry. It opened its eyes, shut them again, yawned several times, turned its head this way and that way as if realising the unfamiliar surroundings and then looked straight at Anne very intently, even seeming to give a faint smile. Anne could not move, she had no recollection of how long she stood there, whether minutes or hours. Suddenly she became aware of another presence in the room. She turned abruptly and her eyes encountered Susan standing

43

just behind, looking quite calm. She gave Anne the ghost of a smile and then said in a quiet voice: 'Now, Anne, that you have had him to yourself for a while, could I have Jason back?'

Anne inclined her head. Susan picked the baby up and without hurrying, disappeared. Anne was rooted to the spot. She looked into the faint indentation the baby's head had made on the pillow and suddenly dissolved into tears.

Next day, Sloane, having obtained leave of absence from his company, took Anne and Stella for a protracted holiday. When they got back the neighbours were gone.

It was much, much later that Anne found out from Sloane the whole story. Susan had been well aware of Anne's tragic vigils at the back window and had ached for her. Feeling she could not carry on in those circumstances she had already decided to move when she unexpectedly inherited a house from her aunt who had died recently. That crucial day she had seen Anne come into the garden and pick up the baby, and had followed her into the nursery. She let Anne adore and 'own' the baby – these were her very words – for a while before retrieving her son. Susan said she had been half expecting something of this sort to happen, but, as she put it: 'As another woman I had to let Anne have this moment of healing. I knew it would help her – it would have helped me if I had been in her situation. I simply had to share with her, if only for a moment, the victory of life over the utter tragedy of a loss.'

XI

Anne's husband, Sloane, perished in an air disaster somewhere over the Atlantic. He was returning home from a business trip which he had been able to share to a degree with Anne. Since part of the conference took place in Jamaica, paying an additional sum out of his own pocket enabled Sloane to have Anne with him for ten days on the northern shore of the island in a delightful place called Occio Rios.

Three days before the end of the holiday, Sloane left for another meeting in Miami. Anne returned home on her own, expecting her husband to follow her two days later. She said goodbye to him at the airport in Kingston, little realising that it was the last time she would see him.

She arrived home safely, opened up the house and started to unpack and generally get back into the normal routines. She found everything in order – no frozen pipes or recalcitrant central heating – which was just as well as her trip took place at the end of February and another cold spell was in progress. She had enjoyed the exotic holiday even though she had had to share Sloane's presence with his various business commitments so that even their farewells in Kingston had been rather short and constrained. Sloane was accompanying the chairman of the company and some other directors. Anne had been a 'company wife' long enough to know that in such circumstances one kept one's place, looking happy and smiling, acknowledging by one's behaviour the importance and seriousness of the occasion. Sloane looked competent and attentive to his superiors. After all, it was up to him to answer all the queries of the VIPs and have all the relevant figures at his fingertips. And so she was left behind on the tarmac and had to be satisfied with a tiny wave of Sloane's hand as he turned back before disappearing into the entrance of the aircraft.

Anne had no premonition or doubts about Sloane's safety. Having crossed the Atlantic the day before in a very pleasant manner, she felt confident and relaxed about air travel in general. She awaited Sloane's return in a joyous frame of mind. When the approximate time of his arrival had passed and began to be seriously overdue, she assumed that there must have been a change of plans and that her husband would be coming on a later flight. To check whether there was any possible delay she phoned Sloane's secretary, sure that head office would be the first to be informed about any new date and time of arrival.

Sloane's secretary sounded rather vague and unsure. She asked Anne to wait and then told her that Sloane's assistant

45

was on his way to her to explain everything. This sounded rather unusual but still Anne did not suspect any major disaster. She tidied the sitting room and was about to finish unpacking a small holdall containing souvenirs and presents for the family, as well as some notes she had scribbled in the hotel in her free time, when the doorbell rang.

As soon as Anne saw Sloane's assistant the first premonition of something very wrong swept over her. Jake, always so jolly-looking, with a ready smile, looked tense and very nervous. He came into the room and, taking Anne's hand, asked her to sit down, then sat down next to her. Looking into her eyes, he delivered the blow as gently as he knew how. He said in a quiet voice, 'Anne – I'm the bearer of bad news. There has been an air disaster. There are no survivors.'

Later, Anne could not recall how long it took her to comprehend the meaning of what Jake had just said. At last she asked, 'Was Sloane on that flight?' And Jake nodded.

'I am here to help,' he added, 'in any way possible.' But Anne could not find it in herself to think what should happen now. She sat there quietly, only wishing that Jake would go. When he asked if he could contact her daughter, Anne made herself speak.

'No, thank you. I will do it later. Just now I would like to be on my own. I'll let you know tomorrow if I need any help.' And soon she showed Jake to the door.

Then she took the telephone off the hook, threw the unpacked holdall into the back of a wardrobe, together with the rest of the items that still needed sorting out, sat down in an armchair and let the tears come.

It was in the same armchair that her daughter Stella, alarmed by the continuous engaged tone of Anne's number, found her early next morning. Anne seemed withdrawn and passive. There was little to be done as Sloane's firm took charge of most formalities. There was no funeral to attend, no customary mourning rites. Anne refused to have any memorial service and all she asked was to be left alone.

Days and weeks passed. In the course of time Sloane's company provided a generous pension as well as giving a lump sum as compensation in recognition of the fact that his death had occurred while he was on company business. This meant that Anne did not have to make any drastic changes in her lifestyle. She mourned Sloane in her own way; she had a feeling of being apart from everybody else and very near her husband. That was the reality for her: Sloane not physically present yet uppermost in her thoughts, not with her yet in all her doings.

Then one day the feeling was gone. And so was any sense of belonging, of actually being part of a union. The long period of desperate longings set in and when it reached its fullness of time – the forgetting began.

It must have been a couple of years before Anne could steel herself to finish the unpacking begun that fatal day of her return from Jamaica. At the back of a large wardrobe, under a lot of discarded clothes, not worn any more now but still not quite ready to be thrown out, Anne found the holdall full of presents and souvenirs, never distributed, never enjoyed, deliberately shunned. One wintry, dull afternoon she made herself tackle this sorry job, having decided to give away all the objects once so carefully chosen in a happy and relaxed moment, now tragic reminders which nevertheless had to be disposed of.

Without much care she placed all the exotic shells, carved animals and other trifles in a plastic bag she had ready; the half-used suntan lotion and assorted make-up was promptly thrown into the dustbin, and then at the very bottom of the holdall Anne found a small folder containing some invitation addresses and loosely written notes which she had completely forgotten about.

The notes were written in longhand and had many crossings-out. They were obviously of an intimate nature. Anne was not quite sure whether she should read them. After all, what seemed a whole lifetime separated her from them. It was another Anne who had put down those words, those feelings. But something made her read on . . .

* * *

47

... I am sitting on the balcony of our comfortable suite (it is called 'Sea Horse') wishing the rain would stop. The sea looks misty and the large drops make a distant sound as they splash down on the waves. One part of me doesn't mind the rain falling – in case, somewhere there beyond the horizon, the thirsty survivors of an imaginary shipwreck scoop water into all available containers, into their hands – laughing and exclaiming: 'Rain, rain!'

I am a divided person, the eternal Libra, always deliberating my preferences and that of other claimants.

Sloane is sitting at the table doing reports for the company (Sceptre Trust – it sounds really royal) and in some way it seems as if it were by royal command of the trust that I am able to sit here at all, instead of in my burgundy kitchen, probably solving a crossword puzzle or something. Sloane is unaware that when working he smiles from time to time; he is so deeply involved in what he is doing that, I bet, he didn't even hear me when I asked for some paper.

Sloane is my shield, or perhaps more appropriately, as I am sitting no more than two yards from the sea, my lifebelt, constantly available to be thrown into the deep sea of difficulties and problems as they come into my life, always reaching me, always dependable in response to a single call 'Sloane!' I am really a very lucky girl. In fact, I would add, I have more luck than I deserve as far as Sloane is concerned. Which is only partly true – sometimes I think Sloane is a thorough pig.

It is still raining. Surely, by now, all those possible survivors should have caught all the water they need and it might be even dangerous for their boat if the rain keeps on falling . . . Here we are, on to my usual preoccupation – worrying. Soon I will start worrying about the phantom castaways.

But to continue. We arrived here very late on Wednesday or early on Thursday – it depends which time zone you are thinking in. A very nice chap met us at the airport. I later found out he was known as Bobby B. Then in quick succession we met the manager and a lot of other people. After

48

that we had drinks and soup and a plate of cheese. Still later I learned that Bobby B. is over seventy (does not look it) and is a friend of Prince Philip – they were in the navy together. Then we found ourselves in this delightful apartment, which is air-conditioned, pleasantly furnished with a mixture of simple modern furniture and some hideous remnants of pseudo-colonial origin. The apartment is on the second floor, facing the sea, and there are several pictures on the walls – abstracts in gay colours – I have named them 'an undeveloped Stella period', a reference to the time when Stella used to draw very intricate 'doodles' – we even sold some of them.

The first morning, with breakfast on the balcony, really turned me into a fan of opulent living, what with the lapping waves and the yellow sand and the grove of palm trees curving along the bay. It is beautiful here, even more beautiful than I could have imagined – and it is so quiet. Like now – the rain has stopped and there is not a soul in sight – just the water and the sand and the palm trees. I can see a chink of blue in the sky and our American neighbours are beginning to stir. I think I would be wise to change into my swimming suit. I am going on the beach . . .

* * *

I don't suppose I shall write much more about our holidays – I wouldn't even be writing this, except that having caught too much sun yesterday I am being sensible and staying out of the sun today, again on the balcony. It is a glorious day; there are some clouds about but the predominant colour is blue, the blue of the sky, the ultramarine blue of the sea at the edge of the horizon and the turquoise blue nearer the shore. The lapping of the waves goes on and on, I can see the waves getting into a queue right there on the horizon, coming nearer, losing their strength as they approach the shore, only to retreat once they have touched the golden sand.

Sloane has gone off to another meeting, but he is coming back at lunchtime and in the afternoon we plan to tour a plantation.

49

I have been crying today, right here, with all the sun and the sand and the sea. I think it has been too much for me, too many nice things, people simply trying to please me. I am not used to this sort of thing, such kind treatment seemed to unlock within me all the dark cupboards and recesses (which we all possess), where all my days and nights of defeat and humiliation lie chained by my instinct of self-preservation, cast out of my memory, rendered dangerous to sanity, forgiven a thousand times in the context of 'Our Father' and yet alive. They all come to the surface, crowding over, demanding attention, exposing scars still tender (do they ever heal?). In fact I was full of self-pity. Is that what is meant by 'killing by kindness'?

Really I am just a hurt, frightened little girl underneath all the so-called composure, my reasoning powers, my self-discipline, my sense. Oh, well, it is all over. I went and dried my tears – fearful lest a maid might see me and perhaps think my husband beats me or something. My fears and defeats are back where they belong.

I am really glad to be here yet I regret I can't share this experience with all the people who for one reason or another cannot take a holiday in February in the Caribbean. And I mean all the people, all over the world. I feel as if I am letting them down, forgetting them simply by being here. (Is this the Libra syndrome again?).

But to continue. In a few days I shall have to pack up and leave for home. On the way back I shall have for company the people I met last night, people who one might say are already enjoying the fruits of their labours, commuting practically all the year round between London and some nice, exotic place. They have a son, very promising of course, and they look happy together, totally committed to having a fabulous time, totally committed to themselves and nobody else.

I probably will not believe it myself in a little while that I have had this extraordinary holiday, I shall probably call it 'the Cinderella fortnight', to be indulged in privately when I have a quiet time to myself. I won't tell too many people about

50

the time I am having either – it might not be very kind, apparently there is another cold spell in England.

It is funny, but it never crossed my mind that marrying Sloane would lead to something like this. I was quite prepared for a rather quiet time – why, when Sloane proposed, he put it very simply, if poetically, 'We shall be spinning our lives very thinly'. Indeed.

* * *

Here I am again, with a sort of PS. I shall be leaving here in two days. Already Sloane has left and half my joy. I am not so much missing him as missing myself – that is, there is less of me when he is not here.

Today I shall meet my cousin's friend who lives here permanently. I hope I shall like her and will be able to spend the day most agreeably, but for the moment it means waiting for her in my room, hence my writing to pass the time.

Yes, this is precisely what most people holidaying here are doing, killing time, voluntarily or not. There seems to be a lot of time wasted – and, from my superficial observation, in a particularly unimaginative manner. They spend quite a lot of time on the beach, getting their bodies brown, and then sit for the rest of the day and the whole evening eating and drinking and talking about their successes – never failures! I like to listen and try to guess what lies behind their confident smiles. It is funny, but places like this require success – you simply do not belong unless you are full of confidence, know everybody and have stayed in a dozen five-star hotels, so that you may compare their respective comforts. I feel totally exposed and gauche with these people because I can't boast of even one five-star hotel, yet revealing my ignorance and the absurdity of it would be bad taste, bad manners.

It seems to me that by a peculiar law of economics the beauty of this island and the beauty of similar places is reserved for the very poor and the very rich. I wonder . . . how conscious are the poor inhabitants of the beauty surrounding them? Do they get any kick out of it?

51

But to continue. I am really very glad I've been here. I have lost one or two hang-ups and I have not gained too much weight. I hope to get home safe and sound and start on the washing feeling refreshed and rested. I hope to be able to listen patiently to all and sundry and not to mind the repetitiveness of it all, since I know now that boredom is not the privilege only of the unprivileged. Gin and wine taste the same here as in Wimbledon, and freedom, once acquired, is the most treasured possession anywhere.

*   *   *

Anne let the pages slip from her fingers to the floor. Her eyes were dry, there was even a gentle smile on her face. A curious thought occurred to her. Surely this is the most fitting epitaph to my marriage years. Should I keep it? Yes, came the answer – I shall never be so happy again.

XII

For a long time after her husband's death Anne seriously thought about selling the house and moving into a flat. She deliberated this question from different points of view, trying to keep sentiment out of her considerations. It was not easy. After all, she had spent all her married life at Number 7 Rosetta Way and anything that happened to her in that period had poignant connections with the house.

It was not a matter of finance – Anne was quite adequately provided for by her husband's insurance and the compensation received on her husband's unexpected, tragic demise. But Anne felt lonely in her comfortable abode, unaccustomed to long periods of silence broken only by the television, of which she was in any case not very fond. Then there was the question of security. A middle-aged woman living on her own in a large, not really much overlooked house. Sometimes her imagination summoned up the most devastating scenarios, which resulted in sleepless nights and a new determination to reach a more satisfactory solution. But months then years passed and nothing happened. To her daughter's pleas Anne invariably answered, 'I'll move when I am ready.'

But then quite suddenly a suggestion was put to her by a friend who had some artistic connections: could there be sanctuary in Anne's house for a young artist, a painter, quite recently arrived from some obscure provincial place. He apparently showed great promise but at the moment was penniless and couldn't really concentrate on his art, having to spend most of his time and energy on moving from one place to another, unable to manage on a very small grant, quite insufficient to meet the very high cost of reasonable lodgings in London.

Anne warmed to the idea. After all, she hardly ever used the second floor of the house – in fact, she could not remember the last time she had visited it. So she agreed to give shelter for the budding talent for a very modest rent, and tidied the rooms, furnishing one as a bedroom. Another, which faced north, she emptied of all unnecessary objects, leaving only a few pieces of furniture which she thought the artist might find useful, providing a large space for an easel and possible models.

Kim moved in within a week. He was a handsome lad with a long, untidy mane of hair, but rather surprisingly was very neat about his clothes. He dressed in the universal style of the young – jeans, tee-shirt and an old sweater. He seemed to have very few possessions – a half-empty holdall and, of course, some odd packages which probably contained his painting materials.

He was quiet in manner and temperament, asked few questions and seemed genuinely delighted with the turn of events. Anne gave him a front door key, told him about the cooking arrangements in the upstairs passage and left him to it. And in this way her tenant's comings and goings did not cause Anne much disturbance and soon Kim's presence blended into Anne's life with the minimum of interference.

As the winter approached, Anne felt obliged to offer some sort of heating to her young lodger as the central heating installed some years previously did not extend to the second floor. To discuss the matter she watched for Kim one morning and invited him into the kitchen (which she used much more often than her sitting room). Kim was very appreciative, though he required very few comforts. Probably the studio would benefit from a heating device, the bedroom really did not matter. He was used to sleeping in a cold room. Anne was greatly impressed by the young man's attitude and decided there and then to put in central heating in the entire second floor and also to install a proper kitchenette.

As might be expected, this venture caused more contacts between Anne and Kim, more visits and discussions. When the workmen arrived, Kim had no way of cooking for a few days and it seemed natural for Anne to offer him hospitality during that inconvenient period. Having a cup of coffee or tea together became a habit. They started to get to know each other. Anne was interested in the young man's ideas on art, on life. Kim, by nature not very communicative, unbent a little. In consequence, even when the work was finished and there was no particular reason to continue the tentative association, a new routine set in. On coming from the art college, Kim would drop in on Anne and have a cup of coffee. Sometimes in the evening, if there was an interesting programme on television, Anne would call up the stairs and invite him down. Quite often he would join her, depending on his mood. If he was working well, he would excuse himself. If on the other hand nothing seemed to come right and a mood of despondency crept upon him, he would accept the invitation, to break out of his depression.

In time Anne began to realise that she was growing fond of the young artist, but her feelings for him were more of maternal concern rather than of physical attraction. Or so it seemed. But there again, not many people are willing to delve into their emotions if they even fractionally suspect an inadmissible truth. So much easier to ascribe them to one's generosity of nature, or goodness of heart. Anne was no exception. She policed her thoughts if they strayed on to the dangerous ground of planning her days so as to give her a greater opportunity of seeing Kim. She dismissed as irrelevant a slight tremor of excitement when Kim's head appeared round the door, as if he half expected to be asked in, to share a meal or just for an hour of gossip. The involvement happened so gradually that at no stage did it look anything more than the natural flow of events.

Kim was more and more relaxed in Anne's company. He became more articulate and found it quite natural to talk to Anne about the progress of his work, discussing with great feeling and seriousness his continuous inability to transfer his perception of reality to canvas. Anne listened and was happy. Sometimes she was not quite sure if she understood the unsolved dilemmas of an artistic soul, but was quite convinced that there was real force and talent behind Kim's struggles to express his truth.

On occasions they had much more prosaic conversations, about things to be done in the house and garden, the shopping, and as the familiarity increased more personal subjects became admissible. One of the things which Anne teased Kim about was his untidy, long hair, difficult to control, permanently (it seemed) in need of washing. And as Anne was quite an expert at cutting hair, Kim allowed her to shorten and subdue it. Anne fetched special scissors and began to comb through Kim's neglected and abundant locks. For the first time in their relationship she actually touched Kim's body. To get a better view of the job to be done she asked him to put his head forward and thus got a close view of the nape of his neck and the top of his shoulders exposed by the loose tee-shirt he was wearing. She actually put her hand on his left shoulder and at that moment, in a flash, the thought occurred to her that this young, unblemished body, so close to her, meant a terrible lot to her.

She realised that at the bottom of her concern for Kim there existed an overpowering attraction, a desire to hold that body, press it against her own, search its lips, wind her arms around the young man's neck and allow a long-forgotten, long-unused rapture to take over.

Anne never knew how she managed to complete the job of

cutting Kim's hair. She went on as if driven practically by instinct and was greatly relieved when it was finished and he left. She sat at the kitchen table, looking at the cuttings spread over the floor and suddenly said to herself aloud, 'I love that boy.' She was aghast at the idea yet overjoyed, confused and happy, devastated and in a way reborn.

What followed seemed to be preordained, not to be avoided. Whether it was the way Anne looked at Kim, or the way she smiled at him or emanated some strange allure, two nights later, lying in her comfortable bed, Anne heard the door half open – and suddenly she put out her arms and welcomed Kim into her bed, into her body, aware only of her need to be loved, to be cherished. Her lips uttered words long forgotten. The poetry of this encounter, its intensity, unleashed in her unknown resources, inexplicably the nobility of this unpremeditated experience obliterated reality.

The facts of her age, her position, the possible consequences were buried for the moment under an urgency and passion which Anne had never known before and could never explain or understand. That night a different Anne determined the course of events, cutting across the pattern of a lifetime.

For the next few days Anne did not see anything of Kim. She was too stupefied and unnerved by what had happened to seek him out. Anyway, she could not face him. Reaction set in. Recriminations within herself began. How could I? she asked herself over and over again. How am I going to face him now? A woman of 50 making advances to a young boy! She felt deeply ashamed and it was only in the far distant future that Anne could see the tragic, the romantic side of the whole incident.

When eventually Anne ventured to ascend the stairs to Kim's flat, she found it empty. Leaning against the wall was a painting. Anne stood before it and contemplated it. It was an abstract composition with a predominance of reds and yellows, somewhat softened by vertical strokes of light blue and deep turquoise. There were also some rare traces of white.

The composition seemed violent yet benevolent. There was a suggestion of sadness tinged with hope. A small card was attached to the picture. It said simply, 'Thank you'.

* * *

On the first-floor landing, facing the stairs, there hung an oblong painting. Abstract in composition, vivid in colouring, it was a suitable embellishment for its surroundings. Anne was not quite sure whether she liked it or not and often thought it should be taken down, yet she never actually made the move to dispose of it. It had meaning for her, although with time its significance had diminished and dimmed like the memories connected with it. Yet at the time she had hung it, she did it as a punishment for her only important lapse during an otherwise admirable, if dull, widowhood. She felt at that time that having to look at it every time she mounted the stairs would be a fitting retribution for straying from the virtue and respectability which she had been brought up to preserve and had practised most of her adult life. The guilt she felt then, the feeling of having betrayed her own principles, was over-whelming. Anne could not help but blush when she remembered the details, the lies she had fed herself on prior to her foolhardy behaviour. Sometimes she wondered if the whole thing was not a figment of her imagination, but just one look at the painting provided convincing proof of her guilt.

Looking at it now, she was able to feel a certain pity and forgiveness towards herself, yet still the painting had the power to make her shudder and wish it had never happened. A woman of 50, she thought to herself, getting so duped by pride as not to recognise the warning lights when they appeared. Where was my common sense? Where was my integrity? To get oneself so entangled as to lose all control! She didn't need anyone to make her feel guilty – she was the sternest prosecutor and judge possible – and yet, and yet, she couldn't take the painting down. Perhaps the memory of this sinful encounter held a certain sweetness at some deep level of

57

her subconscious, so that though it could never be admitted it must nevertheless be preserved.

XIII

There is no poetry in my life, concluded Anne as she momentarily stopped reading, on page 14, a slim volume of poems which a good friend of hers had written and presented to her when they met recently. These encounters happened less and less frequently because, as so often happens in life, their ways diverged as time went by. Since becoming a widow ten years before, Anne discovered that the circle of friends she and her husband had acquired in the past had diminished considerably, had in fact very nearly ceased to exist. So meeting her friend again, after not having seen him for ages, gave Anne tremendous pleasure. The newly published poems filled her with a wonderful longing for beauty and pure, unblemished poetic encounters, now, alas, sadly lacking in her life. Or so she thought.

How fortunate and privileged he is, mused Anne, to have preserved and nourished the capacity for transferring any theme, any object into a lucid poetic form, purged of any unnecessary distraction, but nevertheless speaking of those transient concepts which are difficult to express (or even to notice unless pointed out by a poet): feelings, impressions, reflections.

Anne was full of admiration yet at the same time strangely envious. In a way, it seemed very unfair that one person should be granted so much talent, the ability to do almost anything he liked with words – make them sound different, imbue them with new, unforeseen, unaccountable meaning and emotion – while others lacked the capacity for the simplest expression, or even the need for poetry. Anne envied the author the vast range of aesthetic experience which must have accompanied the creation of the lines she had just read. And yet the factual material of the lines presented here on paper by the poet were in themselves accessible to everyone.

They applied to happenings in which most people participated at one time or another. What, after all, was so extraordinary about the flight of a plane, the description of a forgotten street, a stone, a house one had stayed in?

Yet, in the hands of a poet, dozens of inner associations, undetected meanings and reflections were possible; they sounded authentic, true, engaged one's feelings, spoke to one's imagination. One just stood helpless in admiration not only for the perfection of form, but for what seemed to be the unlimited capacity of human invention.

So Anne thought, and as if in a vain attempt to try to compare and at the same time confirm her own prosaic existence, she recalled her day which had just ended. She was lying in bed now, her 'Bed of Roses', comfortably relaxed with a book in her hands. Her day had certainly been busy: shopping in the morning, cooking her solitary lunch, before entertaining her four-year-old grandson to tea. She collected him from his home, giving his mother Stella a chance to do some literary work – her present interest. The boy liked coming to tea and was easily strapped into his safety seat in the back of the car. On the way Anne stopped to fill up with petrol and, turning round, discovered that her grandson had fallen asleep. When she got home she was in two minds what to do. She knew better than to pick him up, as experience had shown that when woken from his afternoon nap the child would not easily adjust. He would be fractious for a long time, half crying, half dozing off. The only solution was to let him sleep at least for an hour and hope he would wake up by himself in a rosy mood.

Leaving him in the back seat, Anne did some gardening, looking every now and then into the car window. But the boy slept on. Eventually she decided to try to wake him, so, singing very softly, she sat herself next to the child in the back of the car. She unfastened the safety strap and reached for him, intending to give him an ample cuddle and the reassurance of her closeness.

Alas, the child only opened his eyes, stretched his arms to Anne, turned over and settled to another doze in her arms,

59

nestling his head in the crook of her neck and shoulder, pressing against her bosom. The back of his lovely curly head was all she could see. His curls, slightly damp with perspiration, tightened even more, but still retained the golden, angelic colour. His body pressed against Anne's chest with that genuine, trusting abandon of which only children are capable. It felt heavy, yet at the same time full of contained vitality. Anne sensed that she was holding something precious on her lap, not in terms of family relationships, but in wider human terms. A kernel of life, full of potential to be revealed in future, yet already present within this body, at once relaxed and yet abounding with energy. In fact, Anne had a vague feeling that she was holding life itself within her arms.

In her confined position all she could do was to wait for a while longer. She glanced momentarily out of the car window, through which she could see only a rectangle of very blue sky and in one corner some greenery. The thought occurred to her that within her limited vision she perceived a quintessence of the universe itself: a reminder of space, nature and eternal energy. It was indeed a view to behold. I must never forget this experience,' resolved Anne, who was generally a thrifty person as regards memories. But this feeling of things ultimate must never be buried irretrievably. She firmly instructed her brain to comply: this feeling must remain available to be recalled whenever the meaning of life might seem to lose its point.

Anne lay in her bed for a long time with her eyes closed. Sleep was late in coming. Then, she was falling asleep with the open volume of poems still in her hands. She did not finish reading them that evening . . . Perhaps my life is not altogether devoid of poetry after all, was her last conscious thought.

XIV

When Anne received an invitation a couple of years previously to spend a week in Venice, she was overjoyed. The invitation came from her daughter and son-in-law, Stella and Peter, who were going to Italy that summer. Anne knew Venice fairly well, having been there twice with her late husband. She had most pleasant memories of her previous trips and often used to talk about them. It was probably the great joy and undiminished enthusiasm of these reminiscences that prompted her daughter to propose the trip. Anne was overwhelmed by the invitation for several reasons. She had accepted a long time ago that her travelling days were over, yet without realising it herself, she badly needed some change in her uneventful life. This opportunity made her aware of how great her need was. She was also moved by the generosity shown to her by Stella and Peter, who, while not exactly poor, must have dipped into their savings to finance such an undertaking.

For these reasons Anne started thinking about the approaching journey with a zest and alacrity which she had long forgotten. There were so many things to be attended to: lists to be made of what to take, what to remember to settle before leaving. Old habits and procedures, adhered to on previous trips abroad, came to mind, certain do's and don'ts were recalled, her wardrobe had to be examined, perhaps augmented. And, of course, her straw hat had to be looked out and the ribbon, faded and frayed, replaced. The hat had gone with Anne on all her travels, each year refurbished with the predominant colour of her wardrobe. This task and other similar ones occupied the last two weeks before the journey, filling Anne with thrilled anticipation, as if the great event was already under way.

Anne was to meet her family in Venice; they were setting out a couple of weeks earlier, to spend some time with friends who lived permanently in Italy. Travelling on her own only added spice to the already promising adventure. She was to arrive at Marco Polo airport and make her way by herself to the hotel. Whether by design or by coincidence, she was booked into the same hotel in which she had stayed on her last visit, so she could envisage her journey from start to finish.

Things went smoothly enough. The plane was on time and the water bus not too crowded. Anne had very little luggage and could give her attention to the ever-nearing vistas of her favourite city as she crossed the lagoon from the mainland. There was even the slight mist, so common in Venice at that time of day, just before sunset. The familiar outlines looked as enticing as in her memory. 'Nothing has changed – except me,' Anne whispered to herself, and was at the same time both glad and sad.

Later that evening she met her family. They dined together and planned the forthcoming holiday. As everybody seemed to have a different priority as to what to see and when, they decided unanimously to sightsee on their own, meeting every evening to have a meal together and compare notes. This solution suited Anne admirably, for above all else, out of the things she wanted to do and see, was the desire to absorb and carry away with her the special atmosphere which pervades Venice. She was well aware that this would be her last visit, so she wanted to take back home not only aesthetic memories, but something much more poignant. Being more and more confined to the house, not being able to travel even short distances with ease, with eyesight that had started to fail quite alarmingly, for her, Venice was the perfect place to say goodbye to the sight of beauty.

Anne decided to beat the crowds of tourists by going out early in the morning. The local fishermen and vendors did not interfere with her vision of Venice; on the contrary, they were part of the city. For a few days everything was wonderful. Venice, early in the morning, looked fresh and rested. The streets and piazzas – obviously cleaned that very morning – were washed down and still shone with minute pools of water in the bright sunshine. The canals were only beginning their daily trade and most of the gondolas, still tied up at their moorings, were gently lapped by the incoming waves. All around there was still a fair degree of tranquillity – and even the Piazza San Marco seemed to belong mainly to the pigeons and a handful of early visitors.

When the sun became really hot and throngs of tourists obscured the familiar yet unique buildings, Anne sought refuge inside the Basilica. Seated somewhere in a darkish corner, she examined the famous mosaics over and over again, surprised anew by their richness of theme, the inclusion of so many animals and birds into one glorious design. She found similar places to hide, treasures less well known so that in fact she only now discovered them for the first time. Or she would take the water bus to the northern shallows and inhale the smells and sounds of the true Venice.

It also became a habit for Anne to go for a short stroll after dinner, sometimes with her daughter, sometimes alone. Then she would find a convenient stone or a step in one of the small piazzas, still warmed by the now absent sun. There she would sit and watch the people passing by, particularly the young ones, because they put her in mind of her first visit to Venice.

As the night deepened there would be fewer and fewer people about, but that didn't worry Anne. She felt strangely secure, at home. On the evening before the last, when part of her was already beginning to regret the necessity to leave and say goodbye to these rediscovered feelings and emotions, Anne found herself a convenient niche in one of the small piazzas. She sat with her back against a pillar and, hearing rather than seeing the ever-present nearness of water, became aware of a pair of lovers walking, or rather strolling very slowly, with their arms round each other, crossing the bridge, stopping to look into the waters of the canal, where the lights from the adjacent palazzi were reflected in ever-changing patterns. Anne smiled to herself. It seemed specially arranged for her benefit. Memories crowded back: the timing, the feelings, the gestures. The young lovers were obviously not aware of the presence of anyone else and talked rather loudly (in Italian, which Anne could follow).

There was some silly flirting going on, with giggles and laughter. Anne felt that it was too late now to get up and walk away, leaving the otherwise empty piazza to the couple. Flattening herself against the pillar in front of which she was sitting, she became a witness to what became a nightmare. For the young man suddenly started to accuse his companion of duplicity. His words grew sharper and sharper. He quoted

63

occasions on which, apparently, his girlfriend had mis-
behaved, and furthermore he accused her of being in
collusion with his enemies. The girl vigorously denied
everything. At first she sounded rather disdainful, but as the
quarrel progressed and more and more facts were produced
to substantiate the accusations, her tone changed. She
sounded angry, told her companion that she was her own boss
and questioned his right to demand loyalty from her, when he
himself was a known liar and probably a police informer.

Anne didn't know who struck the first blow, but suddenly
there was a loud scream and then another. A fight ensued, and
from the sound of it the girl was giving as good as she was
receiving. Anne was terrified. What if this unsavoury couple
should discover her? She put her dark shawl in front of her
face to lessen the chance of being discovered. She was afraid
that the lightness of her face would give her away in the
deepening shades of nightfall.

The struggle went on. It intensified, came nearer and nearer
to the bank of the canal, which was protected only by a low
wall. There was the sound of a resounding blow, the body of
one of the participants toppled over the wall and Anne heard a
loud splash, followed by a succession of rapid footsteps. A
figure in dark clothes rushed past her. Quiet descended. Anne
could not tell which of the two had fallen in. Both had been
wearing trousers and dark jumpers. Terrified, she could not
move. Was the victim dead, or could he or she have survived
and be trying now to get away quietly? Could they swim?
Eventually, Anne got up suddenly, walked to the bank of the
canal and peered into its dark water. There was nothing to be
seen, no movement, nothing to hear. She didn't know what to
do. Should she report the matter to the police? But what
matter? She had no proof that anything had happened. It was
doubtful that anyone would believe her.

It seemed so unfair that such an experience should happen
to her just a day before leaving. Anne went back to her hotel
room, not saying a word to anyone, and started packing.
Suddenly Venice had ceased to be an enchanted place, an
idealised paradise, and became just a conglomeration of

people, all sorts of people, good and bad, possessing virtues and vices.

'I must go home quickly,' Anne said to herself, 'before I stop believing in beauty.'

XV

With the help of a magnifying glass Anne reread the letter which had landed on the hall mat that morning. The stamp was Canadian and that in itself was puzzling. Offhand, Anne couldn't think of anyone she knew in Canada, but a look at the signature soon provided the answer. The letter was from Veronica, a distant cousin who, having met a handsome Canadian during the Second World War, got engaged to him and soon after the armistice joined him in Canada, to the general disapproval of both families, who considered her action foolhardy. With the passing of years even the exchange of Christmas cards ceased, and to tell the truth Anne had not thought about Veronica for a very long time.

And now here was a letter inquiring after Anne's health and general well-being and mentioning that in the near future Veronica's granddaughter was to be visiting the old country. Could she possibly stay with Anne for a fortnight? The girl was travelling 'on the cheap' and could hardly afford the price of hotels.

Anne pondered over the letter. It was a considerable time since anyone had stayed in the house with her. The last person had been Kim, and that thought brought back some mixed, if not downright sad, memories. Also, having a stranger with her on the first floor was not acceptable because really she didn't think she could bear anybody sharing her own bathroom or occupying what had been Stella's room, because – oh, there were so many reasons. But the most important one was that she simply didn't fancy a stranger being very close to her own quarters – it would mean reopening the second floor, which for years had been left out of anything one could call care and attention.

She could, of course, refuse. On the other hand, the second floor was so self-contained that it wouldn't really be too much trouble having the girl to stay, after the initial cleaning and setting to rights of the place. She would have to ask Stella to find someone to do the job; Anne didn't think she could consider accomplishing it on her own. Stella was bound to be against the whole idea, calling it an imposition and suggesting Anne should refuse to comply with the request. But in a perverse way, after a while Anne began to enjoy the thought of someone staying with her, although she had some reservations as to whether the young person would prove compatible with the slow, quiet routine to which she herself had become accustomed.

But before Anne could put any of her plans into operation, she was woken up early one morning by the prolonged ringing of the front doorbell. It took her some time to realise that it was her doorbell that was being so resolutely pressed. Still full of sleep, she put on her dressing gown and slippers and made her way downstairs to the front door, which she opened a few inches, leaving the chain on. There she discovered the shapes of what seemed to be two giants but proved to be two girls with enormous high-riding rucksacks on their backs. The girls explained who they were and with visible relief put down their heavy burdens. They started to apologise for the unexpected early arrival, which as far as Anne could gather was done for reasons of economy, air fares being due to go up to peak rates in two weeks' time for the holiday season.

Anne asked the girls in, mentioning in passing that she was expecting only one guest, to which her young relative replied that she had 'palled up' with the other girl on the flight, and on finding that she had no place to stay in London had invited her to stay with her 'aunt', at least for a short time till she could get herself somewhere else to go. She hoped she hadn't overstepped the mark, but she was sure Anne would understand.

The girls were very tired, and happily relaxed over cups of tea. Seemingly they felt immediately at home and more or less took over the situation. Anne was no match for them; in some way she was amused and old habits of hospitality reasserted themselves. After their tea she showed them where they were to sleep – apologising for the dusty and fusty look of the rooms, but, after all, they hadn't given her a chance to get ready.

The girls didn't mind. They asked where she kept the bedlinen, made up the twin beds in one of the rooms, had showers and in no time were fast asleep, leaving Anne not quite believing that the whole thing had actually happened. It had the features of a somewhat nightmarish dream from which she would wake at any moment, but the two bulky rucksacks left there in the hall convinced her that her visitor, or rather visitors, had definitely arrived. It seemed that Anne had no choice but to accept the situation and hope that things would look more normal later in the day when she got to know the girls – Lucy and Emma – better.

Anne was to remember the Canadian visit for a long time. Not that the girls were objectionable in any particular way, rather they brought with them a way of life which was utterly alien to Anne, which she could not understand and could hardly tolerate. Transistor radio music (if one could call it music) was never absent when they were around, but that only really worried Anne when they came down into the kitchen to prepare some sort of meal for themselves (she gave up trying to cater for them after one day). The timing of meals was most unpredictable since the girls seemed to start their day around noon and end it in the small hours of the morning. That, of course, could be explained by the relaxed, leisurely mood of a holiday, but what Anne found absolutely incomprehensible was a total lack of respect or decorum in their dealings with their hostess. They often confronted her in a state of semi-nudity, they never asked her how she felt about them bringing their friends (who were they?) in for a meal or to 'doss down'. Anne never knew how many of them were staying on the second floor, nor was it unknown to come into the kitchen and find her larder (poorly stocked at the best of times) completely emptied. It was true that the next day they would try to replace the consumed milk, bread or cheese, but in the meantime Anne had to go without breakfast or substitute it with cream crackers and milkless tea.

Something of the sort happened one evening in the presence of Stella, who had dropped in on her mother. Stella could hardly contain her anger, called her mother a fool and next day, unannounced, let herself into the house, went to the second floor and had it out with the uninvited guests. She was certainly shocked both by the state of the rooms and by the condition of its inhabitants; the floor was covered with sleeping bags and some six or more tousled heads stuck out of them. Some straight talking took place, some promises were made, some excuses and assurances that they would be out of Anne's house very soon, even within the week. Only then did Stella make her appearance in Anne's kitchen, glad to convey the news and saying she would keep on coming in to make quite sure that the visitors had departed as promised.

Anne felt rather relieved, yet at the same time a bit embarrassed. Somehow the virtue of hospitality, which she acquired early in life, made her wince at the drastic means employed by Stella. She devoutly wished there could have been a friendlier, more civilised ending to the whole affair. Now she only hoped the young people would depart speedily, that having been told to go, they would comply and not require further confrontations – perhaps scenes with Stella intervening, or the undignified solution of having to lock the unwanted guests out, as Stella had threatened to do if necessary.

A couple of days passed. There seemed to be a slight diminishing in the numbers of visitors to the second floor, and on the third day the two girls appeared in the kitchen, looking less sure of themselves than usual. After a few hesitant words they disclosed their reason for approaching Anne. They had promised to go and would like to keep their word, but the fact was they had no money for their fares home. When they started their so-called holiday they bought only the outward flight tickets, meaning to work in some capacity in London and earn their fares home. But what with one thing and another, they never really got down to looking seriously for jobs, earning only enough to get by. So now they were in a difficult position. Where to get money for the air tickets? Could Anne lend them the money?

Anne was quite speechless for a moment. She was not sure she had understood correctly, and only the hollow silence which suddenly descended after this extraordinary proposition brought home to Anne the possible alternatives. She could pay or she could let herself in for a stormy, prolonged and extremely unpleasant situation. She thought for a few moments, trying to find a way out that would somehow rescue her from this quite unforeseen quandary, but her mind refused to provide her with any solution. There was the fact, about which there was no doubt, no mistake: the girls were blackmailing her. Under the circumstances, there were only two possibilities: pay and regain her peace and tranquillity, or endure a most upsetting experience – and, who knows, perhaps even abuse.

She gazed for a while at these rather nice, ordinary-looking girls, who though they had often confused her, even shocked her, had never before filled her with such a feeling of distaste, not to say an undefined alarm. Then she asked quietly: 'How much?'

When Stella appeared at the end of the week, all was in order in Anne's house. Stella examined the second-floor flat and pronounced that no great damage had been done; she promised she would see to it that the rooms were cleaned and set to rights. 'You see, Mother' – Stella looked at Anne with an expression of superiority – 'in life you need to assert yourself.'

XVI

That evening Anne retired early. She made her way upstairs as usual, counting the steps and keeping her ailing eyes closed. She had to stop a couple of times on the way to recover her breath. Yes, it was true, the stairs were getting too much for her, the house too – just as Stella had said. In the time it took her to reach the first-floor landing, she had made up her mind. Now was the moment to give up the accustomed, solitary, but self-chosen way of living, to quit, to get rest at last in more convivial surroundings. It was impossible to disregard her ailments any longer, pretend she could go on. At last Anne admitted defeat.

In some ways, once she had made up her mind she felt relieved. For some time now she had been conscious of feelings of breathlessness and tightness across her chest at practically any exertion. These disturbing symptoms had increased lately, making it virtually impossible for her to lead an existence which could be even remotely described as normal. For the last few months, Anne had ceased to cook proper meals, living mostly on toast and tea, supplemented by a few ready-prepared dishes, bought for her by the home help when she came to clean the house. Anne would not avail herself of Meals on Wheels because, as she put it, she 'disliked being watched by do-gooders'. There was still a streak of obstinacy in Anne.

On her last visit Stella had got really upset, called her mother a difficult old troublemaker and refused to take responsibility for any unexpected calamity that might befall Anne if she persisted in her unshakeable determination to live on her own. Stella sympathised with her mother's need for independence, ever-present since the death of her husband – and that was going back a good many years. Yet Stella felt that something must be decided about her mother's precarious existence, not just in the near future, but now. She said that the time for gentle persuasion was over, for all the good it would do, and some drastic action must be taken. She practically gave Anne an ultimatum: either Anne must give way gracefully or else the social services would be contacted and asked to intervene. Anne thought back over this conversation and the memory of the implied threat still made her very angry. She had sat upright in the armchair, sulking, with averted head, listening to her daughter's tirade, knowing full well that she was in the right yet refusing to acknowledge the truth.

She felt that the decision to move must be made by her and by her alone, must come from within her. And quite suddenly, in some perverse way, while making the difficult climb upstairs this evening, this decision became the reality for Anne. It felt as if a bitter and painful fruit had been ripening all this time within her breast, somewhere in her consciousness, and just now, at that very moment, it burst open – and thus inexplicably, miraculously, it stopped hurting. (Or it could perhaps be described as a painful abscess or a tumour that nobody could lance but oneself?)

So be it – Anne made her way into the bathroom. She had to sit down to rest because the pain in her chest had become too intense to ignore. After a while she started the evening rituals of her toilette. She washed her face, put on some night cream and began groping for her toothbrush but could not locate it. 'It must be here somewhere,' she whispered to herself. And in trying to find it, her hand, moving awkwardly, managed to overturn the toothmug and several other objects standing in close proximity on the window sill. They all fell to the floor with a clatter. This is getting impossible, thought Anne, kneeling down and retrieving all, or most of, the fallen items. She was not terribly concerned, she was too tired to prolong the search and, anyway, the home help was coming the next day and would no doubt pick up any remaining bits and pieces.

At last she found the toothbrush and mug, cleaned her teeth and, feeling greatly relieved at having achieved this test of self-reliance, entered her bedroom. She undressed slowly, putting her garments and underwear in orderly fashion on the chair by her bed, so that there would be no frustrating search for stockings and such items next morning. To tell the truth, it was rather difficult to keep her mind on what she was doing, because she felt a bit confused and at the same time strangely excited at the prospect of winding up her abode of so many years, so many memories, so much good and bad that had occurred in this house over the last 40 years. Stella will have her work cut out – getting rid of all this accumulated junk,

71

Anne mused. It seemed to her as being reasonable, even imperative, that if she was to go, then she must leave memories behind, go without taking the long-cherished, now faded and even bizarre-looking memorabilia which had cluttered and filled her house to overflowing. It will be easier that way, she continued her unspoken monologue. If I can't take everything with me, I shall take nothing.

She happily slipped on her nightgown and lay down on her bed, under the familiar 'Bed of Roses' cover, stretched her weary legs and stayed thus for a few moments. She shut her eyes and tried to imagine where would be her new home. Some institution, no doubt, for the elderly; just one room with a television (if she was lucky), meals eaten in the communal dining room, afternoon tea taken in the lounge, days all very much alike, nights rescued by the power of the magic sleeping pill. 'Well, so be it,' she repeated. She smoothed down the familiar counterpane, still full of faded roses, her faithful companion. But I will certainly take that with me, Anne vowed.

She switched on the radio and listened to some music. Never being able to remember the names of particular compositions, she only satisfied her ears with the sound – it was familiar, reassuring, nostalgic. It made her feel more relaxed and ready to take the sleeping pill. She was about to switch off the bedside lamp when something made her stop. She hesitated and, sitting up in bed, took a long, careful look at her surroundings. She saw only shapes because of her diminished eyesight and the poor lighting, but this was perhaps the right way to look at her cherished possessions. They gave the impression of being already in the past, half-forgotten, of having lost their power to tie her down to what now seemed to be an eternity of refusal to accept change. In a little while, Anne switched off the lamp, crossed herself, turned off the radio, and slowly sank into oblivion.

That night she had a strange dream. It was really more than a dream, it was a series of tableaux, extremely vivid, fascinating, galvanising. She was a child again. It was summer and she was wearing her favourite blue dress with a white

72

collar. It was getting late and she was far from home. She was trying to get back from somewhere; her mother was waiting for her in the garden, sitting in the same armchair in which she died. But Anne found great difficulty in getting to her.

She was standing at the top of a seemingly endless staircase, burdened by what at first seemed to be toys and then turned out to be odd-looking packages, cases, bags. She could hardly carry them all, she could not make any progress in descending the staircase and yet she didn't want to let go of any of them. They were very precious to her, necessary, part of her, yet they prevented her from making her way down to where she knew her mother was sitting.

It made Anne feel very frustrated, ill even, the distance she had to cover and the inconvenience of all this luggage she carried with her. The situation was getting beyond her strength. What should I do? she thought feverishly – she could not let go of anything and yet she must have one hand free to hold on to the bannister, otherwise she would never manage all those flights of stairs. In desperation she let go of something and it clattered all the way down, at the same time giving Anne the chance to descend a little. Encouraged by this progress, she let go of something else and quickened her steps. But she still had so many flights of stairs to cover, and she was getting tired. She felt her heart starting to beat more rapidly, the palms of her hands grew damp and clammy. In spite of herself she released some more packages; there was an enormous din as they rolled on, some breaking with a sound of shattering glass. She felt so guilty at letting go of these important, valuable items. Important to whom? Anne asked herself. But there was no answer, only an urgent, over-whelming necessity to get down those stairs because her mother was waiting – she might be cross or worried if Anne delayed her homecoming. Anne was fully conscious of the frantic beating of her heart, the drumming of the pulses in her head; she was getting more and more desperate.

Suddenly, she let go of everything; there was a tremendous clatter and clangour as bags, parcels, toys tumbled down the stairs and Anne followed them, free at last. She increased her speed. The stairs seemed to melt before her very eyes. She was running now, breathing very rapidly, gasping for air, with only one thought in her mind – I'll soon be in my mother's arms.

And at last she reached her. Her mother looked at her and smiled with that smile Anne remembered from childhood. There was love in it and kindness and promises of security. She held Anne to her breast, sat her on her lap and said in a warm, quiet voice, 'I had waited for you so long.' She put her arms around Anne and pressed her to her bosom again and Anne experienced a feeling, long forgotten, of belonging to someone in so many different ways. She picked up the familiar scent which seemed to be part of childhood, the avid trust which had an answer to all problems, all worries. The hurried breathing began to subside, the pressure of her mother's arms upon her, though heavy, made her feel secure, so secure. Her mother's voice sounded reassuringly in her ears and she suddenly recognised the restored spirit of early childhood – free from all constraints. There were no memories, good or bad – they never happened. There were no mistakes and no ugly deeds – they never occurred. There was nothing to regret and everything to delight in. The past had no meaning, there was only sunny today and rosy tomorrow. There was only summer and the blue dress and the future, trust, unspoken hope that life is what one makes of it.

And gradually Anne's heart regained its normal beat and then imperceptibly began to slow down. A pleasant lassitide invaded her body, thoughts grew less and less defined, a certain tiredness set in, the heart beat slower and slower, consciousness reached its limits. Then the heart stopped beating altogether.

AN OUNCE OF LUCK

The number 11 bus was very late. Very late. The three waiting would-be passengers got to such a state of exasperation that they were prepared to take notice of one another, if only to give vent to their frustration. The first to break the silence was Mrs Holt, who was also the first in line. She turned to the youngish chap in a raincoat and announced: 'Shocking, isn't it?' The man, somewhat surprised at being addressed, mumbled something which could have been broadly interpreted as agreement.

The last person in the queue, who looked like a retired shopkeeper, directed a question not necessarily at any one of his companions, but rather at large: 'Is it always so late? I am a comparative stranger here – we only moved in recently.' He looked as if he would be willing to enlarge on the subject, but at that state of the proceedings it was still too early for an actual conversation to ensue.

Silence reigned for a while and then Mrs Holt, seeing that the youngish chap was not going to reply, took the initiative and, half turning to face the questioner, said: 'Well, you will learn soon enough. Number eleven is murder, because it has to cross the centre.'

'Is that so?' The retired gentleman returned the compliment of being noticed.

At which the youngish chap piped in: 'Actually, it does not cross the town centre, it is the eighty-seven that does.'

Mrs Holt didn't like to be contradicted. Assuming a slightly hurt expression, she answered back: 'You must be mistaken, I am sorry to say. I have been taking the number eleven for the last twenty years and I assure you it crosses the town each time round,' she finished, on a rather ironical note.

That put paid to any further discourse, so it was with relief that the trio boarded the bus which had at last emerged from around the corner.

Mrs Holt got on first and made for one of the seats in the front, the youngish chap raced upstairs, but the retired gentleman followed Mrs Holt, and after inquiring if she minded, sat next to her. 'At least one gets a seat,' he added.

'That is because we are near the end of its run. I get out at the last stop.'

'So do I. Do you live here? I ask because we bought a bungalow in Denver Road,' volunteered the retired gentleman.

'Oh, that's one road down from where I live. You're the people who bought old Mrs Kenny's bungalow?'

'Yes, that's right. But of course I didn't meet Mrs Kenny, she passed on well before. We only dealt with the agent.'

'Of course. Poor Mrs Kenny. She was very poorly at the end. All alone and hardly able to move.'

The conversation came to a close, as the end of the line had been reached. The two got off and said their goodbyes, since they were walking in opposite directions.

On reaching the house Mrs Holt quickly took off her coat and put the kettle on. She then pushed off her shoes, and over the freshly made cup of tea considered the situation. She was just back from visiting her husband, George, in hospital. These days, what with short days and the threat of mugging, she visited him in the afternoons. George wasn't getting better as quickly as she would have liked. There was a new setback – a chest infection – on top of other things. She had felt quite put out when the nurse told her. Oh well, with the antibiotics it should clear soon enough.

She forced herself to change the train of her thoughts. This man on the bus seems nice enough, and well mannered. That's good, we don't want just anybody in the neighbourhood. He said 'we' when he mentioned buying the bungalow,

76

so there must be a wife somewhere. I hope she is nice.

Next morning Mrs Holt rang the estate agents who had sold Mrs Kenny's bungalow. She knew one of the girls in the office, so it was fairly easy to discover the name of the purchaser. The new owners were Mr and Mrs Arnold, and he was a retired greengrocer.

On Sunday afternoon, when Mrs Holt went to the hospital, she found George rather poorly. The antibiotics didn't work. They were switching him to another one, but in the meantime George felt very sorry for himself. She stayed longer than usual, trying to cheer him up, and it was getting dark when she left. In her haste she nearly collided with Mr Arnold, right in the entrance. They were both unsure how to behave but Mrs Holt, being rather forthright in her manner, asked him straight away what he was doing in the hospital.

'Visiting my wife,' came the reply. 'She was taken ill soon after we moved in. Are you on your way home?'

'Yes,' said Mrs Holt, and so they set off together, discussing the state of health of their respective spouses. They were lucky with the bus, and soon reached their destinations. They were about to take leave of each other when Mr Arnold said, 'By the way, my name is Arnold,' to which Mrs Holt replied, 'And I'm Mrs Holt.'

From then on these two people, temporarily left on their own, often met on the way from the hospital. In a way, they enjoyed their bus ride back home and became quite friendly. In fact, Mrs Holt was several times on the point of inviting him in for a cup of tea, but was afraid of being miscontrued, so she decided to forgo her generous gesture. That is, until one afternoon, a particularly nasty, rainy day in October, when she chanced on Mr Arnold at the bus stop and noticed that he looked rather depressed, upset. 'How is your wife?' she inquired, but all Mr Arnold did was shake his head.

When they alighted at the last stop, she went up to him and suggested he came in and told her all about it. To her surprise he agreed, and soon was warming his hands around the mug of hot, strong tea. But he didn't say much. Apparently Gina, his wife, had had a breast removed five years ago. Since then

77

she had been fine, so they had sold the business and moved to the seaside for their retirement. But on a recent check-up a new shadow was discovered on her lung. She had some treatment, and seemed stable, but the outlook was poor.

There was little Mrs Holt could say, especially as she had been given rather good news that afternoon concerning George. He was recovering quite well now; the hip replacement was a success, the chest infection over, he should be coming home soon.

Mr Arnold didn't stay long. He thanked her most politely and left, taking with him the sad uncertainty which he had no one to share with. Mrs Holt was quite upset. Poor man, she thought, uprooting himself and not quite knowing where to turn.

So she was quite glad to see him on her doorstep one morning a week later and, with great sincerity, asked if she could help him in any way. 'Yes,' he replied, 'that is why I'm here. I have to go and see my married son who has got himself in some financial trouble again. There is a small baby there, so we can't let things rip. Would you be so kind as to visit my wife while I am away? It will only be for a few days. Perhaps you could get her some flowers, or grapes. Here is some money. I know it's asking a lot, but you are at the hospital every day anyway. Would your husband spare you for a few minutes, do you think?'

'Of course, Mr Arnold. I shall be glad to meet your wife and make her welcome. Don't worry a bit. You go and sort out your son's problems. I promise I shall keep my eye on your wife.'

And indeed she did. George was coming home by the end of the week and did not need her uninterrupted attention all afternoon. He was now fully mobile, though still using a crutch. The very first afternoon she was in hospital she went to Ward 3, having bought a few roses on the way, and introduced herself to Mrs Arnold.

Mrs Holt was quite unprepared for what she found. Although not looking at all well, Mrs Arnold was obviously a beautiful woman. Her hair, full of tight curls, looking like new growth, provided a perfect setting for Gina Arnold's face. A perfectly oval face, distinguished by a straight, narrow nose and eyes of exceptional brilliance. They were deep violet, framed above by regular brows, while the long curved eyelashes completed the picture. As she smiled, accepting the flowers, she seemed to exude such vitality, buoyancy and joy that Mrs Holt's heart contracted at the thought of the vulnerability of this extraordinary creature. She did not stay long, but promised to come each day and keep in touch – perhaps do some laundering – till Mr Arnold's return.

Several days passed, but there was no sign of him. George came home, and Mrs Holt found herself obliged to visit Gina, as she started to call Mr Arnold's wife, particularly as the poor woman was getting quite worried about the lack of news from her husband. She asked Mrs Holt if she would get in touch with her son to find the reason for the delay. But when Mrs Holt managed to get through, she discovered that Mr Arnold had not been to see him. As the rather unfriendly young man put it: 'The old stick has not been near us for the last two years.'

That certainly caused consternation all round. What was going to happen? Gina was seriously ill, George was still convalescing at home and Mrs Holt was right in the middle of some drama. She discussed it at length with George and next day with Gina, who couldn't give any explanation. 'Excuse me, Gina,' said Mrs Holt, 'has your husband ever done anything like this before?'

'No, never . . . that is, yes, once, ages ago. I had quite forgotten. He stayed away for two or three weeks when his first business collapsed. It was a nervous breakdown, or something.' Gina thought for a while and then, since she was a plucky woman, in spite of her many troubles, announced that she would try to get into a convalescent home. The hospital didn't want to keep her any longer. 'I'm sorry for the inconvenience Arnold caused you. I shall be as quick as I can in arranging my affairs.'

Next time Mrs Holt saw Gina, practically everything had been settled. The only thing needed was for someone to go to the bungalow to fetch some warmer clothes and a coat, and it was decided that Mrs Holt and George would do it next day.

'I will need the key,' said Mrs Holt.

'But I haven't got one,' exclaimed poor Gina, and for the first time she broke into tears.

'Never mind, please don't worry,' – Mrs Holt tried to sound reassuring – 'we have a locksmith friend who, I'm sure, will oblige.'

And so the next day George drove his wife to the Arnolds' bungalow. The locksmith was late, and Mrs Holt waited in the car for his arrival. 'The lawn certainly needs cutting,' remarked George, getting out of the car and with the help of a stick proceeding towards the front door. He gave it a push and, surprisingly, it gave way. It was on the latch. George went in, stayed for a few moments and then rushed out as quickly as his condition would allow him. Mrs Holt started to get out of the car, seeing him to be in such a hurry and visibly upset, but he shouted, 'Get back, get back, this is a job for the police.'

The police took over. On the way to the house George explained that there was no doubt Mr Arnold had committed suicide. He had left a note – 'Can't face Gina's end'.

'What shall we tell Gina?' asked the terrified Mrs Holt.

'Nothing, let her think he is coming back. She might not last all that long.'

And George was right. Gina suddenly took a turn for the worse and died three days later from a massive heart attack.

Mr and Mrs Arnold were cremated on the same day. There were only three mourners – the objectionable Arnold junior, who seemed to be more upset about there being a delay in putting the bungalow on the market because of some sanitary regulations than at the loss of his parents, and George and Hanna Holt, the providers of the only floral tribute.

Hanna wept right through the service. When it was over, and they were speeding home in a taxi, she sat enclosed in George's arms and still wept. 'It's all over, dear girl,' George kept saying. 'It's all over for them. In a way they were lucky to have found you. What would they have done without you? Hush, dear.'

But Hanna only drew nearer to him and kept repeating, 'Thank God you are still here. Thank God we are still together.'

THE RED DRESS

Ellen had not felt so bad for a long time as she did that morning. As soon as she woke up she knew it was going to be a bad day, and was sure it would get worse as soon as her feet touched the floor. She made an effort, and stood hesitantly by the bed. The usual nausea immediately appeared and so did the ringing in her ears. And then the feeling of panic. Unaccountable, but pervading her whole body.

I must take my pill as soon as possible, she mused. She directed her unsteady steps towards the bathroom, clutching at convenient objects on the way. She knew from experience that if she did not give in, things would improve as the day wore on.

Why do I feel so ghastly? she wondered. Particularly now, when the situation was on the mend. True, she had been under considerable stress for the last few weeks but, things being equal, she could expect a much easier passage in the near future. Leonard's bender had taken place a fortnight ago; he was now safely home, recuperating. They were well over the painful stage of remorse, anguish and excuses. The placatory flowers arrived a few days ago and Leonard had promised to mend his behaviour. It seemed they would be able to pick up the threads of life again . . . and hope for a miracle.

Leonard was a good husband, father, provider. In the long days of their marriage it would be difficult to find a particular time when Ellen had been unhappy. Then, at 55, Leonard, a successful businessman, having amassed a small fortune, sold his business and retired.

It was from that moment that things went wrong. No more than a social drinker, he let the bottle acquire supremacy. It started with prolonged visits to the pubs nearby. Then in the last few years it had deteriorated into monthly benders, when Leonard would disappear for two or three days, arriving back in a sorry state, his clothes soiled with dirt and vomit, fit only to be thrown into a dustbin. He would be unshaven, very smelly and invariably deeply sorry. Ellen tried to remonstrate, lock him out of the house. She contacted AA, doctors, psychologists, all to no avail. There would be a slight improvement, perhaps a pause in the frequency of Leonard's behaviour, but sooner or later things would deteriorate. There was nothing left for Ellen but to wait for his return (sometimes wishing it would not happen) and then, when he appeared, run the bath, throw away the soiled clothes, and keep her thoughts to herself.

I should have left him as soon as I realised that he was an addict, she sometimes regretted. But where would she go? How could she reveal the truth to the whole world without feeling humiliated, a total failure? As long as her mental stamina and nerves could endure such an existence, it seemed a preferable choice. Particularly because Leonard was never violent. On the contrary, he sought Ellen's forgiveness on many an occasion, promising to change, to break the vile habit which spoiled their life.

Ellen decided to go out. It was sales time. Perhaps she would distract herself from her ailments by taking a look at some clothes and seeing people, break the continuous trend of her thoughts, which sooner or later would lead her to contemplate the future. She knew from experience that if she stopped to put on her make-up or hesitate over what to wear, her resolve to get out would falter, even disappear. So, putting on her coat and snatching up her purse, she made for the station and the West End.

The stores were packed. Ellen felt a bit confused and was unable at first to find the right department. She wandered here and there, not quite able to focus on any particular display. But after a while she regained her bearings and stopped at several stands which boldly advertised fantastic reductions. One stand in particular attracted her attention. It contained a selection of French dresses, rather pricey, even though offered at a 50 per cent reduction, but nonetheless dresses of undeniable distinction.

Ellen examined them for several minutes and regretfully decided they were too expensive. She moved on, but somehow found the merchandise on nearby rails, by comparison, lacking in elegance, of inferior design, uninspiring. She went back to the selection of French dresses, handled one or two, admired their style, but decided against trying any of them on, mentally attempting to impose the discipline of her usual thrift.

But she started to waver. There was one in particular, a coral-red dress, which especially appealed to her. It had a most delectable neckline, a sort of crossover, ending in three buttons, a half-belt in the back and deliciously flowing folds right down to the hemline. A dream dress.

An eager French assistant approached and politely inquired if madam would like to try the red dress, which only showed its remarkable merits if draped over a person, being cut on the cross-weave.

Ellen acquiesced. Why, she argued with herself, trying on doesn't mean buying. The dress might lose its appeal when actually on one's body. But, of course, the opposite happened. Ellen looked at herself in the mirror and realised she must have that dress. For some unexplained reason the dress acquired a mysterious quality, somehow connected with her state of mind. It seemed to become a good omen, heralding a change in her circumstances. Wholly instinctively Ellen imbued the dress with magical properties. She could actually distinguish a voice in her head saying: 'As long as you wear this dress Leonard will keep sober.'

And indeed, wear it she did. As soon as she got home she changed into the red dress, swearing never to take it off. Leonard complimented her on the new acquisition; so did others. Ellen wore it proudly, every two or three evenings washing it and putting it on next morning, since the dress dried very quickly and did not require ironing.

One week passed, and another. Ellen's panics totally disappeared. Leonard stayed quietly at home, spending a lot of time in the garden or on some maintenance jobs around the house. Ellen made an appointment with the hairdresser, bought make-up to match the dress and made contact with some of her friends, invariably wearing the red dress. She became more and more convinced that as long as she wore it, nothing bad would befall her or her husband. If it occurred to her that this blind faith in her dress bordered on an obsession, she soon put the thought out of her mind. So what, if it sounds crazy – it works, doesn't it?

A month passed, another was practically over. Ellen's confidence grew by leaps and bounds. She was now quite used to the washing and wearing routine, which seemed in fact to have become the norm.

And so she found herself one afternoon attending a matinee performance of a musical, the rage of the town at that moment, in the company of a congenial friend. When she returned home in the late afternoon, humming a catchy tune, she was rather surprised to find the house quiet, as if deserted.

A look in the bedroom revealed the situation. It was strewn with Leonard's belongings. Ties, underwear, socks everywhere, and she read the signs correctly. Leonard had been searching furiously for his cheque book prior to disappearing on a bender.

Funnily enough, Ellen did not react as she had in the past. She did not pick up the mess and retire to bed, as she would have done before. She still held a conviction that as long as she wore her red dress things could be arrested in their motion, reversed, prevented from becoming a nightmare.

She felt a powerful surge of energy. She decided to look for Leonard, the action she had promised herself in the past she would never undertake. Since the car was in the garage, the chances were he was in one of the local pubs, and so, quickly grabbing her bag, she ran to the nearest one. There were a few people propping up the bar but alas, no Leonard! She quickly

85

retraced her steps and tried the pub at the opposite end of the street, drew a blank, then hurried to the third one further on, without success. She tried to recall the location of other drinking establishments, visited all of them, and was equally unlucky.

He might have gone up to town by train, her agitated brain suggested. So, not quite sure how she would deal with the problem, Ellen, with great speed, reached the station and approached the ticket collector.

'Excuse me, I am looking for my husband. Have you noticed a grey-haired man, in grey flannel trousers and blue blazer boarding a train this afternoon?'

'Lady, how can I tell? Dozens of men dressed like that have boarded trains since I came on duty. After all, we look at their tickets, not the clothes they wear.'

'But you might have noticed. It is very important that I contact him. I know I can find him with your help. After all, I am wearing my red dress.'

'And a lovely dress it is. But what is your hurry? He will come home all right, don't you worry!'

Some people wanted to enter the platform and obviously the ticket collector was getting a bit impatient.

'Please help me, try to remember,' said Ellen, quite unaware of the strange looks directed at her by the bystanders.

'Lady, you are stopping me from doing my job. My advice is, go home and wait for your hubby. He will turn up – they always do.'

Ellen retreated. Her agitation increased and so did her determination. After all, she was wearing the red dress!

She accosted several people, drew polite or rather impatient replies. She pointed out to all and sundry that she must find her husband and that anything was possible because of the dress she was wearing. It was getting dark and chilly. Ellen started to shiver, but was now too hysterical to react to bodily discomfort.

She walked along the street past a church where a group of people stood in front of the porch talking to the vicar, probably after a service. Ellen approached them and asked, in a voice verging on tears, if they had any news of her husband. The surprised cleric, realising he was dealing with an emotionally upset person, replied that he did not know her husband, but what was the trouble? And so came the story of the lost husband, the red dress, the danger of Ellen's only chance of happiness being lost if she did not find him straight away – now!

Trying to be helpful, he suggested that she contact the police. It seemed a most reasonable idea and so, not even saying 'Thank you', Ellen ran to the police station, losing her handbag somewhere on the way, her hair getting dishevelled, her make-up rather smudged.

She breathlessly accosted the constable on duty with a request that he, or someone else, go with her to look for her husband. The officer, rather taken aback, asked Ellen to be more precise. 'Would you give me your particulars and explain what seems to be the trouble?'

'There is no time for all those questions! Please, I need help in locating my husband, before it gets too bad. I know I can find him, my red dress tells me, so if only someone will drive me about . . .'

'Madam, what you are asking is impossible. Can we start with some details? When did your husband disappear?'

Ellen blew up. 'For Christ's sake, help me!' She stretched over the counter and seized the man's shoulders. 'I need help, my dress will help me.' She started crying, becoming quite incomprehensible.

The startled officer took a couple of steps back and called to someone behind him, 'Tell Cathy to come.'

Soon, a young policewoman appeared, but Ellen was beside herself. Half resisting, she let herself be led to a small room, where Cathy suggested a cup of tea and a moment of reflection. 'We are losing time,' screamed Ellen.

'Not at all,' said the policewoman. 'Drink your tea and start at the beginning.'

That was too much for Ellen. She hurled the mug containing the tea to the floor, then snatched the girl's

87

notebook, tore it up and threw the pieces into the air. She then started to scream with an intensity that penetrated the walls. She lost all control; the fury of many years exploded, the frustration of her life communicated itself in her total abandonment and in the way she was pounding the walls with her clenched fists.

Somebody must have sent for an ambulance, and the next thing they were leading Ellen towards it. She caught the word 'hospital' and in her distraught state assumed that that was where Leonard was.

When escorted to the ward, she was asking, 'Where is he? What have you done with him? Lead me to him. So I have found him. It is the red dress I am wearing!'

The nurse in charge tried to explain that she was tired and needed rest. Why didn't she undress and leave things till the morning? But Ellen refused. She drew her arms protectively to her sides, asserting in a hollow voice, 'Never, never. If I do, my hope will be gone.'

'You have got to sedate her,' someone said. The needle entered Ellen's thigh. Suddenly the whole world exploded, and she was falling into nothingness.

It took two nurses to ease the red dress off Ellen's inert body.

THE FIND

I have two friends at home. Both of them live in the basement, and come to life twice a day: at 6.30 each morning and at 4.30 in the afternoon. I mean, of course, the two central-heating boilers who, so to speak, bring to life the whole house, dispensing instant welcoming warmth during the cold, unfriendly winter months.

My bed companion, Joe, is a very bad sleeper. He gets up two or three times during the night and falls really soundly asleep after four o'clock. Therefore, if I wake early on those dark, wintry mornings, I dare not even switch on my bedside lamp in case I wake him. Instead, I wait for my friends to start working, as I can hear them distinctly from my bedroom. Then I know it is 6.30, a fairly respectable hour to get up quietly, shut the door to the bedroom and get myself an early cup of tea.

In the afternoon I usually take a rest between three and four o'clock, because it is then that the chill in the house becomes noticeable. When at 4.30 my friends start working, I know I can get up, since soon the house will be gloriously warm again, a proper haven against the elements.

I live in a Victorian house, over 150 years old. Those houses were not necessarily models of heat conservation, amongst other drawbacks, about which Joe, given half a chance, would enlighten anyone within earshot with great aplomb. I say, 'But those houses have an atmosphere.'

'What atmosphere?' asks Joe, and points to the warped floors, walls, windows.

'Atmosphere is an abstract term,' I correct him.

89

'Well, you can keep it,' he replies. 'Give me a straight, tight door any time.'

When we first moved in, the lovely Victorian garden was overgrown, and what was not overgrown was spoilt by the last, careless owner. Joe went to work on it straight away and, bit by bit, the old look was restored. Except for the bottom of the garden. Here, chaos reigned supreme, though there were one or two pointers that some time in the past it was a separate unit, perhaps a child's garden. This winter, Joe had a go at it. He had to dismantle a virtual hillock of rubbish mixed with earth and rotting vegetation. A tremendous job, back-breaking. Nearly through, he had a bit of luck. One day he came to lunch, and handed me a piece of yellow metal chain. I had a close look at it. There was a chance it was gold, since there was no sign of rust. I washed it with soap and water and examined it. It was a bracelet with a broken clasp, consisting of links, beautifully shaped. There were two heart-shaped links, followed by a plain one, the pattern repeating itself throughout the bracelet.

Really, I should have taken it to a jeweller to have it tested and valued, and perhaps establish its age, but I didn't. I preferred to imbue it with a past and a story suited to my imagination.

I found from the deeds of the house that it was built for a Doctor Morex, who lived in it for close on 40 years. On his demise, it then passed to his unmarried daughter Louise, who herself inhabited it for nearly 30 years. After her death, the house was sold. But we need not bother about what happened later. This story is about Louise.

I firmly maintain that the bracelet belonged to Louise. She was an only child, pretty, pensive and inclined to bouts of depression. Her mother's prolonged illness might have had something to do with it, as well as her father's serious turn of mind. Having private means, he devoted little time to his practice, preferring to indulge in scientific research on various subjects. One of the downstairs rooms, known as 'Father's study', was permanently out-of-bounds to Louise, on penalty of severe punishment.

90

Margaret, Louise's nurse and later companion, because of Louise's mother's ill health, was the person who attended to all her needs and schooling. She was also the person who, each Saturday and on the eve of holidays, put Louise's slightly wavy hair into curlers, thus enhancing her pleasant appearance. The bottom of the garden was Louise's domain. She held tea parties there for her dolls, cultivated some flowers and, shaded by a larch tree, read books on sultry summer afternoons.

For Louise's home had to be quiet at all times. Her parents impressed it on her often enough. Either Mama was resting or Papa was working were the usual reasons given, so it was only on rare occasions that Louise could entertain children in the house. But she did not mind. Curled up with a book in front of the blazing fire in the marble fireplace in the drawing room, or on her own in the pleasant first-floor nursery, which is now Dominic's bedroom, she had enough resources to entertain herself.

Of course, she was taken sometimes on visits to her cousins, or walking in the park, but for Louise, staying at home didn't mean boredom because, quite early on, she started to invent stories, and when she had mastered writing she put them down in her exercise books.

Her father liked to read those literary efforts, but was rather puzzled by the fact that their endings were always unhappy. He tackled Louise about it, yet never got a satisfactory answer. Louise would put her head down and look demure. She knew the answer, of course, but preferred to keep it to herself. She wrote in the only way she could because she was sad. The house was always quiet and now, after the death of her mother, the house was sad, and so were her stories.

When Louise reached 17 years of age, her aunt insisted that she should spend more time in her house, meeting her cousins, other girls of her own age, and some young men, many relatives by marriage. Louise started to attend dancing classes; her hair was put up in the most fashionable manner. But, to tell the truth, she was not an instant or general success. Being rather shy and prone to daydreaming, she must have missed quite a lot of opportunities – besides, her cousins were so much better instructed in the social graces.

It was when Felix, a far-removed cousin from the provinces, appeared on the scene that things began to change. Felix discovered Louise. He had enough gaiety for two and, being a bit of an outsider himself, took this opportunity to establish both of them. Louise was warned against him. He was apparently reckless and, to top it all, he was penniless. These were two very important disadvantages in the eyes of sensible young ladies, and their chaperons. He was on a longish holiday prior to a voyage to India, where the family had been able to procure a job for him in the civil service. Louise knew that time was short, and was determined to make the best of it, particularly as she felt herself strangely attracted to Felix. His sense of humour, the way he would sweep her off her feet in a more lively dance, even the way he looked into her eyes, unabashed, were all novelties for her, whose normal behaviour relied on two main qualities: self-restraint and modesty.

At a picnic in Richmond Park, he boldly approached her, asking if she would take a walk with him, and as soon as they were out of earshot, his smiling countenance changed to a serious one. 'Louise,' he said, 'we have not much time, but there is something I must tell you. You are very dear to me, in fact I have fallen in love with you, but at the moment I can't offer you much. I am only on the way to establishing myself, yet I know I will succeed. Will you let me write to you?'

Louise was more than ready to enter into a correspondence with Felix. As it was, she dreaded his departure. She put her hand through his arm and said, 'Yes, of course, and I will wait for you.'

Felix reached into his pocket and placed a thin gold bracelet made of entwined hearts on her arm. 'This is my troth.'

Louise could not wear the bracelet – there would be too many questions asked – but she kept it in the drawer under her silk stockings, together with the frequent letters from Felix. She often read them and wrote back, posting the letters herself so as to be sure they were really sent. She asked her father to give her permission to install a lovely white wrought-iron garden seat under the larch tree, and spent many hours dreaming about the future.

About a year later, one of her cousins went out to India; it was at that time quite an acceptable way of finding a suitable husband from amongst hundreds of single officers in the army or the administration. She started to correspond with Louise and from time to time mentioned Felix. He was quite distinguishing himself in India, the Viceroy having taken a liking to him. He was also being pursued by a large number of marriageable young ladies, but as yet was unattached. Louise enjoyed the news, but was rather disturbed by the attention paid to him by the society girls. Will he be faithful to me, she asked herself, with all this competition? Won't he forget me? She started to devise ways in which she could influence her father to let her go to India, but did not get very far. Apparently she couldn't be spared.

When, eventually, Louise learned in a roundabout way that Felix was married, she was all but prepared for it. There had been fewer letters lately, and even those that came were written in a hurry, in a superficial manner. She couldn't say anything to anyone, because there was so little to say – no engagement, no ring, just this golden trinket in the drawer, never worn. So, next day, Louise proudly put the bracelet on, but nobody noticed. Then she repaired to her seat at the bottom of the garden and pretended for a long time that things had worked out differently. But in the end, her pride asserted itself. She tugged with great force at the bracelet, broke the clasp, and then hurled it into the shrubbery.

She never again visited that part of the garden.

TRIALS AND ERRORS

Something must have disagreed with me, realised Philip, having woken up at two in the morning, feeling queasy and bloated. He had had a late supper in an Indian restaurant after seeing a play in the West End in the company of Sylvia and Adam, his friends. It must have been the curry, Philip decided. He got out of bed and, putting on his dressing gown and slippers, repaired to the kitchen, where he drank two glasses of water and felt marginally better.

Why do I accept these late invitations? he regretted. Particularly coming from Adam and Sylvia, who were not even as convivial company as might be expected. After all, some time ago Philip had come near to marrying Sylvia, and in their subsequent meetings he was always aware of a certain undercurrent which required real skill to navigate.

Philip switched on an electric fire in the sitting room and, having made himself comfortable in his favourite armchair, cast his mind back to the past. Sylvia – the girl he had nearly married. Why hadn't he? He supposed he was not quite ready for a permanent commitment. He had teetered on the brink several times and always, at the last moment, found a reason why not . . . Yes, he had missed his chance with Sylvia, who probably came to the conclusion he was not the marrying type. She had certainly found a substitute in record time. Before he knew what was happening, Adam had proposed and carried Sylvia off. Didn't that imply that she wasn't as much in love with him as she had maintained? Was she, after all, only looking for security and position? He would never know. Just as well he hadn't got himself shackled to her, or anybody else, for that matter. His lids drooped on this self-congratulatory note, and Philip nodded off.

In distant Ealing, in one of the semi-detached houses facing a tree-lined street, light came up at about the same time. Sylvia woke up feeling decisively unwell. Blaming it on the curry, she sat up in her marital bed and surveyed her husband, fast asleep and snoring with extraordinary vigour and regularity.

Sylvia got up. There was no earthly chance of falling asleep with that noise going on, and shaking and turning Adam to one side was a fruitless task. Much easier to go to the spare room and try to go to sleep, having stopped on the way in the bathroom for a dose of Alka Seltzer.

The cool sheets of the spare room bed enveloped Sylvia, but sleep would not come. She put her mind back to the previous evening and considered the outing dispassionately. It had not been too bad; anyway, it was worth the bother of cajoling Adam into participating. He wasn't a social person at all – to him, his work and playing games on the home computer were the limits of his interest. Not like Philip . . .

Philip – her thoughts went back to that still painful subject. The man she loved, and would have married, had she been asked. But she had not. There was the rub. Why did she still want to see him? To prove to him that she was settled, cherished, happy? Was she happy? Sylvia had her doubts. It would have been different had there been any children. But Adam didn't want children – he had made it clear from the start. 'Get a dog,' was his advice, 'if ever you start feeling broody.' And she did so. The two dachshunds even now lay on her bed, one on each side. Sylvia absent-mindedly stroked their silky, elongated heads. Their relaxed posture and the emanating pleasant warmth soon induced the sought-after repose.

At noon next day, the flowers arrived as usual, and a thank-you note from Philip. They were exceptionally pretty, long stems of stocks, grown out of season. Normally, Sylvia would have left the matter at that, but on this occasion, the sensual scent of the blooms and the lateness of Adam's return from the office made her pick up the phone and dial Philip's

95

number. They chatted amicably, reviewing the night before, and then talked about a book that had recently been published. Philip offered to lend it to Sylvia, and the upshot was that they agreed to lunch together one day the following week. They made a date and rang off.

The lunch was a success, and proved to be one of many over the next few months. Sylvia did not tell Adam about her dates and, frankly speaking, Adam would not have been very interested to know. But matters got out of hand one particular day when, instead of having coffee in the restaurant, Sylvia went to Philip's flat for coffee, with an open mind. It was unavoidable that the old relationship was re-established on the old footing, which meant, pleasure, yes – commitment, no.

Sylvia had just reached her fortieth birthday, so when she missed her time twice she put it down to the early warning of the change of life, but when she started to feel persistently sick in the mornings, the warning bells rang. She visited her doctor, had the test done and unexpectedly found herself three months pregnant.She was shocked, but at the same time curiously unable to come to any decision. She found herself preoccupied with her body, became inward-looking, relaxed, putting the reality out of her mind. There was a peculiar dichotomy in her attitude. She knew she would have to tell Adam, but how it should be done, she could hardly envisage.

It was Adam who finally broached the subject in a most peculiar manner. Apparently there was a cottage for sale in the Dordogne, fully functional and equipped. He thought it would be a good investment. So he put it to Sylvia – would she like to go there for the rest of her pregnancy and then put the baby up for adoption? 'That way, with the minimum of fuss and inconvenience, we will get out of our fix. I suppose, being your age, you relaxed the precautions. I quite understand your silence on the subject, knowing how I feel about children. Leave it to me. I will see to everything. But you must leave here before it shows.' Sylvia inferred from this long speech that Adam considered himself to be the father of the forthcoming baby, and she left it at that.

So, after disposing of the dogs to some friends in the country, Sylvia and Adam left for the Dordogne, hoping that their plans would succeed.

The cottage was charming. Surrounded with greenery, high on a hill, it boasted a small garden and even a trout brook, of which Adam took full advantage. Sylvia experienced a peculiar state of mind. On the one hand she was relieved at not having to take a more active role, on the other she felt manipulated, deprived of her right to decide for herself. It was in that rather rebellious mood that on her last day before leaving she phoned Philip and told him bluntly that she was going to have his baby, but because it was too late for an abortion, she was going away to France and, when the baby was born, would have it adopted.

What bothered Sylvia was Adam's attitude to her pregnancy. He was very considerate, much as if having started a job, he was going to see it was well executed. The baby had to have a good start, therefore no effort must be spared to attain this goal.

And that was where Sylvia's role came in. As far as she was concerned, Adam treated her waiting time as some sort of complaint which would clear up in due course. Everything was being done to bring about total success, an approach very much in line with that employed in Adam's business.

After a fortnight, Adam departed by train, leaving the car behind as well as a whole list of contacts in case of need. He also stocked Sylvia with enough foodstuffs as was reasonable. The rest he left to Sylvia's common sense.

It was the height of summer. Sylvia enjoyed every moment of the splendid weather, spending much time in the shade in the garden, reading and dozing to her heart's content. And that was how Philip found her, not long after Adam's departure, arriving unannounced in his smart sports car.

Sylvia was astonished, and rather apprehensive, afraid that Philip's visit boded no good tidings and was bound to complicate an already tricky situation. They went indoors, where, over a cold beer for Philip and an iced lemonade for herself, Sylvia inquired how on earth he had found her. To this, Philip replied nonchalantly, 'That was quite easy – I phoned Adam.' Sylvia didn't know whether to laugh or to be outraged. Apparently Philip had told Adam he was going on a touring holiday in France and wouldn't mind looking up Sylvia as well as seeing the cottage. Adam thought it was a splendid idea to cheer Sylvia up in her boring exile, and supplied directions. He also explained the situation to Philip, trusting him as a good friend not to broadcast to all and sundry the present botheration in which he and Sylvia found themselves.

Some time later, Philip explained the real reason for his visit. He found it impossible to accept that his child should be given up for adoption. So he wanted to adopt it himself, and then foster it out with reliable candidates. Failing that, he proposed to acquaint Adam with the truth, precipitate a divorce and settle with Sylvia and the baby.

Sylvia felt outraged. It did not escape her notice that Philip's first preference was to recover the baby, and only as a last option did he envisage them coming together. She exclaimed, rather angrily, 'You only want the baby – don't you? You don't want to include me in your life unless there is no alternative. Stop meddling in my affairs – you have done enough to complicate them as it is. Leave me and Adam alone!' And she refused to discuss the subject any further. When Philip left next morning, the matter remained unsettled.

As the time for the confinement drew near, Sylvia became really confused about the whole issue. She wanted to keep the baby, but could not see how she could bring it about. The whole mechanism of adoption was set in motion – the adoption agency was informed and a place booked in the clinic connected with it. Sylvia expected Adam any day now. She was unhappy beyond belief, regretting her involvement with Philip, yet unable to change the course of events to which she had given her approval.

Shortly afterwards Adam arrived, looking rather jubilant and determined. As soon as he had settled in, he announced, 'There has been a change of plans. We are going to keep the baby. This is what you always wanted – so be it.' Sylvia was speechless. She had never expected such a diametrical reversal of opinion – had not thought it possible.

She went for a walk and spent a couple of hours considering the whole matter. Now that they were going to keep the baby, the question of who the father was became important. She decided she must inform Adam about the possibility of him not being the baby's father. She could not go on for ever with this deception on her conscience. It was not fair to Adam, and anyway she could never sustain the stress that her guilt in foisting somebody else's baby on an unwilling Adam would cause. She said as much to him, having thrown caution to the winds, having stopped really caring what would happen to her and the baby, as long as she was out of this improbable nightmare.

If she had thought Adam would lose his temper, or do something violent, she was greatly mistaken. Adam laughed, slightly sardonically, and said, 'I know all about it. Philip came to see me a week or so ago. He wanted me to facilitate his quest for adoption, and told me the reason. Now that he wants the child so much, he will not get it. That's how I am going to get even with him.'

A fortnight later, Sylvia gave birth to a bouncing, strapping boy of over nine pounds. He was the living image of Adam.

WHAT TO DO ABOUT THOMAS?

Thomas was born prematurely. He spent the first six weeks of his life in an incubator, causing a lot of anxiety to his mother and the staff of the hospital. He looks more like a skinned rabbit than a baby, thought Monica, when she was allowed to see him for the first time. She watched him tenderly. His tiny fists closed, his lips curved in a minute fashion in an involuntary sucking action. He was monitored closely. There were wires attached to his chest and head. Monica was appalled. What chance has he got? The question within her stayed unanswered. But the doctor and nurses thought otherwise. 'Wait a few weeks,' they kept telling her. 'You will not believe your eyes.'

And they were right. After being discharged from hospital, Monica visited there daily, to extract milk for the baby, and slowly, slowly that little miserable-looking scrap of humanity started to look like a handsome baby. After two months Monica was allowed to take Thomas home, if the superior-looking house of Monica's parents, Colonel and Mrs Roberts, could be called that.

Her father fetched mother and baby. He was obviously moved, for all his gruff manner. At least the baby is alive, he thought. Small consolation in the circumstances. Still, he felt quite proud to be a grandfather.

The reason why Monica didn't take Thomas to her own home, by which she meant the cosy, if small, flat in Clapham, was the untimely death of her husband Ronnie a week before Thomas's birth. Ronnie had been killed instantly in a car accident and the ensuing shock in all probability had caused the premature labour. Monica had not been to her flat since that awful moment when a young policewoman appeared at her door and, after a few cautiously chosen words, broke the news which shattered her world. She then telephoned her parents, who immediately fetched her home and she had stayed there ever since. Monica had not even attended Ronnie's funeral and neither had her mother, because at that very time Monica was halfway through her labour.

Ever since then, Monica had not functioned in any proper sense of the word. Never very assertive, she now simply did as she was told, spending most of the time sitting around with a blank look on her face, unable to comprehend the enormity of her loss and the grief which overwhelmed her. She had been married for only two years – on the whole, happy years – and the misfortune which had befallen her plunged her into utter chaos.

Nobody blamed her. 'It was the shock,' everybody said.

'She needs time and affection,' was the verdict expressed by her family. Monica's two sisters – married and with children – as well as her parents, surrounded her with love and comfort, but for the time being it seemed to have little effect.

And so Thomas entered the world fatherless, but with enough mothering, and some to spare. Even disregarding the two doting aunts, he certainly inherited two mothers – his own, and Mrs Roberts. It goes without saying that this was an unavoidable outcome. Left to herself, Monica would have probably starved herself and the baby. Her mother took command but, as often happens in life, once a position of supremacy is thrown on to one's shoulders, it is not easy to relinquish it. That was the problem in Monica's case. It certainly prolonged Monica's inertia, and made it more difficult for Mrs Roberts to assume the role of grandmother – fond, but not possessive, loving, but not obsessive about Thomas. Having been blessed with three daughters but no sons, the experience of mothering a little boy had been denied to her in her own life.

Monica stayed with her parents for over a year, until she had recovered sufficiently to return to her own flat, taking Thomas

101

with her. She regained her physical, but not financial, independence. Ronnie's life insurance, which she received as a lump sum, when invested, paid the rent but no more. She had to rely on her parents for an allowance, and that gave them a certain right to monitor the way the money was spent. That, in turn, created embarrassment when some items of expenditure did not meet with their approval. Particularly if as a consequence Monica had to ask for an extra cheque.

The decision to move back to her own flat Monica justified as the only way in which she would regain her independence. She was not denying that the year spent with her parents had been necessary. Somebody had to take over when she was thrown into a state of complete confusion, depression, utter misery. But, as time went by and Thomas began to change into a delightful toddler, her senses couldn't remain frozen for ever. She still felt deeply wounded, but knew that if she was on her own, she would recover more quickly, simply because there would be the need to take up duties and responsibilities. So long as she stayed in her parents' house, she would just drift, because it was easier. That had to stop. So, even if she could not claim full independence, at least she was on the right track. Thomas became her main preoccupation; she established herself as a mother in the full meaning of the word, and began to plan her future.

To give Monica's parents their due, they made no difficulties about the move. Mrs Roberts, being a mother herself, understood the need for Monica to put a more clearly defined structure on family boundaries. Which didn't mean that she did not feel a terrible wrench when the actual parting took place. While packing Thomas's clothes, she kept behind one outgrown baby coat, and could be seen (if anyone was interested enough) holding it to her face, or cradling it in her arms. She promised herself she would assume the usual role of fond grandmother, and on the whole succeeded. She visited Monica once a week, stayed to lunch – which, incidentally, she brought with her – encouraged Monica to take this opportunity to venture on her own for a few hours' outing, and did not offer advice unless asked.

When Thomas turned two, Monica began to look for work. It was not easy, but the bank where she had worked before her marriage eventually offered her a position. Not as good, perhaps, as the one she had held before, but the offer included a bonus for a nursery fee. Monica jumped at the chance, and considered herself very lucky.

She unfortunately miscalculated her parents' reaction. They felt hurt that Monica was entrusting Thomas to some paid help in preference to her own family, who were willing to look after the boy, and mentioned it from time to time. Not much was said, but Monica was left in no doubt about what her parents thought.

Thomas didn't take easily to this new regime. He suffered lots of colds and ear infections, and willy-nilly Monica had to ask her mother to step in at very short notice to look after the sick child when he wasn't well enough to be taken to the nursery. Sometimes even the grandfather looked after Thomas, particularly if Monica occasionally joined someone from the office for an evening out. After all, she was only 25, and as time went by couldn't resist an invitation to have some fun with her contemporaries.

Therefore it was no wonder that Thomas divided his affection between his mother and grandparents and, as he developed, so, too, did a certain kind of rivalry between the three grown-ups, each motivated by the best intentions, each in a way a victim of circumstances.

But, in truth, such a situation had an adverse effect on Thomas's sense of security. It manifested itself in the only way he was capable of showing. He became very suspicious of any change, however small. At the nursery each morning, he had to be forcibly parted from his mother's arms, with accompanying howls of fury. A similar thing happened when he was left in the evening, even with his grandparents, should his mother venture out for an evening. Granted, he settled down, once his mother had gone, but as likely as not he would wake up on her return, and then nothing would help but being allowed to spend the rest of the night in her bed.

All these emotional upsets registered with Monica's

parents, who kept their opinions to themselves with increasing difficulty. For them, the solution was obvious. Monica should return home and allow them to participate in rearing young Thomas, giving him a broader base, a more stable background.

So it was with great disquiet they learned of a new proposal concerning Monica's life. Being fluent in French, she was offered a job in Paris in the bank's French branch. It was a considerable promotion, bringing forth monetary advantages as well as an enhanced status in the hierarchy. To their horror, Monica's parents discovered that she proposed to take Thomas with her, enter him in a French crèche and 'go it alone', without family backing.

There was a rather heated exchange of views between the parties involved, but Monica's decision was firm and unshakeable. Early in September, she left for Paris. She was taken to the airport by her father, not her mother, who refused to have anything to do with this – as she described it – mad venture.

Monica settled in Paris quite easily, being helped by the other members of the local staff; she enrolled Thomas in the nearby crèche, feeling that her decision was the right one. However, she soon discovered that although, in one sense, she had achieved a full freedom and established herself as the principal character in Thomas's life, the practical side of this arrangement left a lot to be desired. Thomas, once again, found himself in new surroundings difficult for him to understand – new language, food and customs. It made him bewildered and confused. He suffered a whole series of colds and infections, which forced Monica to seek help from agency nannies. The same problem arose if she wanted to go out in the evening. She had to employ babysitters, who on the whole did not speak English. All hopes that it would be only a question of time before Thomas settled down proved false. If anything, Thomas grew more unhappy, inclined to cry at the slightest provocation, became listless, fractious and generally difficult.

With Christmas festivities in the offing, Monica suddenly

experienced a hefty dose of homesickness. Having listened to the exciting plans of her office colleagues, she came to realise that in all probability she would be spending Christmas on her own with Thomas, alone and rather neglected. On top of that, the feeling of independence, so valiantly fought for, began to pall. Yes, it was very enjoyable to be entirely free, to carry through all her decisions without having to account to anyone, but it also meant constant rush and hassle, getting Thomas ready to go to the crèche on those dark, night-like mornings, at the same time as getting ready for the office. It also meant leaving the office, sometimes at a very incon- venient moment, to collect Thomas from the crèche and then struggle in the rush hour on the metro on the way home. Thomas would sometimes fall asleep, complicating matters. It also meant not being able to accept any impromptu invitation for a drink or a meal out, since a babysitter had to be booked in advance. That proved particularly galling when one of her office co-workers, Jean-Pierre, started to pay her considerable attention, which Monica would have liked to encourage.

So, having obtained an extension of her Christmas leave, she boarded a plane on Christmas Eve, to be met by her father at Heathrow, beaming with goodwill, all differences forgotten. She received the same treatment from the rest of the family, very much the prodigal daughter returning home. Jean-Pierre, having discovered Monica's plans, inquired whether she could include him in her holiday, perhaps spend New Year's Eve in his company, should he be able to arrange a long weekend in London. So Monica was doubly pleased – she would have some respite from looking after Thomas, and have a chance to promote a promising relationship on her home ground.

Thomas, surprisingly, after an initial shyness, quickly adapted to the new situation. He might have remembered some of the surroundings from his past; he also found himself to be the centre of attention willingly provided by Monica's parents, aunts, uncles and cousins. It was a very pleasant Christmas all round. The family gathered together, there were

105

children everywhere, and Thomas found it very much to his liking.

Monica, released from her 24-hour duty of motherhood, spent a lot of time shopping and catching up on the entertainment scene. In a way, she started to appreciate the perks of being on her own, unencumbered by a loved but rather demanding child. The ten days passed quickly; it was time to make the return journey and here, perhaps encouraged by the three days spent in the company of Jean-Pierre, Monica surprisingly quickly fell in with her parents' suggestion to leave Thomas behind. After all, it would only take her an hour on the plane to come to visit him as often as every other weekend. Meanwhile, he would be well looked after by the family, in well-liked, stable conditions, with lots of love and tenderness.

As she was going back with Jean-Pierre, she did not feel the wrench from Thomas as much as she had feared. Thomas took it quite calmly, waving her away with great gusto, and in the circumstances it seemed a sensible solution.

On the whole the new regime worked quite well, except that Monica's visits became less frequent. This was understandable, because she spent more and more time with Jean-Pierre, who appeared to be quite serious about their relationship. They set up house together and when, the following year, Monica discovered she was pregnant, a quiet marriage ceremony took place in a civil registry office. The newly-wed couple came to England for their honeymoon and there, while meeting Monica's parents, Thomas's future was discussed. Monica, preoccupied with setting up a new home and the coming of the baby, was quite willing to leave Thomas where he was temporarily, on condition that in a year's time he would come to live with her and Jean-Pierre.

Monica's parents, anxious not to cause any friction, accepted the proposal, relieved that at least for the time being they would not have to part with Thomas. As to the future, who knows? Monica might have another baby; she might come to the conclusion that Thomas was really better off with her parents, remembering the difficulties of her earlier attempt to transplant him.

But from that time on, a certain change emerged in their behaviour. His mummy and new daddy were hardly ever mentioned and, without actually expressing it, an idea was communicated to Thomas that he belonged to his grand-parents. The battle for Thomas's loyalty had commenced.

Colonel Roberts, using his long-standing connections, was able to put Thomas's name down for one of the more prestigious public schools, taking out an endowment to pay the fees. In the meantime, he was sent to a good infant school, where his education was begun in a familiar, traditional manner.

Thomas seemed settled, hardly mentioning his mother. In fact, he started to address his grandparents as Mummy and Daddy, to which Monica's parents did not object.

Monica, having given birth to a daughter, came to England to show off the baby, and was rather upset by what she discovered. Thomas was not really interested in her or the baby, he was full of stories about his friends and television heroes. As to the question of address, a compromise was reached: she was to be known as 'Maman' and Mrs Roberts as 'Mummy'. Jean-Pierre was rather uncommunicative about the future of Thomas. He left it to his wife to sort it out, neither encouraging her to precipitate action nor dissuading her from claiming Thomas.

A second daughter was born to Monica in less than a year. She welcomed the baby, but at the same time could not help feeling rather despondent. As it happened – she rightly acknowledged – this was another obstacle in her ever-increasing tussle with her parents over Thomas. Had she produced a boy, it might, in a way, have made up for the acute longing she felt for Thomas. As things stood, the new baby gave her parents another reason to postpone the handing over of Thomas, and it rankled. What should she do? Resign herself to her first-born living outside her life, or, overlooking the difficulty of looking after two small children, claim her son and hope for the best? She changed her mind on this matter frequently, and when she discussed it with Jean-Pierre, he was not at all helpful. Confronted with two children under two, he did not share her anxiety. He was rather inclined to leave the existing arrangement for the time being, quite unaware that the longer Thomas stayed in England the more difficult it would prove to integrate him in his new family in the future.

Monica had by this time, quite understandably, put aside in her memory her parents' help in the early years of Thomas's existence. She saw them now only as formidable rivals for her son's affections, with all the advantages on their side. Sometimes she came near to hating them. And, funnily enough, Monica never considered her parents as separate entities. For her, they were basically a monolith, with little or no life of their own, save rearing Thomas. Perhaps because she felt so beleaguered and largely defenceless against their stable, well-entrenched existence, she couldn't envisage them as two individuals still capable of actions not directly concerned with the aim of depriving her of her son.

Therefore she was quite unprepared for Colonel Roberts's telephone call one evening the following spring. Her father sounded rather apologetic, and disturbed. He went straight ahead with his extraordinary news.

'Your mother has left me.'

Monica started to laugh. 'Don't be silly, how could she? You are joking.'

'I wish I was, but it is true. She found a new companion and moved out a few days ago. I've tried to manage on my own but find it impossible. Can I bring Thomas out to you as soon as it can be arranged?'

Monica was speechless for a moment. Then she blurted out, 'But, Father, what happened?' Somehow Thomas's future, the need to reclaim him, became a secondary issue. She failed to comprehend the enormity of her parents' calamity. 'But Mother will come back,' she shouted. The idea that she would be deprived of the permanent source of support, be it at times disagreeable, seemed to her monstrous. 'It must be some mistake. Did you talk to her? Could I come over and try to sort it out?'

'It is no use. I should have acted earlier, but it seemed so preposterous I simply paid no attention.'

'Who is this man? A younger one? Where has she found him?' Monica got quite agitated. 'At your age, it is simply not on, can't you see?'

'Calm yourself, Monica. It is more complicated than you think. The man is a widower with four small children, all boys. His wife died two years ago and ever since he has been struggling with a whole host of helpers, none very satisfactory. Two of the boys often came to play with Thomas. The father would fetch them and sometimes stay for a while to discuss his difficulties with your mother. They became great friends, the subject of children being their main preoccupation. Frankly speaking, your mother knew that sooner or later she would have to part with Thomas. Deep down she knew she was in the wrong, keeping him away from you. His future had to be resolved because she sensed your distress, frustration and resentment. In a way, she was giving Thomas back to you – but at a price. She joined a motherless family where she will be able to love and cherish children without feeling guilty.'

THE LAW OF NATURE

In retrospect, only one outcome was possible. The one which actually happened. But hindsight is a dangerous game. It adds bitterness to the people involved, and an undeserved feeling of being more perceptive than others to the bystanders.

Barbara and Andrew were a handsome pair, both tall, with strong faces. They were determined kind of people, the ones who get to the top. And even their cultural background was of the same sort, so often the saving grace of marital break-ups. They had two handsome children, planned and bred to perfection. Both boys enjoyed their uncomplicated childhood. They were brought up in the country, aware of all the possible diversions to be pursued there – riding, rambling and so forth – and made conscious of the beauty of the surrounding scene. Why, then?

Let's start at the beginning. Andrew's job was the satisfying, if demanding vocation of country veterinary surgeon. He chose this calling, and approached it wholeheartedly. Barbara made a good wife, aware of what the duties of her husband involved, and prepared to put them before her personal needs. She thoroughly enjoyed living in the country, and even more enjoyed the rewards of Andrew's labour. They were twofold: material, which gave her independence; and personal, namely the satisfaction of achieving precisely those circumstances she had envisaged in the past – leading a healthy, relaxed and stressless life in a comfortable setting.

In fact, they were this rather seldom-met family – completely satisfied with life. Self-satisfaction was the word to be stressed here. For in a paradoxical way, it was the realisation of having reached the optimum of their goal that became Barbara's and Andrew's undoing.

After the boys had started boarding school, the working day in the household used to begin quite early. Andrew, fortified by a cooked breakfast, prepared on time by Barbara, would drive well before eight o'clock to the nearby town, where he would hold surgery for a couple of hours. Then he would answer calls from the neighbouring farmers, and return home around seven to bath and have supper, often in front of the television.

Barbara, having seen Andrew off, would put on rubber boots and as much warm clothing as the weather demanded, and take their two red setters for an hour's country hike. She would purposefully empty her mind of all intruding thoughts concerning the running of the house, or suchlike, and tune in to the prevailing mood of nature. She could thus achieve practically a symbiosis with the physical world surrounding her, following the winding country lanes, noticing the changes and permanency of all living organisms on the way: trees, hedges, the odd rabbit, the scent of newly cut grass, the mouth-watering bramble.

Thus refreshed, she would get back and start on her chores, but would make them as short a spell as possible, to make room for her preoccupation with the garden. If there was a special word describing the love between a human being and his or her garden, it would be called for here.

Barbara's garden was her kingdom, which she had ruled wisely for the last ten years. The mature look of the plants, shrubs and trees was the result and pride of countless hours and days spent on all sorts of tasks. Nothing was overlooked, a great deal added. With the growing children, a need for a swimming pool arose; later on, a tennis court.

She had a special gift. Her floral schemes were most unusual, extraordinary. She would place the plants or shrubs in such a way as to achieve the most eye-catching designs. Then again, she would do something surprising, like planting the flowers in the colours of a rainbow. It was precisely the vision she had, even before embarking on a new venture,

111

together with the proverbial green fingers, that gave Barbara's garden a distinctive look which couldn't be repeated or copied.

Therefore it was no wonder that she badly needed an audience to admire her achievements, and this was not necessarily forthcoming from her husband. And so Barbara sometimes had the niggling thought that it was a pity that there was no one to share her overwhelming enthusiasm, somebody as deeply devoted to growing things as she was.

Andrew liked the garden, and provided help if necessary, but his main interest was his work and animals in general. He undoubtedly had a way with them – the most recalcitrant animals became putty in his hands. Even the highly strung, overbred mare of Major Clifford would be gently assuaged into giving birth to yet another healthy foal. For this reason Andrew was highly regarded by the farming community in the vicinity, and greatly sought after. So much so, that he had to take on a partner to be able to fulfil all his obligations.

Barbara, too, profited from this new development. She found in Andrew's partner a person who, being a dedicated gardener himself, showed a most eager interest in her enchanted garden. Should he call of an evening to discuss some professional matters with Andrew, sooner or later he would drift into the garden, accompanied by Barbara, and spend the remaining time before darkness set in in admiring, suggesting and encouraging her to more, or better, ways of presenting the unquestionable beauty of her domain.

Then just as the future looked settled and full of promise, Andrew developed a strange complaint. It started with a couple of unexplained driving accidents, which happened in perfect conditions, for no apparent reason. Andrew blamed the car, but after it had been thoroughly examined, the mystery remained. Next, he noticed that he had difficulty in focusing, on quite a lot of occasions. This began to interfere with his work. He consulted the doctor, had an eye test – there was no explanation. But an increased amount of headaches, together with other symptoms, began to make sense. The dreaded word 'trachoma' was mentioned, soon to be confirmed by a rapid deterioration of Andrew's eyesight. Yes, it was true, Andrew was going blind. Trachoma is the highly unlikely, very rare disease, which can be contracted from animals – a quiet dread of anyone working in that field. Soon, things got too difficult to pretend otherwise. The future looked bleak.

Both Barbara and Peter rallied to Andrew's side. Together they engaged another assistant, and by common consent a deal was struck. Andrew retained a fraction of his income by remaining a consultant in special cases, but the load of the work was taken over by the other two men, as well as the title of partnership.

It is too painful to describe the agony and bitterness which became Andrew's lot. On the surface controlled, he raged internally, and all efforts on Barbara's side did not amount to much. Andrew spent most of his time at home, listening to music and making an effort to fight back by learning Braille. He kept in touch with his partners, often being asked for advice on some tricky problem. After all, he had a whole accumulation of experience behind him, and an uncanny insight into animal behaviour. But these were sad times for Andrew and Barbara.

She, needing some release from the blow fate had dealt them, spent even more time in the garden and, little by little, a certain distance grew between husband and wife. After all, Barbara was a dynamic, ambitious person and somehow felt let down by Andrew. She was leaving him behind.

Peter's frequent visits assumed a new meaning. He, with the circumstances in his favour, replaced to a certain degree the pathetic figure of Andrew, who more and more receded into the background.

Barbara came to rely on Peter for support. He proved to be very resourceful and, above all, with him she could indulge her abiding obsession of ever more enhancing her garden, whereas Andrew, not able to see, was of no use to her. How soon her friendship with Peter became an emotional involvement is difficult to say. But it happened. Barbara was not even feeling guilty. She needed a forceful, ambitious partner in life and her rational make-up had little time for failures.

In a way, Andrew sensed it. Maybe he would have felt the same, had Barbara failed him in his pursuit of success and advancement. He recognised the law of nature which rejects the weak, the impaired, the not fit to survive. He still had in his dispensary enough remedies to use in such cases. He was not even sorry for himself. He simply admitted that his life was not worth prolonging. So he availed himself of these means.

A PUZZLE

When did it all start, this misunderstanding that had pursued me most of my life? From the very first day of my life, when obeying my instinct, I put my fate into the hands of my mother. She too, obedient to her maternal instinct, reinforced my faith, my unquestioning trust in another human being. And so it went on. Never being let down by the person nearest to me, the arbiter of my survival. Later this was reinforced by my other parent, my family.

My childhood was spent in a stable environment. Seasons passed, years accumulated, and my faith in humans grew with me, gradually transferred to people outside my initial contacts. The books I read, the teachings I imbibed in church, all these, in one way or another, built in me an enormous potential for trust in the human race.

If the reality did not always tally with my credo, I was encouraged to disregard it, to pay back evil with good, to forgive 77 times, and notwithstanding the facts, trust. Always trust.

I suppose it worked in a peculiar way. From time to time some occurrences of great importance have reinforced the fundamental cornerstone on which my character was built. Then, the contrary experiences did not seem to matter, they were put down to human weaknesses, to be understood.

Yes, this was the other word from my vocabulary responsible for the way I dealt with life. 'Try to understand' was the unending cry. And I tried, with the inevitable loss, from my point of view, of my desires, my dreams. Today I doubt very much if in reality my deliberate, freely given

115

acquiescence made any difference to those who were the recipients of it. Except to make them thoroughly selfish. And demanding. And fuel my resentfulness.

Where, oh where, did humanity invent the myth that goodness is its own reward? In face of such blatant contradictions, one is brainwashed into believing it by the wise men, so that it requires a superhuman honesty to stand up and say 'This is a myth.'

* * *

David closed his diary. He felt much better for committing to paper the thoughts which had crystallised themselves in his mind in the last few years. Thoughts he had had no courage to write down before, even in his private diary. He felt that by committing them to paper, he had finally and irrevocably repudiated the very substance of his life. It seemed like a betrayal of the principles which had guided him for most of his life, and now, practically in the last chapter of it, left him robbed of even the satisfaction of justification. The structure of his (sometimes heroic) endeavours lay crumpled around him. He was left with nothing.

But how much longer could he pretend? He wanted badly, very badly, a pay-off, a recognition of his value, and did not feel ashamed of wanting it. If he wasn't as idealistic as he had always supposed himself to be, at least he was honest. He felt reprieved from the increasing weight of the realisation that he was not what he had made it his business to be, by virtue of inherited rules, accepted in good faith.

I have lived too long. I have been taken advantage of once too often. I have trusted in vain once too often. David pondered and pondered, and only the set, straight line of his lips denoted the frantic inner line of questioning that went on in his mind.

Is it like this for everybody? Have I been a fool all my life? Or do other people prefer a fool's paradise to the devastating truth? And what now? How, if at all, do I change my outlook, my dealings with other people? I am too old, too set in my

116

ways. The reputation I acquired, together with the duties and loyalties I accepted, preclude me from making a drastic change. People will conclude that, in my old age, I changed for the worse, became self-centred, sterile, and will not even give me the benefit of taking a considered decision based on rational propositions.

Therefore there is nothing left but to proceed along the old lines, but bereft of the convictions that carried me through my life. What a prospect!

But what David did not take into consideration was that once he had admitted the discrepancy between what he did and what he wanted to do, he opened a real Pandora's box, with all the consequences emerging. Subconsciously, a shift occurred in his dealings, and his reactions to people underwent a change. And so he found himself not available to do all the repairs with which he had formerly obliged friends and neighbours. He also refused to lend money to his nephew, on the grounds that at that particular time cashing in his savings would be detrimental to their value. In the same way he brought to an end a long-outlived friendship with Charles, who, for a long time, had been getting on his nerves, because Charles always seemed to imply that David's endeavours were either ridiculous, or plain stupid. Now he had the strength to say 'No' on many occasions and surprisingly he didn't feel particularly guilty about it. He was neither happy nor unhappy, he simply *was*.

At the same time, David discovered that he had more time on his hands, and resolved to use it in clearing out some old papers which, for many years, had been gathering dust in the attic. Sorting out these old relics, he came across some watercolours which he had done a good 20 years before and, on impulse, put his hand to some ideas which appeared in his mind from nowhere.

He became very engrossed in the project, set aside special time for painting, and discovered, as time went by, a great liking for this occupation. His technique improved, inspiration seemed to be unending and the results quite pleasing. David showed some of them to the owner of a small

117

gallery in the vicinity, and was pleasantly surprised when two were accepted. He was even more surpised when both pictures were sold in a comparatively short time, and he received an offer for more. Soon, people around started commenting on David's luck; he became a celebrity in the neighbourhood. He even lived to see a very complimentary article in the local paper.

Things started to move. One of his watercolours was bought by a well-known art collector, then another, and in a couple of years, David's income was supplemented to a considerable degree by the sale of his efforts. There was even talk of sending some of them to the Royal Academy Exhibition.

David was nonplussed. After a life-long attempt at being of use to others, largely overlooked, now, when he concentrated on his selfish pursuit, he obtained what he had really always wanted – recognition and acclaim.

AN EPITAPH FOR HENRY?

After the funeral, since no relatives had been present, no wake had been arranged. The group of mourners, consisting mainly of some office colleagues and friends, quickly dispersed. The office people had to get back, having got only a few hours off, the others went on to whatever was next on the agenda. Angela had driven herself to the cemetery. Now, greatly relieved that it was all over, she returned to her car. She wound down the car window but did not start the engine. She waited for others to leave, she wanted a moment of repose.

It was a glorious May day, such as only happens on rare occasions. The silence was blissful, there was no one in sight. If that is the foretaste of everlasting peace, for which the priest so earnestly implored God, I am all for it, the thought occurred to her. One could even hear a bird or two. The sun bit down on the ground with ferocity, the shrubs and trees had that fresh, newly donned look. But soon another funeral party entered the cemetery gate and Angela started the car. 'Oh well,' she said aloud, 'that is that.'

As she had the day off from the office, on the way home she stopped at the corner shop to get some food for lunch. Ham, French bread and some pickles. Only after paying the bill did she realise that nobody would be coming any more, asking, 'Where are the pickles?' She felt a bit weepy but shrugged it off. After all, for the last year or so her affair with Henry had been practically over. There was no sense pretending otherwise. After the last bust-up she had really made up her mind to put a stop to it.

119

I still have my key to Henry's flat, she mused. Better send it back to that executor of Henry's will, that tall man at the funeral – what was his name? . . . Nesbitt, yes, never met him before.

Next day Mr Nesbitt telephoned. Would she be good enough to meet him in Henry's flat? He was the executor of Henry's will, but he had not much knowledge of his more mundane affairs. He would like some pointers, as he knew she was his close friend. There was also the matter of Henry's will. They made an appointment for early afternoon two days later, Angela stipulating it must end by three o'clock, as she had to fetch her son from school.

When they met, there was really not that much to discuss. Mr Nesbitt explained that, though he had known Henry well, back in the army days, recently they had seldom seen each other. He also told Angela that the flat and all other effects were left to Henry's estranged wife Nicky, except for a legacy of £1,000 which had been left to Angela.

Angela was speechless. She had not known anything about the existence of a wife. In a second, the missing piece of the puzzle, why Henry would not marry her, fell into place. He had a wife. Angela became very angry. 'I don't want any money,' she blurted out.

'As you wish, as you wish,' came Mr Nesbitt's conciliatory answer. 'Think it over. I suppose Nicky will sell the place, but if there is anything here you would like to have, I am sure it can be arranged.'

'No thank you.' And then suddenly Angela asked, 'What is the wife like?' She did it impulsively and regretted it as soon as the words were out of her mouth.

'I don't really know what Nicky is like now. I met her in the old army days, when one met brother officers' wives as a matter of routine. She was a nice girl, vivacious, even flighty, but really quite harmless. Of course, when the boy died, that put the lid on it. Henry hit the bottle, Nicky felt doubly deserted and so they drifted apart. He was very fond of the kid. Soon afterwards Henry left the army. I stayed on and our ways parted.'

120

'I must go,' said Angela. 'Here is the key to the flat. Please don't involve me any more in this business. I am really an outsider.'

She picked Toby up from school, and when they got home she had to put up with another reminder of Henry, this time coming from Toby. 'Now that Uncle Henry is dead, what about the boat? Who is going to sail it?'

Angela suddenly realised that she had quite forgotten about the boat. She and Henry had been co-owners of a small sailing boat, not much more than a dinghy. It was Toby and Henry who were the chief sailing enthusiasts. As soon as the weather became reasonable they used to spend every weekend sailing the hospitable waters near Southampton, where the boat was moored.

'I suppose we could buy out the ownership,' answered Angela, 'and sail it ourselves.'

'But you are not good enough,' complained Toby. 'We need a man!'

'We'll see. Don't worry, it will be all right, somebody will turn up.'

And indeed somebody did, but not necessarily the person Angela would have liked to meet. A week later the phone rang and a woman asked for Miss Wilson. 'Speaking,' replied Angela, in her neutral voice.

'It is rather difficult.' The voice seemed unsure of reception. 'This is Mrs Gill, Nicky Gill. I would like to meet you. I know Mr Nesbitt told me you didn't want to be involved, but perhaps you could spare me an hour or so. I am staying at Henry's flat – would you like to come round sometime?'

Angela wanted to refuse, but something in the woman's voice made her hesitate. 'Yes . . . all right.' She paused. 'But you had better come here. It is easier that way because of Toby. I work all week and could only meet you at the weekend.' They settled for the following Saturday.

When Nicky came in, she looked quite different from what Angela had imagined. She was of medium height, rather on the plump side with short, cropped hair turning grey. She sat down, not quite sure of herself, and looked around the room.

And then Toby took over. He was the great communicator of the family. Soon Nicky was presented with his latest craze to admire: the Dr Who assortment, Daleks, Cybermen, the Tardis, Dr Who himself – the lot. Nicky seemed to be totally absorbed, asked the right questions, made pertinent comments. Nobody even noticed when Angela slipped out to the kitchen to get the tea.

After tea, when Toby retired to his bedroom to watch his favourite programme on television, Nicky smiled and said, 'You have a wonderful child, Miss Wilson.'

'Yes, on occasions,' replied Angela, nonetheless quite pleased.

'Is he Henry's son?' came the direct question.

'Yes.' Angela was not prepared to elaborate.

Then Nicky added: 'He looks like Henry – especially the eyes. I am so glad.' And soon she got up and was gone.

Nicky arrived at the flat in a despondent, even sombre, mood. Obviously the girl didn't like her. No wonder. If she had been in love with Henry she probably resented all his previous relationships. And goodness only knows what Henry had told her about his marriage. He could have made her into a real harridan. But that boy. Oh, what a child! So much like Mark. She winced. It still hurt. If Mark had lived, perhaps she and Henry would have solved their difficulties. After all, it was Mark who had held them together.

Now Nicky knew what she was going to do. She would sell her shop, which in the last two years had been losing money anyway, and move to London. What was the point of fighting a losing battle? Ever since the marina had been built the competition of larger, better equipped stores had proved too much for her little souvenir shop. Her sailing days were as good as over, and the winters on the exposed Norfolk coast were really grim. Her arthritis got worse each year. The damp and windy climate put too much pressure on her health. If she moved, perhaps she could, in some way, get to know Angela and have the privilege of watching Toby grow. Yes, Toby was the decisive factor.

Angela, washing up, also gave a thought or two to her

122

visitor. On the surface, she looked harmless enough. Toby had taken to her straight away, not always the case. Why, then, did she dislike her? She didn't have the appearance of the proverbial wronged wife. But there was something – Angela could not quite put her finger on it. And then the reason suddenly surfaced. Nicky had something that Angela had wanted for a long time. She had Henry's name. The realisation made Angela sit down. Am I plain jealous? It seems so. I would have given a lot to have been married to Henry, to give Toby a name. He could have got a divorce. But the bastard wouldn't. I wonder why. I shall probably never know. Never mind, though. Nicky has the name, but I have Toby, and will do my best for him, on my own. It seemed that this emotional scoring ended in a draw.

During the summer Angela took Toby sailing on several occasions, but it was not the same as with Henry. Some rigging had to be adjusted, or replaced; Angela was not sure just what should be done. Not being sure, either, that the boat was safe, she wouldn't venture far from shore, to Toby's disappointment. It became more and more apparent that she needed some professional advice, which was not forthcoming. Either that, or the boat had to go. Toby would take it badly, but Angela was not affluent enough to engage a permanent expert for the whole season. She left it for the time being, promising herself to solve it next year.

Sometime in September Angela received a note from Nicky. She was now settled in Henry's flat and going through his papers. She had discovered some photographs of Angela and Toby – would they like to have them? Perhaps they could join her for a cup of tea one afternoon?

On being told of the proposed visit to Nicky, Toby was not all that keen. But when Angela mentioned that perhaps they might settle something about the boat – after all, half of it belonged to Nicky – Toby eagerly accepted the invitation.

The flat had changed out of recognition. There was a slightly nautical feel about it. Most of the furniture had been replaced, and now there were glass-fronted display cabinets containing models of ships, boats, yachts and other craft. There was one full of trophies, probably also connected with sailing. The walls were covered with enlarged photographs of various boats and their crews. Toby was visibly overwhelmed. He went from one exhibit to another, demanding explanations, thrilled and impressed. He was obviously quite unprepared for such a show and could not conceive that all these trophies had a connection with Nicky. 'Are you a sailing fan?' he asked eventually.

'I used to be,' Nicky replied. 'At one time I represented England at international competitions.'

'This is incredible,' exclaimed Toby. 'After all, you are a woman!'

'Toby, don't be rude,' Angela intervened. 'Mrs Gill –'

'Nicky,' corrected Nicky.

'All right then, Nicky is a champion, as you can see.'

Toby still had to verify a few things. 'Are you better than men at sailing?'

'I hope so. Anyway, as good as most of them, and perhaps better than some.'

The tea was served, and the two women exchanged some remarks. Then suddenly, halfway through, Toby exclaimed, 'Mummy, Mummy, don't you see, this is it! This is what we were looking for – a partner!' And the whole story about the boat tumbled out – Uncle Henry's dexterity, the present difficulties, the unsure future.

Nicky listened intently and then suggested that she might have a look at the boat and try to bring it up to standard.

'Mummy,' Toby implored, 'say "Yes".' His eyes were sparkling, his face excited and eager.

Angela felt herself being drawn into a new relationship which she was not sure she wanted. But there was Toby, beaming and animated, and there was Nicky, just as keen as Toby. Perhaps I owe it to Toby, and to Nicky – and even to Henry – she thought.

She pondered for a while and eventually said, 'Shall we give it a try, then, next weekend?'

A SALUTE TO FAIRIES

From the world of storytellers we are given to understand that at the christening of practically every princess a fairy godmother would appear (sometimes more than one) and, depending on the gifts bestowed, the future of the child would be determined.

Why not try to simplify things a little? Let's argue that at every baby's birth a fairy or two are present. It seems just as good as any other way of explaining the character of the child in question and a great deal more romantic.

There would be, of course, the most important fairy – the life-giving fairy, who is obliged to witness every birth on earth by the ancient law in the statute book of fairies. It would be the waving of her wand that allowed the baby to draw his or her first breath and, should the life-giving fairy fail to appear or not make the gesture with her wand at the right time – it could spell trouble and would end in a mishap.

Then there would be the second most important fairy, the fairy of beauty, together with a number of minor fairies by the name of handsome, pretty, presentable, and so on. The beauty fairy is a perfectionist, inclined to be narcissistic, spending a long time viewing her own image while other helpers attend to her duties. She is inclined to sulk for long periods, should she notice some discrepancy between what her vanity requires and reality shows. But should she be in a good mood, pleased with herself, and decide to go on a job – my goodness – can she perform miracles! From the most unpromising material, just by waving her wand, a beautiful child would evolve. Some say such a child is as beautiful as the fairy herself (or even more so) but that sort of talk is rather kept secret.

The fairy of goodness, together with her cousin the fairy of good intentions, next come to mind. Both are doing as much as possible, but as there are only two of them, and having so many calls for their presence, they are sometimes, alas, absent from the moment of birth! Should that happen, history well demonstrates what it could lead to, with devastating results.

Then there are, of course, the fairy of faith and the fairy of truth – on the whole avoiding each other, explaining that they are not compatible; closely followed by the fairy of chastity, demoted lately to the status of secondary fairies, and being rather cut up about it.

However, there is no fairy of love; this quality has to develop from the ingredients received at birth and can't be bestowed on an infant in a purely magical manner. Therefore, it is rather a question of luck, of which fairies attend the baby's entrance into this world, that determines the ability to love and be loved.

Nobody was ever able to explain why – perhaps because the mother of the baby to be born had believed in fairies long past the age at which children stop doing so, or maybe because, when she had grown up, some people called her fey, as she was aware and capable of hearing and seeing something others possessed no faculty to discern. But a few weeks before the end of that year, each and every fairy received a memorandum:

7 DECEMBER 1984 – NURSING HOME. A boy to be born, to be called DOMINIC. Your presence is absolutely essential. This is a three-line whip.

Signed: THE REGISTRAR OF FAIRIES

No wonder the midwife complained that the labour room seemed to be full of static electricity, and an Irish nurse had a slight suspicion that a strayed fairy might have wandered into her ward. The happy mother held her little son proudly, smiling in that faraway way only she was capable of. Who

126

knows what she was thinking? Was she wondering what gifts the baby brought with him into this world? That was for the future to reveal. She could have been sure of only one gift he had certainly received – he was a beautiful baby.

HOLIDAY POLITICS

'Two women in the kitchen,' her mother used to say, 'are one too many.' Admirable sentiment, Veronica sometimes reminded herself, particularly after a prolonged session of preparing a meal together with Miriam, her sister-in-law. Try as they might, things didn't seem to work out. Surprisingly, the meals would be late, cold as often as not, and not to the standard one would expect from two experienced house-wives. Had there been any post-mortem – but there never was – the reason for such a poor showing would probably have been put by each of the participants at the door of the other. But such is human nature.

Miriam, when alone, entertained similar thoughts. Supposing, she mused, I had to share a kitchen with Veronica all the time, and she shuddered. It was bad enough on holidays, when one knew it was only a temporary arrangement.

Neither would admit in public that they found the current state of affairs unsatisfactory, and change it to shifts. One day one, and the next the other. It would have been considered a sort of failure, marring the 'perfect holiday' (the term applied by the respective husbands of these two entrapped cooks). Their husbands, close and loving brothers, seeing their families together, couldn't conceive of any undercurrents.

Miriam was Jewish. She did not keep a strictly kosher kitchen but still adhered to some dietary rules passed on to her when she was a child. That was the reason behind the decision to have her always at hand when meals were prepared, so that no glaring mistake would be committed.

128

Miriam's husband, Paul, not being Jewish, couldn't care less what he ate, and their twin sons, Robert and Larry, seemed, if anything, to be put out if their mother expressed a final decision as to the contents of a controversial meal. The rest of the family, by which we mean Paul's brother John, his wife Veronica and their three little daughters, all viewed it as a mild eccentricity on the part of Aunty Miriam, to be indulged good-naturedly.

But, food apart, the holiday was really shaping in the most enjoyable way. Paul and John, so much alike except for a few minor quirks, spent hours by the pool. Because of the nature of their work, they seldom saw one another for any length of time. Now they had an opportunity to catch up on the news and engage in lots of discussions on various topics, learning about one another and their respective development, if any, since the last time they had had a chance to talk.

The subjects ranged from economics to philosophy; in fact, anything that at that particular time occupied the mind of either of the brothers. There was only one subject which, if not entirely banned, did not appear high on the agenda: politics, particularly with regard to the immediate past and embracing the Second World War.

The brothers knew from experience that there was a certain danger in tackling that subject, and for rather an unusual reason. Miriam's grandmother's family had perished in the Holocaust, whereas Veronica's grandfather was German – a prisoner of war who, having fallen in love with an English girl, did not go home after his release but stayed in England, married the girl and, in a most unobtrusive way, blended in with his surroundings.

These events were far enough removed from the present time not to have caused an outright animosity but, as often happens in families, should a purely personal dislike occur for any particular member, it is so much easier to attribute it, consciously or unconsciously, to some propensity inherited from the past.

Therefore, the whole family, for all the good time they were having, and with plenty of space in the two comfortable flats, a heated pool large enough to accommodate the gregarious and the solitary, awaited with some disquiet the arrival of an extra guest to join them for the third and last week of their paradise.

He was Veronica's nephew, living in Germany, now on his way home after a year spent in Israel working on a kibbutz. Hans was 17, well endowed with brains, rather sensitive and, in common with many of his compatriots, somehow compelled to do something for Israel, as if in reparation for the many foul deeds committed by the Germans during the Second World War.

What was he going to say? How did he view the present dilemma facing that beleaguered nation? What would his politics be? These, and other questions, intruded from time to time into the minds of the otherwise relaxed members of the party. (Of course that did not include the children, who were immersed in their own more or less vocal, pursuits.)

John and Paul went to meet Hans in Palma, and tried hard not to let the forthcoming visit impinge on their mood. Since the plane was late, they spent most of their time in the bar, fortifying themselves with a concoction made of rum and Coca-Cola, and consuming large quantities of peanuts to dispel the cumulative effects of their imbibing.

When at last the passengers started to emerge from the customs hall, the brothers looked in vain for a tall, blond youth. Everybody they encountered seemed to have a companion, and at last they realised that Hans, too, was not on his own. He had a girl with him, dark-looking, and very Semitic. Both of them had haversacks on frames and held in their hands plastic bags filled to overflowing with duty-free drinks.

'You must be John and Paul,' said Hans, in good, if rather heavily accented, English. 'I hope you will find room for Esther at the villa. She is coming with me to Germany for a two-month stay.'

What could anyone say? Of course, they were delighted to meet Esther; there was plenty of room at the villa, the more the merrier. What the thoughts of the two brothers were was another matter. It might have occurred to them that the situation, already difficult, was about to become even more complicated than they had anticipated.

Introductions completed, a shared room settled, and a long dip in the pool accomplished, they all sat down at last to their first meal together. First, the family's news was exchanged, but it was rather scanty, since Hans had not been home for over a year. The young people immediately started to talk politics, and wild horses wouldn't have driven them away from the subject.

While Hans approved Miriam's dietary rules, Esther considered them practically primitive throwbacks to ancient superstition. She made a point of mixing meat and dairy products, to the annoyance of Aunty Miriam, who rather expected an ally in Esther. On the other hand, she did not care for the approval coming from Hans, because of his nationality. Miriam's children, of course, joined in, feeling vindicated, while Paul didn't know what he should do.

Hans proved to be a fanatic about the right of Israel to build the settlements on what he considered to be their sacred heritage land, a position which Veronica and John regarded as a bit drastic, having read in the press about the plight of the Palestinian Arabs. The fanatical opinions expressed by Hans met with disapproval on the part of Veronica, who dared not think what his parents would say, once he got home. They were well-renowned for their even-handed approach to all problems, and Veronica deemed Hans's present state of mind as an hysterical symptom, bordering on brainwashing. She put it down to the excitable company he had kept in the last year.

It was a relief when the meal was brought to a close. But, over the next day or two, two distinct followings of political involvement emerged. One, consisting of Miriam, Hans and Paul, under duress, being champions of everything Jewish, and a second faction made up of Veronica, John and Esther, rather pro-Arab, highly critical of most of Israel's ventures in politics.

Since this change in the preoccupations of the adults, the

131

children really enjoyed themselves. The grown-ups could easily be distracted by their unending arguments, and so the children had the run of the house and pool, with all rules in abeyance.

John and Paul finally decided that something must be done. The easiest way, of course, would be to prevail on the young troublemakers to put forward their departure. Yet, somehow they were unwilling to pursue such a drastic solution. But what was to be done? After all, the young couple would go anyway, leaving behind the hitherto united family in disarray.

The solution, when it came, was perhaps more than anyone had bargained for. One of the girls, Eva, strictly against orders, since the pool did not have any lighting, went for a late swim when it was already dark. Her parents thought, in retrospect, that this foolish action might have been a dare coming from one, or all, of her cousins, but what really happened certainly proved to be an ordeal for everyone. Eva jumped into the pool and, whether she miscalculated the depth, or the dark pool frightened her – anyway she appeared to be in difficulties, shouting for help. Robert and Larry jumped in to give her assistance, but Eva was pulling them down. The other girl, Sara, followed them into the water and only contributed to the ensuing chaos. It was left to the youngest girl, Lucy, to run for help and tell the grown-ups about the possible disaster. She did it in the most dramatic way, bursting on to the veranda, where drinks were being served, the conversation still in the throes of politics, with a cry, 'Everyone's drowning – help! Help!'

They all rushed to the pool; they could hear splashing and thrashing but could hardly see anything. Hans shouted, 'Get some light!' and dived into the water, followed by Esther and Paul. John rushed to the car, drove it as near to the pool as possible and switched the headlamps on. Veronica looked for torches and towels, while Miriam, not a good swimmer, rushed round the pool alternately imploring God's mercy and berating the children.

Soon the children were out. Eva and Robert were in a bad

way and Hans and Esther concentrated on giving them artificial respiration. At last they succeeded in making them sick, thus starting their gasping, strenuous breathing. There was an absolute rumpus going on. The parents claimed their offspring. It took the better part of the evening to settle them into bed, and it left the grown-ups thoroughly exhausted. When, eventually, they gathered for snacks and coffee, Miriam exploded: 'Look what we have done to our children! We nearly lost two of them. And how the hell would that have helped the political solution in the Middle East? I forbid, absolutely forbid, any more discussions on that subject.' Then she rushed out, crying, and slammed the door behind her.

The last two days of the holiday were spent in sightseeing and buying presents. On the last Saturday the party dispersed; some went by plane, some by car, all, perhaps, a little wiser?

THE TIDE

Like an incoming tide . . . Life has been to me like an incoming tide. This comparison occurred to Fiona, deep in thought, taking a stroll along the shore, in a quiet, small, seaside resort.

It was very cold. She wore an anorak with the hood up, a scarf wound twice round her neck. Her hands, in woollen gloves deep in her pockets, still felt cold, and so did her feet, though encased in sturdy lined boots. But Fiona was not conscious of the prevailing temperature. Her eyes were far on the horizon, mesmerised by the force and the unstoppable progress of the incoming tide.

As it was out of season, she had the beach to herself – much to her liking, since the reason for a few days' break from her home surroundings was precisely that: to be on her own. To take stock of the past and, if possible, to get some bearings for the future.

The sky was overcast. Thick, grey clouds accompanied the towering, turbid waves on the way to the shore, where they pounded against it at a measured and relentless speed. The sea looked angry, very much in accord with Fiona's mood. She kept taking a few steps at a time, stopping to face the force of the wind, then resuming her walk again.

Life took everything from me I held dear, like this tide, except that I am not the passive, compliant stretch of sand, submitting with resignation to the superior force of the tide. I resent it. For Fiona was a proud woman. That was her strength and her weakness. She faced with dignity the blows that life aimed at her but she did not know how to bend with the wind,

134

and when a position because untenable she retreated, with bitterness and bad grace barely contained within herself.

Fiona was on the wrong side of 50. She already had behind her 20 years of a fairly successful marriage – that is, till it broke up. David, her husband, was rarely home – he worked abroad as a salesman, and was good at his job. Ten years ago he had told her bluntly that he wanted a divorce. He had been offered a permanent position in Italy. He had met somebody there who captured his emotions. He was sorry, but that was it. David was very accommodating about the divorce. He left the house to her and custody of the children, and promised maintenance for as long as the children needed schooling. But he wanted freedom.

Fiona's pride took over. There were hardly any tears and, if there were, they were shed in private. She told David, 'Don't tell me anything more about it. You want to go – then go.' And she left it at that. But she agonised inside, and the hurt was bad. But, of course, there were the children, Susan and John. They needed her now more than ever before. She must make a go of it. This was not the time to feel sorry for herself.

Then she met Jeff. Funnily enough, she fell in love with him. He moved in, but never got round to marrying her. Fiona's pride kept her from making an issue of it. Surely the children were old enough to understand that she had some private needs of her own. But Jeff was not a prudent choice. Not being the marrying sort, he was also not the fatherly type. He was full of ideas, changing them rapidly. He wanted to emigrate; soon afterwards he wanted to move into the country and try his hand at farming; then again he was all for setting himself up in business. None of these schemes materialised because, as he put it, 'Fiona puts the children first.' Yes, it was true. So Fiona couldn't really blame him when, on coming home one evening from her part-time job, she discovered two suitcases and some bits and pieces in the hall. Jeff was moving out. He explained that he had to make a break while he still had some spunk in him, some initiative. If he waited till Fiona's children were old enough to fend for themselves, he himself would be too old to have a go at some exciting

135

enterprise. He was sorry, but that was the score.

Fiona's pride came to her rescue. 'Of course, Jeff, you go ahead. I wish you luck' – and cried herself silly on a number of nights, but kept a brave face for the outsiders. Life must go on, except that she suddenly felt old, and used.

After Jeff, there were no more men in Fiona's life. The children were to have all the attention. They were on the brink of making some important decisions. They needed her guidance and the fruits of her experience.

But, again, she was badly mistaken. John joined the navy and only told her about it when he was ready to leave, and Susan! Susan was a confused, superficial fool who couldn't and probably never would make up her mind what it was she really wanted. Fiona was usually called upon to pick up the pieces after some – yet again – disastrous venture. She talked to Susan, tried to help, to give some direction to the girl's disorganised attempts at planning her future. She warned her against foolhardy decisions taken on the spur of the moment to get involved with men, only to be told, 'What about Jeff?'

A week ago Susan had told her mother she was going to join her father in Italy. Fiona knew the children kept in touch with David, even thought it decent of him to show some interest in his offspring. But that last bit of news knocked her out. She was going to lose Susan too. She would be all alone. Submerged, like that sandy beach, which was now no longer to be seen. After a life of caring, life like the savage mimic of the oncoming tide, took all.

That night Fiona had a dream. She was shopping for a dress. She knew exactly what she wanted; the cut, the embellishments. It had to be black, for it was a very formal, important occasion which necessitated the purchase. She visited a score of shops, eagerly examining the rails full of dresses. They had lots of dresses of the kind she was looking for, but none in her size. Fiona had no time to wait for the shop assistant to order the size she needed. She had to have the dress that very day. There was only one more shop she could think of and, surprisingly, they had the dress she wanted in her size, but in different colours – pink, yellow, red, green, blue, but not black. Fiona was devastated.

Then the dream became confused, as dreams are prone to do. It seemed that Fiona bought the lot – the pink, the yellow, the red, the green and the blue too. She had this enormous parcel, which she could hardly carry – and then she woke up.

It was very early; there was the promise of a sunny, mild day in the air. Fiona was highly relieved that it was only a dream and that she had not committed the folly of landing herself with a purchase which was beyond her needs and means.

She went over the dream in her thoughts – she remembered it in detail. An association occurred to her. Perhaps she had been looking for the wrong colours, only a few selective values in her life? Perhaps there were different colours of joy and fulfilment from the ones she had pursued all these years? Things that would give her personal satisfaction – and a new outlook.

What if she joined a painting class? She had always wanted to. Or took a foreign language course? She might divide the house into two flats and take in a young family with a child. It might be fun to hear a child's voice again in the garden.

She grew more ambitious. She might learn how to parachute or ski, or take up old-time dancing. The more she thought, the more possibilities came to mind.

Fiona packed, and on the way to the station stopped for a moment at the point where, only yesterday, she had spent several hours assessing her past. The tide was receding. The beach grew, with every minute, larger and larger in size. The freshly washed sand glistened in the rising sun, virgin in appearance, save for some contours left by the receding waves. There was nothing and no one on the beach except for a few seagulls, mewling in unison.

Fiona left her suitcase on the promenade and stepped on to the sandy beach. She started to make new tracks in the sand, delighted with the results – like a child.

MARY AND MARTHA

There was nothing extraordinary about Abbot Street. It consisted of a long row of semi-detached houses, similar in style though different in some embellishments. Mary and Martha lived in adjacent houses, their gardens separated by wire net fencing. It was there, at the fence, that they met, soon after Martha and her family moved in. They liked the look of each other and instantly became friends.

Soon the autumn term started and both girls were sent to the neighbourhood school, sharing the same form, desk and, quite often, their sandwiches. Their friendship was to continue for a very long time, through junior school and grammar school, and it was only after passing their exams that the separation occurred. Mary did not want to go to college; she had set her heart on going into a business, and so started as a shop assistant in the best department store the town could boast. Martha had been offered a place at university, not far from where she lived. It was, however, their first separation, and they both felt quite unhappy about it.

For the two, now young women, still felt the same about each other. Their friendship grew with the years and was, in a way, much stronger than the ties they felt towards their respective siblings. There wasn't anything that one of the girls didn't know about the other. When separated, voluminous and frequent letters were exchanged, bringing them up to date with the small and the significant happenings in their lives. They were so close that often even their thoughts seemed to interchange. It was quite remarkable.

When Martha graduated, she returned home for some

time, overjoyed at being with Mary again. She did not know what to do exactly with her degree in humanities, and soon solved the question by marrying a handsome graduate who had fallen in love with her in her last year at college. Regretfully, she and her husband had to move north, but that was where his job was.

Mary, not long afterwards, married a local tenant-publican, and so had her wish fulfilled by becoming a full partner in the business.

That did not mean that the friendship of yore vanished, or even diminished. There were letters, telephone calls and meetings. Each year, on the last Sunday in August, which was the date they had first met by that wire fence, both women made a journey to a town more or less halfway between their respective homes, and met for lunch at an hotel called The Four Feathers. They would spend the whole afternoon together, have tea, and then leave, promising to meet in a year's time. And they kept their tryst for a good many years. The appearance of children in Mary's life did not deter them from the yearly pilgrimage – any kind of holidays were out of the question at that particular time. Their husbands accepted it, and made it easy for them to be absent from home on that particular date.

On the tenth anniversary of their meetings, Mary arrived first. She got herself a drink and watched the door impatiently. But Martha failed to put in an appearance. Mary waited for nearly three hours, then, in desperation, phoned Martha's home, to be told that Martha had left at the appointed time to meet her. Disappointed and apprehensive, Mary left for home and on arrival immediately phoned Martha's husband. But not surprisingly, there was no reply. Mary jumped to the conclusion that there must have been an accident. She spent an uncomfortable night, waking several times, and tried to contact Martha's home the next morning. But again there was nobody at home.

She was so worried that, asking her mother to look after the children, she was getting ready to travel to Martha, when the telephone rang and Martha's voice sounded in her ear.

Martha apologised for Sunday, said she had left her husband, and would be in touch when she had a permanent address. Then the line went dead. Mary was dumbfounded. She was not sure what she should do – whether to pass this message to Martha's husband, or to keep out of this rather tricky situation. She decided to do nothing – after all, her loyalties lay with Martha, who might have good reasons for leaving her husband. She would wait for Martha to contact her and then, when she knew more, decide. But no letter ever arrived. Martha vanished completely.

Overwrought – more, broken-hearted – Mary went about her wifely duties, helped in the bar, looked after the children; but her thoughts continually went to Martha and her disappearance. She reread Martha's letters, particularly the more recent ones, looking for clues. Since they had had no secrets from each other, Mary knew that Martha's marriage had not really worked satisfactorily for years. Charles had proved to be one of those husbands who, for all the charm and sweet words, was a selfish, self-centred man, prone to violent outbursts and long sulks. He was also rather mean and kept Martha short of cash, and even the little she got had to be accounted for in minute detail. However, things had not got any worse in recent years and Martha, a resourceful woman, was quite philosophical about her spouse. She had found herself a part-time job, to be more independent, and, if not happy, she certainly did not seem to contemplate a separation or a divorce.

Mary was quite prepared to go to any lengths to find anything about her missing friend. She wrote to Charles, anxious for any news, but the letter was returned with a laconic annotation 'Gone Away'.

Still, life had to go on and Mary, immersed in family affairs, couldn't brood for ever. In a way she felt let down by Martha; her silence seemed an uncalled-for gesture towards a person so close and devoted as Mary had been over all those years.

With Christmas approaching, there was a lot of talk in the papers and on the television about the plight of homeless people. Viewers watching a programme on the subject were presented with a group of down-and-outs warming themselves round a blazing brazier on a cold December night. There was a short interview with one of the group and Mary, watching the programme, cast her eyes over the rest of the people appearing on the screen. In a corner, sitting rather apart, was a woman who, to her astonishment, she recognised, or thought she did – Martha! It lasted only a few seconds, then the camera moved to a studio discussion, leaving Mary thoroughly worked up. Was that Martha or, rather, a gross distortion of the old Martha? She couldn't decide, alternating between accepting and rejecting the idea . . . Anyway, she felt she must investigate, and had already started to make mental preparations for rushing to London in search of her friend when Stewart, on being told, absolutely forbade the idea.

'What are you going to do when you reach London? You are not even sure it was Martha. Will you comb those unsavoury surroundings at night, alone, risking being mugged – or even worse? And even if you find her – what then? She is probably on drugs, or drink, changed out of recognition.'

'But at least I could speak to her, find out why, perhaps help her to make a new start, give her some money. I won't rest till I find something about her. You know she is the closest person to me in the whole world!'

'And what about me, the children, the business? I can't do without you. I rely on you for help now that the Christmas holiday season is here. The children are looking forward to the celebrations. Get your priorities right, Mary. I categorically forbid this reckless venture.'

And so Mary acquiesced. But, getting into her comfortable bed at night, in the well-heated bedroom, she couldn't get Martha – or the woman like Martha – out of her mind. She felt she should do something, but did not know what.

The opportunity to search for Martha came about sooner than she expected, and in circumstances Mary wished had never arisen. Her youngest daughter, Clare, had not been well for some time. She was suffering severe headaches and had lost weight and, soon after Christmas, started to have some sort of fits. Alarmed, Mary consulted the family doctor and on his advice and recommendation was immediately referred for advice to a children's hospital in London which was renowned for its specialised facilities and surgical skills.

A tumour on the brain was suspected, and Clare was admitted to hospital for tests and, if necessary, a brain operation. Mary, of course, went with her daughter, and was given accommodation in the nurses' wing. Striken with anxiety, she spent long hours waiting for results, her nerves stretched to the limit, unable to eat, sleep or even think.

To relieve the tension, after she tucked Clare up for the night, and on the advice of the staff, Mary would leave the hospital and venture out for a few moments' relaxation. Having found out from a friendly nurse the possible places where the down-and-outs congregated at night, she set off to find Martha.

Incredibly enough, she was lucky at her third attempt. She was just thinking of giving up her search on that particular evening when, in an obscure cul-de-sac somewhere behind Victoria Station, she located a solitary woman sitting on an orange box, with her back against a disused doorway. It was Martha. She had a blanket thrown over her shoulders and a woolly hat brought well down to her ears, so that little showed of her features. But Mary could see the overall expression on the face, because of the convenient street lamp on the other side of the road, and was appalled. That face was absolutely blank, immobile, with eyes closed. Martha might just as well have been dead. Standing across the street from Martha, Mary considered her next move. The thought of lice, even vermin, crossed her mind, for Martha looked dirty, unkempt, with matted hair escaping from that ridiculous hat.

But the pull of friendship asserted itself. Mary crossed the street, touched Martha's shoulders and said, 'Martha. It's me, Mary.' There was no response. Martha seemed to be far removed from reality. Mary crouched by her old friend and was suddenly so overcome with grief – her own and Martha's – that she started to cry, releasing all the bottled-up emotions of the last few months. She spoke of her distress, her terrible anxiety, the possibility of losing Clare, the dread of the operation the next morning. In a way it was like old times, emptying all the hurt and worry on to Martha.

While she was talking, she was conscious of some reaction on Martha's part; she opened her eyes, her features acquired some life, and then she said, 'It will be all right, Mary, your child will live. I give you my word. I know it will be all right.' She put out a dirty hand and gently stroked Mary's cheek.

Mary didn't know how she got through the next few days. Clare stayed barely conscious after the operation, her poor head bandaged, her face pale and drawn. Mary stayed with her day and night; she couldn't risk going out in case her child needed her. She wanted to tell Martha that she was right – that the tumour was benign, and that she had found in the contact with her friend that extra ounce of courage that allowed her to withstand her ordeal.

As soon as Stewart came up, she left him with Clare and rushed to the place where she had found Martha that night. But Martha was gone.

THE NEED

He stood with his back to the window, hands deep in his pockets. He looked so handsome with the fair hair, showing just a hint of receding, and features deserving a second look. The picture was, alas, spoiled by the twist of his mouth in displeasure. 'Why did you do it?' he asked, and when Inga did not answer, repeated, 'Why did you accept the invitation to Radlings, when I told you after last time I don't want to go there any more?'

Inga, sitting at the table, looked more indifferent than guilty. She put her folded hands in what could be described as a half-supplicatory manner and replied. 'I don't know – at the time it seemed a good idea. Radlings were very pressing. They like you.'

'But I told you never to accept an invitation from them!'

'Well, I didn't think you meant it. After all, it is such a small matter. Look, I'll phone them and cancel the date, say I didn't check with you beforehand, and now find you are busy on the day.' Inga reached for a cigarette and lit it; she was getting a bit rattled.

'You never pay any attention to what I say!' The grimace on Nigel's face grew even more pronounced. 'Mind!' he shouted suddenly. 'You will spill that ash!'

And indeed Inga spilt it. It lay offensively on the table's shiny surface, all in a heap. She got up and went to fetch a duster.

'Not with a cloth, you will only smudge it. Pick it up first with a piece of paper, like this.' Nigel came over and, reaching into his pocket, drew out a small card. It looked like a visiting card. He scooped the ash back into the ashtray, then, taking the cloth from Inga's hands, dusted the offending stain. He gave a quick shine to the surrounding area and handed the cloth back to Inga.

She left the room, and leaving the duster in the kitchen, used the back door to get away into the garden. This was the best way of bringing to a close a tricky situation.

It was mid-March. The daffodils were fully in bloom, except for three right in the middle of the flowerbed which were only half-grown and spoilt the overall effect. No doubt I shall hear about it, mused Inga. After all, I planted them. I must have dug the bulbs in a bit deeper than the rest.

She heard Nigel start the car. He had taken a day off from the office and volunteered to pick the children up from school. It would be easier once they came home. Nigel was very good with children, quite a different person, really. He had extraordinary patience and could manage them in a most efficient way. Better than I do, Inga smiled a bit sadly.

Nigel was a professional grumbler. He held a grudge against his superiors at the office, the neighbours, the greengrocer who called twice weekly, the man who came to clean the windows – in fact, everybody he came into contact with. Inga sometimes wondered if God, too, was included. But on the other hand he was a dependable, steady husband, devoted to the well-being of his family, a handyman who could put many so-called experts to shame. There was nothing he could not fix, mend or put right. And if he couldn't do it at first, he found out all about the problem and would accomplish it in the end. He was also generous to a fault, and if only he smiled more, he would be a very handsome man into the bargain.

Inga loved him dearly, but then she was rather inclined to foist her loving propensities on anybody within reach. She respected Nigel for his principles and steadfastness but, if hard pressed, would admit that he was very difficult to live with.

But the main – the most important – reason why Inga was prepared to put up with a lot of things was her need of Nigel.

145

Like you need your eyes, or hands, or feet. He was that part of her life which she could not absolutely dispense with. She needed Nigel to share her thoughts, to have an intelligent conversation, to make plans. Which often got her into trouble, because she was sometimes rather capricious. Inga was the sort of person who, as likely as not, would start a sentence with, 'Let's do this . . .' or 'Let's go there . . .' 'Let's ask XYZ in . . .' and Nigel's careful scrutiny saved her from many possible mistakes. So, making allowances for the differences in character of husband and wife, things had worked well, on the whole.

And probably they would have gone on working, had not Inga decided to go to the summer sales. Buffeted and pushed by a crowd of determined women, she escaped to the relative peace of the restaurant. It had only one seat empty, at a table for two – one being already occupied by a middle-aged woman with an ample bosom. After a few remarks about the sales crush, Inga recognised that her companion had an American accent. She asked, rather surprised, whether the American lady had come over especially for the sales.

'No,' the lady replied. Apparently the reason for her being in London was an attempt to introduce and establish in England a particular religious sect called Christian Friends. Soon the lady introduced herself. 'I am Mona Daring. I am also a deaconess in my church. We are trying to establish a centre in England, and this is my mission.' She delved into her enormous handbag and fished out a pamphlet. 'Here is the introductory literature, inviting everybody to our first meeting on Friday night at the Royal Hotel.' She handed Inga some pink sheets of paper full of information. 'Why don't you come? And bring your husband or friend. You might be surprised, but our meeting here could have been contrived by God.' And with that, Mona left.

Inga read the pamphlet. There was a short description of the aims and methods propounded by this new sect, imported from America. There was nothing new in it on the theological side, just the usual platitudes. But one sentence, particularly, caught Inga's eye. The sect was especially aimed at people

146

who were in a no-win situation, where there was no escape from the status quo and the existing conditions had become beyond endurance.

So, on Friday evening, Inga went, with mixed feelings. She was not a churchgoer as a rule, but she had an open mind and from time to time she longed for some sort of commitment. Would this be it?

She liked what she heard, and eagerly participated in the singing of some hymns, copies of which had been distributed. She also found interesting the practical advice to those who found life intolerable. It came as a selection of short songs or ditties, applicable to different needs. It was recommended that, when faced with a critical situation, one should shut one's mind to everything and burst into song. Nobody could object to singing – after all, it was a sign of joy, and such action was guaranteed to bring relief and escape from whatever one had to endure. Then, at weekly meetings which had to be attended, the members were to relate how successful they had been with their 'singing weapon', thus encouraging one another.

And so Inga started attending the Friday meetings and would come home determined to put into practice this new method of dealing with Nigel's pernickety behaviour. But she was rather afraid to do it quite openly – the most she would do was to hum the prescribed melody *sotto voce*. After a few days of qualified success, she ventured to pronounce the words, still at a reduced volume. Strangely enough, it did not seem to upset Nigel. He glanced at Inga from time to time, but seemed reassured that the singing was only a sign of light spirits. Inga grew bolder. After a particularly bad bout of Nigel's complaining, she did not argue, as she had been known to do in the past, but broke into a song. Its message usually depicted the beauty of Creation and God's benevolence towards the whole human race. And so it would go on. Nigel was puzzled, but, try as he would, there were no more arguments to be had.

The success of Inga's new approach to her life's tribulations made her even more keen to attend the Friday meetings, where she would compare notes with other participants, and by getting thus involved she began to make new friends. With their support, she became more and more dependent on other recommended exercises, like Bible reading and general discussion. She transferred, bit by bit, her need for company from Nigel to other members of the group, sharing ideas, problems and suggestions. Nigel became a peripheral figure and, to a certain degree, so did Inga's children. Without meaning it, her allegiance shifted away from her family towards this group of people from whom she received attention and support. All this happened quite painlessly, and so gradually that Inga at no time felt guilty. She embarked primarily on this new venture to facilitate her home life. But, in consequence, her family receded in importance as her personal involvement grew and other people claimed her loyalty. The need for support, for fulfilment, shifted to another source.

Nigel, of course, noticed the change, and tried to discover the real cause of what he called Inga's 'indifference' to him and the children. But by then Inga was too much taken up with the activities and proselytising of her new source of strength to allow herself to be drawn in to a confrontation. At the least sign of the impending danger of an accusation she would break into a lusty, rousing song, and kept it going until Nigel was forced to leave the room.

Soon, Inga announced that she had to go to America, to undergo a two months' course, prior to becoming a deaconess. She engaged a housekeeper and, with a triumphant song on her lips, departed one morning, leaving her family in God's care.

BORN TO LOSE?

At last I am fully prepared to admit, before all and sundry, that I am a born loser. I have been toying with this idea for quite some time and, regretfully, I have come to the conclusion that this is my lot. I have met a number of people who have displayed the same unlucky quirk. Therefore, I assume, there must be a fairly large number of us – the admitted and unadmitted losers who, even if winning some battles, unremittingly lose the wars.

Born in fairly comfortable circumstances, the youngest of a family of four boys, I enjoyed, one might say, the privileged position of being the baby of the family. Should one add to this the fact that nature had endowed me with a pleasant physical appearance, I was totally unprepared for the stark reality which confronted me as soon as I left the secure environment of my home.

It was not too difficult in the beginning. There were my older brothers to fight the battles for me, should an aggressive youngster try to bully or hurt me in any way. But as they grew up and dispersed, I had to look after my own interests, and soon realised that luck eluded me.

The most traumatic experience of my early adolescence happened in front of crowds of people. I took part in an inter-school cross-country run and had great hopes of winning, or coming near the top, since I was the best runner in our team. The race went all right for me for most of its duration. I was leading in the last stretch when, suddenly, I discovered that my shorts had begun to slide down. The elastic was giving up on me. I stopped in my tracks, absolutely frozen with apprehension. What should I do? Run, and risk my pants falling down and entangling my ankles? While I considered the options I was conscious of other runners overtaking me. The crowd of people gathered round the last 50 yards at the finish soon figured out from my anguished demeanour that I was in difficulties. Some tittering broke out and, yes, you have guessed, I was the last to cross the finishing line, holding on to my shorts with both hands.

It took me a long time to live down my mishap. I earned the nickname of 'pants-loser' and, hard as I tried later on, I never recovered my previous form in running. I was never again included in my school team. Perhaps they were wary of my bad luck.

I was a good scholar, but showed no particular aptitude in any subject. I was what is commonly referred to as an all-rounder, which is all very well, except that it makes it more difficult to choose a future career. I decided to leave school at 16 and enrol at the technical college, since I was good at working with my hands as well as at drawing.

Changing school, meeting new people, I was prepared to work hard. The first term went smoothly enough. My instructor liked me and provided me with a lot of encouragement. Unfortunately he left, for some reason, and the new man had very different methods and approach to the studies in question. Not being very experienced in dealing with people, I mentioned on several occasions the methods of his predecessor. Consequently I became unpopular with him. He paid special attention to my work, often criticising it in the extreme. He gave me the more difficult assignments, making sure I followed his ideas to the letter. Soon, a battle of wills developed between us, while the rest of the student watched in quiet amusement. I was naive enough to think I could win.

The finals came up soon after my eighteenth birthday, which proved to be, as things turned out, my most unhappy one. My parents, not a strikingly devoted couple, nevertheless had in the past provided a fairly steady background to my life (my brothers having by then left home), but apparently my parents had agreed to part as soon as I had reached maturity. My father, it transpired, had a long-standing relationship with another woman, but had given a pledge to stay with the family until the children had grown up.

And so, one day after my birthday, he packed his bags and went, leaving my mother absolutely broken, since she had never really believed that he was serious about the compromise she had agreed to, years earlier.

I failed my finals – to the great satisfaction of my instructor – not being able to concentrate on my studies in the emotionally charged atmosphere which reigned in my home as a consequence of Father's departure, as well as the changed financial circumstances. And, of course, the shock to me personally. It was too much. I refused to resit my exams, left home for a time, and just bummed around for a year. Then I returned and found employment at the local garage, with a view to becoming a qualified mechanic.

My years in this new setting were not to be envied. I was considered by my workmates to be a general dogsbody most of the time. In a way, they resented the way I spoke, my manners and general behaviour, and vented their own frustrations in life on me, who, as they put it, had had it easy from birth.

But it was also at this garage that I met Zena, the owner of a splendid sports car which often broke down and had to be brought in for repairs. Zena herself had first noticed and singled me out. I think now, with hindsight, that her flirtatious nature required some sort of mild involvement in all possible contacts with the opposite sex and, as I have mentioned before, from a promising young boy I grew into quite an attractive young man. That must have caught her eye. She always found a way for a short encounter with me. On several occasions we met after work and sometimes she took me for a spin in her prestigious car – even let me handle it for a bit, on a straight, fast road, where we went at full speed to the limits of the engine.

It was therefore not surprising that I fell in love with Zena, and her car, not paying any attention to the differences which existed in our social standing. Zena was older than I, the only daughter of a successful businessman. I was 21 and had no education to speak of, no real trade or profession, and no money. In fact, the only thing I was good for was a light-hearted relationship, the sort of thing that Zena liked to engage in, changing her partners with frequency.

One evening after work, I volunteered to deliver Zena's car, which had just had a service, to her home address. Her father answered the door, as Zena was out. I got into conversation with him about the frequency of breakdowns; the vehicle, being an expensive model, should have been more reliable. Zena's father blamed her bad driving habits. I started to defend her. As it was a hot day, her father asked me in for a drink, and I took this opportunity to make a detailed sketch of what I considered to be the intrinsic fault of the model under discussion.

Zena's father was quite impressed; he was the chairman of a company distributing sports cars all over the country. We had a most interesting conversation about sports and racing cars. He suggested that I visit one of his showrooms and, in a relatively short time, offered me a job at one of his retail outlets. One thing led to another. Soon, I was made a salesman, earning a fairly good wage and commissions on cars sold. I discovered a special aptitude for that kind of work, my looks and manners proving an advantage in dealing with customers. In a couple of years I was voted salesman of the year.

I continued my relationship with Zena all this time on an on-and-off basis; we took several holidays together, but she was unwilling to settle down and from time to time, would engage in short-lived affairs, which I had no choice but to overlook. I was deeply in love with her, and short of losing her altogether, I had to agree to her terms. Which I did – hoping that sooner or later her unpredictable behaviour would cease and I would be the one to win her for good. I hoped she would realise that I was the best man to accommodate her mercurial temperament. And so I dreamed of the day when I would marry her and embark on one long, joyful celebration of fast living, fast driving and intense love making, for which I had developed an insatiable zest. I felt that Zena would one day be mine, and I bided my time. I knew that her parents were on my side, maintaining that I was the only sensible boyfriend Zena had ever had.

The unexpected death of Zena's father had a sobering effect on her. It looked as if she had finally reached maturity. She inherited the whole business and, for the first time, had to face some responsibility. Soon after the event she spoke to me on the subject. She described the difficulties she was encountering, and of her own free will suggested that we should marry and so 'give a new lead and impetus to the rather unsettled state of affairs which had arisen in the boardroom'. She expressed herself quite openly. 'My father trusted you, and I do, too. My feelings for you are probably the nearest I could ever experience to what could be called love. Shall we chance it?'

And so, at last, I achieved my dream – Zena for a wife, and a seat on the board of a prestigious company. A total success.

It would be good to finish my story on this propitious juncture, to relate that my dreams had been rewarded with a matching reality. But it soon became apparent that, as a wife, Zena was a total fiasco – and a bore. She had accepted the new role perhaps with good intentions, but the truth was she had no idea, no notion, of regularity, order and stability. Soon our household began to resemble a battlefield. Were it not for her mother's fortnightly visits, our house would have been chock-full of unwashed crockery and unemptied wastepaper baskets. I never knew what I would find when returning home from the office. There she would be, in a beloved old dressing gown which was worn out beyond description and long overdue for dry-cleaning. We lived permanently on pizzas and Chinese takeaways, which I had to fetch on my way home from work. Then, suddenly, on returning home, I would find a laconic note saying 'Gone to the races', which meant she would come home early in the morning, the worse for drink. She even started drinking on her own, so adding to the existing disorder and general confusion.

What had happened to the butterfly girl, the enchanting creature of limitless surprises? Where was Zena of yore, her wit and coquetry as natural to her as breathing?

And so, I lost again. Not in a material sense, not in worldly advancement, since I had just been appointed chairman of the company. But, somewhere along the way, I stopped loving Zena. And I lost my precious dreams.

DOUBLE BILL

Some people thought it strange that, after 20 years of marriage and a similar number of years of motherhood, Emily had not acquired a habit of anticipating the possibility of even the best laid plans coming adrift. Her marital experiences surely must have made her realise that faithfulness in husbands had to be approximated, and, likewise, the bringing up of three children must have prepared her just as much for hope as for despair, while the bliss and drudgery of being a mother unfolded.

Yet Emily emerged curiously unscathed after being accountable to her family for 20 years – that is to say, she was fully prepared to consider and act upon her conviction that the time had arrived to put into action her latent notions. For now Emily intended to put herself first, and join the happy breed of fulfilled women with a job, or a vocation, having accomplished the dignified, if irksome, duties of understanding wife and all-embracing mother.

How she was going to direct her energies and inclinations was not altogether clear to Emily, but the idea was there, coupled with strong determination.

She encountered no opposition from her family. On the contrary, her husband and the three teenage children encouraged her in this new resolution. Some might even suggest they were glad that Emily would, so to speak, get off their backs and so allow them to pursue their lives in their own fashion. So the prognoses were favourable, the time ripe and the financial circumstances encouraging.

Emily did some research into the various possibilities open

155

to her; extramural degrees, different courses at the polytechnic, some vocational training. If anything, there were too
many openings. Even going into business in some small way
held a certain promise, because a whole branch of her family
was engaged in commercial activities. So it was really an
excellent opportunity to spread her wings and acquire a new
status in her own name.

Her choice finally fell between two possible outlets. She
joined the highly prosperous family business, connected with
marketing and general distribution of goods of various
descriptions, and at the same time enrolled in the business
studies course at the local polytechnic. Thus she was set up for
the next two years, highly activated, filled with enthusiasm
and prepared to do the utmost to acquit herself well.

Some months into the new venture, however, a tiny shadow
began to cloud Emily's well-being. The shadow grew more
menacing from week to week, and it did not take very long to
put a name to it. Emily was pregnant.

This realisation proved to be a serious blow to her. What on
earth was she to do? She was quite shattered, and put under
pressure, because she knew a decision must be taken soon and
carried through within a specific time limit, otherwise things
would get out of control. Never before had Emily found
herself in such a quandary. Her past pregnancies were, on the
whole, welcomed (reinforced by her general convictions) and
hitherto she had held no clear view on the subject of abortion,
since it had not arisen in her circumstances. Thus it remained
an issue outside her particular interests. Now, however, the
issue forced itself on Emily and put into the shade all other
considerations. Her work suffered as well as her demeanour.
She found it difficult to look at her plight in a detached,
objective way. The idea of the child she was carrying in her
womb had not thrilled her at all. It was more an obstacle to
fulfilling the goal she had set herself and wanted to achieve at
any cost. On the other hand, actually getting rid of her child
seemed to Emily a preposterous act which made her feel a
cold, calculated person, which she certainly was not.

The soul-searching went on for a week or so. Emily made

some inquiries as to possible means of termination. On the surface it seemed a reasonable and most realistic way of dealing with her predicament, and in the light of day, when her reason functioned at its best, she deemed this solution the only way open to her.

However, when Emily retired for the night and found herself in a way in direct confrontation with what, for the time being, was no more than a tangle of cells, but possessing the potentiality of becoming a child like the other three of her brood, the issue was inclined to acquire a different aspect. Strange to say, Emily already felt responsible for that source of life, and her curiosity and some atavistic impulses absolutely refused to be a party to the drastic solution of terminating her pregnancy.

The time factor forced Emily to make a choice and, as a preliminary move towards it, she decided to discuss the matter with her husband, Darren, the following weekend. She was therefore none too pleased when her daughter Jeanny, announced over the phone, at very short notice, her wish to come home for the weekend, bringing along her boyfriend, Boris. It would certainly complicate the situation, thought Emily, and she nearly suggested to Jeanny that she postpone her visit to the following weekend. But Jeanny would not be put off. And here the matter rested.

On Sunday, after a leisurely breakfast, when most of the family were perusing the Sunday newspapers, Jeanny suddenly asked for a moment of attention. Looking rather apprehensive, yet determined, she announced in a somewhat quivering voice that she was pregnant. That her boyfriend fully accepted the responsibility, and was very much of an opinion that Jeanny should get on with the pregnancy and keep the baby. This pronouncement was reinforced by Boris's vigorous head-nodding. Jeanny apologised to her parents, in fact was quite contrite, but after all she and Boris would now try to put the matter right. Jenny appealed to her parents for advice and help, as understandably some changes would become unavoidable. She would have to give up her studies but – and here was the plea – if her parents continued her allowance she and Boris thought they could make ends meet. In the meantime, they would get married and Boris could carry on with his degree, which required another year at university.

Emily and her husband took some time to absorb this rather alarming news. Emily, in particular, found herself in an unforeseen position. How on earth would she now deal with her own problem, while confronted with a similar one on the part of her daughter? The idea of sharing the experience of motherhood with her daughter did not appeal to her one little bit. It made her feel ridiculous, and rather obscene. However, she felt something had to be said, if only in recognition of the courageous and mature approach of the young lovers.

Darren glared at Emily and directed his first question at Jeanny: 'It is all very well. I appreciate Boris's motives, but what about you, Jeanny, yourself? Do you want to have this baby? After all, it will be you who will have to make the most adjustments. Giving up your studies, getting married rather early in your life, and under certain pressure. Have you thought about it?

'Yes,' replied Jeanny, 'and I love Boris and want to have his baby, but' – and here she looked directly at her mother – 'I know a lot will depend on whether Mummy will support me in a more general way. If she thinks I am doing the right thing.'

Emily recovered her composure. 'Of course, dear, you may rely on my support. If you feel you want this baby, I am sure the rest of the difficulties will be resolved, and I am sure Father will provide financial help until Boris gets set up in a job.' Inwardly she thought: but what about me? Is it the right time to reveal my dilemma to the family? Or should I simply go ahead and get rid of the baby and, at least to a certain extent, try to simplify the situation?

Soon afterwards the young couple left, Jeanny's affectionate hugs demonstrating the intensity of her feelings and a sincere gratitude to her parents. She was not disappointed in them. They, as usual, stood firmly behind their offspring.

Darren and Emily saw them off and then turned back to walk into the house when, suddenly, Darren asked Emily in a

158

rather humorous way, 'How do you feel about being a grandmother?' He knew Emily was rather fond of her youthful appearance.

It is now or never, thought Emily. 'How would you feel about being a father again?' she replied in the same teasing tone.

'What do you mean?' Darren stopped in his tracks and turned sharply towards her.

'Well, you should know,' Emily continued. 'Remember that weekend in Wales when I forgot to pack the precautions . . . ?' She left the sentence unfinished.

'Are you sure?' Darren was visibly upset and yet, as if in an afterthought, strangely moved. 'Oh, well,' he said finally, 'in for a penny, in for a pound.'

SWINGS AND ROUNDABOUTS

Sleep was very late in coming. The effect (if any) of the sleeping pill must have worn off a long time ago. It was well past two o'clock in the morning and the stillness of the night did nothing to soothe the disorderly thoughts which ran rampant in Carol's brain. She twisted and turned in her bed, too hot, then too cold, then hot again. She felt thoroughly uncomfortable, and rather cross. What made it worse was the realisation that she faced an early start in the morning, to set off for London in time for the wedding. Jill, her only daughter, was getting married at ten o'clock in a register office and, as a belated gesture to her parents, had invited them to attend the ceremony.

Carol was in two minds whether to go. She felt hurt and disappointed at the way Jill chose to announce her plans. They differed so much from the ideas she had envisaged about her daughter's wedding day. She knew she was being sentimental but, rightly or wrongly, Carol had always imagined a proper white wedding for her daughter, in church, with bridesmaids, perhaps with music, and all the trimmings, followed by a sumptuous reception and later . . . a dance, perhaps.

But it was not to be. Carol knew she was being silly. Nowadays young people managed their affairs to suit their preferences without considering the family, and yet . . .

In fact, there was more to it. Carol had not told anyone, not even her husband Joe. But for a long time now – to tell the truth, ever since Jill was little more than a toddler – Carol had engaged in a fantasy, a dream about her daughter's nuptials.

Over the years, as her financial circumstances improved, the dimensions of that wedding went on being embellished. She had started a special, secret fund, and each month had contributed to it from her salary. It was to be a reparation, a squaring-up of the rather raw deal fate had dealt to her when she herself was getting married. The wedding fund stood now at over £1,000, and Carol, when confronted with a show of wedding dresses or on seeing a photograph of a fashionable bride, invoked again and again her determination to realise the fulfilment of her fantasy – a wedding of a dream-like quality, something quite extraordinary, for her daughter.

Carol could not help recalling, in those sleepless hours on the eve of the marriage, her own wedding day experiences. The circumstances had been so different, close on 30 years ago. She still remembered her desperate attempts not to mind the austerity, and yes, why not admit it, the downright penury of that day. There was no new dress, let alone a white one. They had enough money to pay the priest and ask a few friends along for a sandwich and a glass of wine. The only extravagance they had allowed themselves and their guests was the strawberries and cream – the wedding had taken place at the height of the strawberry season.

On that particular Saturday, Joe had had to work till 12 noon – he could not afford to lose the money he earned in his holiday job, still being a student. Carol had volunteered to go and get the strawberries from the market. It took more time than she had anticipated. It was already 12 o'clock and the wedding was set for 2.30. She had waited in the long queue for the bus, which was late, glancing from time to time at the clock on the town hall opposite the bus stop (she did not possess a watch), getting more and more anxious.

At last the bus arrived. The people started boarding it and Carol desperately hoped she would be able to get on. She got as far as the door, mounted the step, to be told by an irascible conductor that she must get off. There was no more standing room. Carol felt utterly dejected. She appealed to the conductor to let her on the bus, explaining that she had an important appointment to keep and must get home. But the

161

conductor was not to be moved. 'If you are in such a hurry, take a taxi,' he said with some sarcasm.

'But I haven't enough money for a taxi.'

'Well, that is too bad.' The conductor was quite adamant. He refused to start the bus until Carol got off. Carol clung to the handrail and would not budge. She quickly calculated that if she waited for the next bus she would not even have time to wash her hair – the bus ran only every half-hour.

The passengers were getting impatient. The conductor looked at Carol threateningly. In the end, Carol blurted out, 'For heaven's sake! I'm getting married at half past two, please let me on.' Most of the passengers became involved in the issue, some believing her, others expressing the opinion that it was a put-up job, just an excuse. After all, what was a bride to be doing on a bus a couple of hours before her wedding? She should be at home, getting ready, surrounded by her family and friends, beautifying herself, taking a long bath, relaxing.

Suddenly an older woman got up. 'You go on, love,' she said. 'Take my place, and the best of luck to you.' Then she got off the bus, and when passing Carol, gave her an encouraging smile.

The story has a postscript.

Some time later, Jill told Carol what had happened after the civil ceremony, as there was no reception. After saying goodbye to everyone, the newly-weds went to the local playground and there, dressed in their usual jeans and tee-shirts, drank champagne from paper cups, while swinging.

SUNDAY VISITORS

On the way from church, Mrs Runcie decided to drop in on her lifelong friend, Miss Ellie Grant. It was not taking her too much out of the way – she had to pass the cul-de-sac where Ellie lived to get to her own house – and she knew that her friend would be delighted to see her, since there had been no sign of her in church. Poor Ellie, she mused, obviously there was nobody to give her a lift today. For Ellie Grant was housebound, her hips and knees were badly damaged by arthritis and she was not able to take more than a few steps at a time in comfort, even with the help of two sticks. So, although Ellie was a practising Christian, if there was no offer of a lift, she had to stay put, at home.

Mrs Runcie knew from experience that on such occasions Ellie liked somebody to visit her and tell her all about the service, perhaps recount some of the homily; and whether the visitor had managed to exchange a few words with Reverend Tellard, or anybody else, for that matter.

The door to Ellie Grant's ground-floor flat was always on the latch so that visitors could get in without the invalid having to undertake a painful and slow trip to the front door. Mrs Runcie, well aware of it, let herself in and looked into the sitting room, but Ellie was not there.

She is probably at the back, Mrs Runcie decided, in the garden room. And she was right. Ellie sat in the comfortable, straight-backed chair, a book on her knees, but giving the impression that she had dropped off to sleep in the heat. Not wanting to startle her friend, Mrs Runcie made a lot of fuss over shutting the door to the garden room.

Her friend opened her eyes and exclaimed: 'Oh, I am so glad to see you! I wondered if you would drop by on your way from church, this being such a sultry, hot day. Cathy and Colin are away for the weekend, so I had to resign myself to missing the service. How was it? Tell me all!'

'In fact, you have not missed much,' reported Mrs Runcie. 'It was a very small congregation today. I suppose the weather has to answer for it. Even Mr Tellard seemed to be overpowered by the heat. It must be really hot wearing his vestments on top of the cassock. He seemed sluggish, and so did everybody else, including yours truly.' She laughed.

'What was the sermon about?' inquired Ellie.

'Well, it was all connected with forgiveness. That was the main theme of the Gospel, too. Reverend Tellard said one strange thing, though, which frankly had me foxed. He implied that the most difficult task in forgiving people who have hurt us is when we know that we ourselves have contributed to the injury . . .'

And here her voice trailed off. She suddenly realised that she might have been tactless. Her memory had recalled various rumours circulating at the time of Ellie's misfortune, in her distant youth. And so she quickly attempted to change the subject.

'There were two strangers in church,' she resumed. 'One, I would say, a man of sixty or more, and a youngish chap, perhaps around thirty. Never saw them before at St Michael's. Have you?'

Ellie shook her head. 'No, I can't recall. They might be visitors or just passing through. Remember, this is holiday time.'

'They sat well to the back of the church, so I only caught a glimpse of them when leaving. I spoke to Reverend Tellard for a moment or two, hoping they would come out. But they stayed inside. In the end I had to go.'

'Would you like a drink?' asked Ellie.

'I would, please,' replied Mrs Runcie, 'but on condition that I fetch it.'

'There is no need, I have it here by my side in the cooler.'

And she reached inside the coolbox and brought out two glasses and a pitcher of lemonade. The conversation switched to general topics. The two friends spoke of their mutual acquaintances, about the garden, which looked at its prettiest at that moment.

Some time later, Mrs Runcie took leave of her friend, while Ellie made her slow way into the kitchen to eat a cold lunch, prepared by her help, who came every morning and evening to attend to her.

Fortified by a glass of wine with her lunch, and overcome by the oppressive heat, Ellie retired to her bedroom and soon was fast asleep, staying that way for a good couple of hours. She woke up hot and sweaty, so refreshed herself in the bathroom, smoothed her hair, and was on her way back to the garden room, which would by now be well in the shade, when the bell rang. Ellie was very surprised. All her friends knew about the latch. Who on earth could be calling on her on Sunday, in this heat? It must be some mistake.

She was glad that she was relatively close to the door. She opened it, having first slipped on the chain. Two men stood outside. The older one studied Ellie for a moment and then said, 'Ellie, I've come to ask for your forgiveness.'

Ellie felt quite faint. The bad, angry emotions, buried for such a long time at the bottom of her soul, now began to force themselves to the surface. She wanted to shout, but when her voice actually emerged it was more like a whisper. 'How dare you? Go away this very minute!' She trembled all over and had to lean against the door.

There was a moment of silence and then the younger man stepped forward and said in an earnest way: 'Forgive us, Miss Grant, it was my idea to approach you. I am a man of God myself. Let me introduce myself. My name is Thompson, and I am the chaplain of released prisoners, and in that role I suggested that we approach you. Peter here has been in touch with me ever since his release ten years ago, and the injury he inflicted on you has been preying heavily on his mind all that time.'

Ellie only now realised that the younger man wore what one

165

might describe as modified clerical attire. She looked from one man to the other and then, in a more controlled voice, explained that she couldn't stand any longer, she must sit down, so they had better come in. She released the chain and, supported by Mr Thompson, made her way into the sitting room. Peter followed, not quite sure if the invitation included him. He did not sit down, he just stood close to the door, nervously fidgeting with his hands, which he kept behind his back.

Ellie kept her eyes averted from him. She knew she must say something, but in her mind just one idea circled round and round – this was the man I was going to marry – and then her mind would go blank.

Mr Thompson inquired if he could get her something – a drink, or a cup of tea. Ellie motioned him towards the back room. 'There is some lemonade there in the cooler,' she heard herself say. Then, as the door closed behind him, trying to soften somewhat her earlier, violent outburst, she faced Peter and quietly asked, 'How are you, Peter?'

He did not answer. He was obviously moved, and unable to switch to a more mundane conversation.

Ellie raised her eyes and, with a sad smile, continued, 'I forgave you a long time ago. I might have been at fault too. So eager to become your wife, I encouraged you and then, when you took advantage of me, I panicked. Very much as your lawyer maintained at the trial. But nobody believed it, and I could not admit it – not to my parents. I myself came to this conclusion very much later. That is why it hurt more. But now, please go.'

And so Miss Ellie Grant was left in her sitting room, the lemonade on the occasional table getting tepid, her eyes closed, but her spirit wide awake.

THE APPRECIATION OF NATURE

When Brenda lay in bed, she could see a hawthorn tree through the window. She used it as a private calendar, noticing the seasons in progress, and the one approaching being proclaimed. Of course, she saw more of it in summertime. Then, the days were longer. In late autumn and winter it was already dark when she went to bed, and just as bad when she got up. Except at weekends. Then she would, on waking, draw back the curtains and spend a couple of hours lazing about.

The small, square-shaped panes of the window were particularly useful in winter. Each made a frame for a section of a grey-brown maze of twigs, giving it the appearance of a picture, some abstract composition of strokes and lines. From time to time a bird would alight, spoiling it in one way, but enhancing it in another.

Then, in April, the green lush would appear, only just visible at the beginning, growing fast, with a singular determination. That meant spring. In June it was one great mass of reddish-pink flowers, with hardly any green visible. That meant summer. By the end of August a yellow tinge would begin to compete with the green, gradually driving it away. That meant autumn was on the way. And then back to the austerity of the winter look. The cycle was completed, a year had passed.

Brenda was a great lover of nature. This was rather surprising, for neither her parents nor her siblings had shown any interest in that direction. They were not brought up on country walks – the furthest Brenda was ever taken was

Streatham Common, and that on rare occasions. But Brenda loved all living organisms, was good at biology in school, and would not miss any nature programme on television. She found it fascinating, the existence of a whole world of nature, well regulated, sometimes, perhaps, cruel, but always purposeful: to maintain a species, to assure survival, continuity. Till men interfered. Then, as likely as not, things would get upset, the balance disturbed and the smooth path of evolution stopped short or misdirected.

She did her best to put into practice what she believed. She went on countless country walks, took some trips abroad to discover for herself examples of exotic floral beauty or of special significance in the animal kingdom. And now she treasured her memories, because ill health stopped her from taking part in the pursuit of her lifelong activities.

Now Brenda had to spend quite a lot of time in bed. She did not get up before ten, rested in the afternoons and had early nights. Some days, should her temperature go up suddenly, she spent the whole day in bed, nursed with great devotion by her husband Dick.

The hawthorn tree became a focus of long-lasting gazing, particularly as it was questionable whether Brenda would see the next stage in its attire. But often her fever also had another effect. It didn't make Brenda delirious; on the contrary, it sharpened her perceptions in regard to that living organism which she could still observe and comment upon – her own body.

She observed it at leisure, be it the quickened beat of her heart due to fever, or the insistent, all-engulfing agony of pain, near the time of taking another painkiller. Sometimes she would surrender to it and, after a while, could ignore it. It was, up to a point, mind over matter.

When she was well enough, Brenda would take a mirror and examine her face. It had seen better days, true, but the composition was still there. The result of thousands of years of evolution. Brenda would trace the lines of the eye sockets, and be surprised anew that there, under her skin, existed a hard structure, giving shape to her face. A comment, overheard in

168

the past, came back to her. Someone had remarked that although she was not pretty, she had good bone structure, whatever that meant. She traced the line of her jaw. It was reassuring, this hardness, it gave her a feeling of permanency. The eyes . . . what could one say? Brown, sad, yet thoughtful (I hope I am not flattering myself, Brenda qualified), but as for being a reflection of my soul, as the saying goes – I don't know. It seems to be an exaggeration. And, of course, the wrinkles. By the mouth, dragging it down, two deep furrows running from nose to chin, a score by the eyes. They were the visible marks of the invisible hurts, defeats, disappointments. Oh, well, what do you expect, life is like that. It imprints itself on your features.

The neck also had a history. A French friend of Brenda's, warning her against ageing, used to quote: 'Old age always grabs you by the neck.' How true, yet undeniable. Let it pass.

My arms and legs, with veins standing out as if ready to part company with the rest of the body, the brownish specks of age staining the back of my hands, that was another of nature's tricks. And my poor left leg, damaged in a fall. With the alien replacement of my own, natural hip. It never accepted it, really, revolting in the only way it could – by hurting if put to too much use. As if wanting to demonstrate that anything men invented, when put to the test, was not as good as the genuine, nature-provided equipment.

Not to mention other, more personal parts of my body, which on top of sagging, gave dubious hospitality to those maverick cells that ravage the body.

But, come to think about it, my body gave me good service in the past. The astronomical number of breaths I took, the steps I executed, the weights I lifted. It has been good to me. It gave shelter to my two babies when they needed it, without which they would never have been brought into this world, and sustained them with nourishment in the first months of their life. Also provided a comfortable haven for a good many years – my lap – when tears and hurts could be made better. And the speed with which I could follow my partner in a dance, the clear voice with which I could join in a thanksgiving hymn, and oh, the ever readiness of my eyes to absorb life around me!

Brenda could hear Dick, coming upstairs with the tray full of tempting morsels. She must try to eat, if only to please him. Dick was such a marvellous partner in life. But when the time came to part, for her body to be put to rest, she would be able to repay her first, foremost debt. Offer her body back to nature.

THE USES OF EMBROIDERY

Vicky rang the bell. As usual, she wondered for a moment whether she had come on the right afternoon. The momentary panic was cut short by the appearance of Sally's smiling face. 'Come in, come in, how nice to see you.' Vicky could hear the voices from the front room – yes, it was all right, she had come on the right day.

Sally was leading the way to the back room, when somebody else rang the bell. She turned to Vicky. 'You go and take your coat off, if you can find the space.' Vicky did as she was bidden. There were quite a few coats and jackets piled on the two available armchairs. I hope there will be a vacant seat for me, the thought flashed through her mind, to be immediately answered by her brain: Don't worry, there is always a spare chair. You must go in and mix with others. It is all part of the therapy, going out, mixing with people.

Clutching a plastic bag containing her embroidery, Vicky entered the front room. It was full of other members of the embroidery class, of which she had been a member for the last two months. When Vicky had her breakdown, the psychiatrist recommended taking up a hobby and joining a group to overcome her fits of panic. Vicky had always been fond of embroidery and had spent diligent moments between her appearances at the nightclub working on it. So it seemed the right way to start her rehabilitation.

Meanwhile, Vicky sat down on a straight chair near the fireplace, having answered several questions about her well-being. 'I am fine, thank you,' she replied brightly, wondering at the same time what the effect would be on her companions if she told them how she really felt. Never mind, her brain again interrupted the flow of her thoughts, you are safe for the next couple of hours. Just relax.

And, indeed, it was quite pleasant to join this group of well-meaning people, even for such a short time. It made them all into a whole, a unit, pulsating with talk and laughter, only to be shattered at the end of the meeting into small fragments, each going its own way. But, for a short time, it gave the impression, the feel, of a common endeavour, a semblance of belonging.

The conversation flowed easily. A television programme was being discussed and Vicky regretted that she hadn't watched it last night, as it would have given her a chance to join in. She was very impressed by the ease with which the other women remembered the names of the particular actors, comparing their performance with earlier ones. With what self-confidence they expressed their opinions on the relative merits of that programme. They were certainly well-informed and discriminating viewers. But Vicky was not. She hardly ever watched television, because of her restlessness and the vague – and perhaps even imagined – similarity in some programmes with her last job, that of a stripper, which had been responsible for her breakdown.

Now, due to some new royal anniversary, the conversation shifted to the subject of the Royal Family. Again Vicky was struck by the knowledge of the more or less intimate history of various Royals. And again she found herself unable to contribute. She knew, of course, the name of the Queen, and had some idea of the royal princes and princesses. But as for their other relatives and offspring, she was totally ignorant, so that the most she could do was to look interested, and keep quiet.

One of the ladies, trying to include Vicky in the general conversation, came over and inquired about her embroidery. Vicky showed her the printed picture of how the finished work should look, and was soon earnestly exchanging views on different stitches, different types of threads. She liked this involvement, and her pale, drawn face acquired a bit of

172

colour, a certain animation showed in it.

Vicky looked at her watch. Already an hour had passed, and she had been able to stay put the whole time. Tea was brought in, biscuits passed round, one of the ladies was telling a funny story which produced a great wave of laughter. How I envy these people, thought Vicky. They are here under their true colours; they have nothing to hide. I wish I was one of them.

Somebody else embarked on another story, slightly racy. It concerned a stripper, past her best, who faced redundancy. Vicky froze. Have they guessed? Are they looking at me? With the best will in the world she could not join in the ensuing laughter, not at all aware that this singled her out as rather a prim person. But the moment passed, and the conversation became more personal, on a one-to-one basis. Vicky spoke to her neighbour on the safest topic imaginable – the weather – followed by some reference to the forthcoming holiday season. She felt safe again.

And then it was time to gather the frames, balls of wool and all sorts of sewing paraphernalia. The people started to leave, on their own, in twos. They exchanged a last word with Sally on the doorstep, and then vanished into the darkening world. Vicky was the last to depart. She was already missing the unforced togetherness she had encountered in the last two hours. She shut the gate and sighed. This warm feeling she was aware of inside herself would have to last for the next fortnight.

A REFLECTION

If only I could stop for a moment the ideas which, like an avalanche let loose by some unspecified force, race under my scalp! They have a life of their own, beyond control, tumbling into one another, overtaking, changing direction, contradicting each other. They feed on events, associations, dreams, delve into past experiences – my own, and other people's – then suddenly drift into the present, dart even into the future. They remind me of an early autumn day when a horde of cumulus clouds, driven by the first cold wind of the season – a precursor of its wintry brothers – chase with tumultuous speed across the sky. They never rest, they change shape continuously, then alter direction, never spent, outstripping one another.

This chaotic activity of ideas in my head at some point reaches a limit, a close. A particular idea comes to the fore – just an idea, a pointer – and begins to torment my thinking mechanism, without let-up. One desperately tries to give it some direction, because there is always a danger of letting it lead to a particular experience or event that one has done one's best to bury in one's subconscious. It may dig out something that is best forgotten, and should such a memory be exposed, it requires all available will-power to quench the unwelcome confrontation. It can be a painful exercise.

On the other hand, one must allow that particular pointer to carry on with its destiny, as any honest man or woman of letters will tell you. One just hopes that it will progress in the direction which at this stage is more or less felt, rather than fully conceived. Like a slightly lost traveller, reasonably sure

174

he is driving in the right direction, yet still searching desperately for the physical proof of a signpost to confirm his intuition.

This time I am lucky. The idea settles on a happy and serene episode from the past which, for some unknown reason, engendered a lasting memory. It concerns a holiday in the Basque country.

There were three of us. Joe, myself and a friend. Joe, dependable, eager to please, with his hand seemingly permanently in his pocket, looking for his purse. So often left behind to expedite problems of parking, luggage and all human comforts. With few demands for himself, except to be left alone when painting. And there was the friend, a glittering personality, his sensitive 'antennae' extended all the time, to receive and absorb into his computer brain all sensations, all changes of mood, all visual phenomena. This unparalleled ability to absorb, analyse, process and then deliver his deliberations made him a raconteur par excellence. The ability to present reality instantly, so to speak, as it unfolded in terms of poetry, drama or wit, put him in a special category as a companion. Finally, there was myself, on the whole the least revealing personality, trying to hide, behind wry humour or a short comment, the excitement and joy I was experiencing.

On that particular Sunday the weather let us down. Our country retreat being deprived of sun, and rather murky, made us decide to drive into town, to Biarritz and somehow disperse the gloom of the day by civilised means. It rained all the way. We left the car and made for the seafront. The promenade, constructed probably in Biarritz's heyday, runs right along the rocky coastline, more or less embracing its shape, suspended halfway up the soaring cliffs. At one point it juts out, a sort of man-made promontory. At the end of it, a statue of Mary, Mother of God, is situated, looking outwards to the open sea. The whole promenade is bordered with a high, broad parapet, on which one can lean and contemplate the ocean.

It had stopped raining, but a cruel wind from offshore whipped the waves to an incredible height, and then crashed

175

them against the rocks. This was the Atlantic in its true form – not some quiet bay protected by a harbour wall. One could not help but be overawed by the unleashed force of the elements. The inimical sounds accompanying the virtual inferno at the point where the seas met the land, right under our feet, added to the menace of the moment. The shades of lead-grey interlocked with the off-white crests of the waves as they were nearing the end of their race, unrelenting, were mirrored in the leaden grey sky and made me, and perhaps my companions, aware of our insignificance.

The promenade was deserted. There we were, three chance-thrown travellers, under this towering statue, exposed to the elements and showing it, witnessing the eternal duel of nature – yet feeling strangely safe. Why was that, I asked myself? Was it because we were united by what was such an unlikely alliance, friendship even, between the three of us? Or was it perhaps the presence of this calm figure, elevated on the tall plinth, apparently a point of reference for fishermen and sailors returning from their voyages, that provided us with a sense of security?

I picked a pebble from the top of the balustrade and hid it in my purse. This puny stone must have been deposited there by a giant wave. I wanted to take it back with me, something that represented a feeling of peace in the face of raging elements. The pebble is still in my possession.

PROFESSOR SCHNEIDER'S GAMBLE

The old adage 'one should never say never' is widely known and documented. In time of stress we are quite likely to use it and, what is more, mean it. But life, being a most unpredictable gamble, plays so unfairly with our resolutions.

Take the case of Professor Leon Schneider. An eminent persona if ever there was one, internationally known and respected. He had held several important professorships at the best universities. His books are still considered unparalleled in the field of historical criticism, and even now, in his retirement, his articles in learned publications furnish more often than not a starting point to many a controversial discourse.

But what about his personal life? Professor Schneider married rather late in life and, by prevailing standards, quite disastrously. His bride, much younger than he, notwithstanding her justified claims to beauty, failed in providing a necessary background to Professor Schneider's position. It was one of those hasty marriages, an outcome of a frantic romance, conducted in circumstances highly conducive to emotional entanglements, during the professor's vacation in Italy. They were staying at the same hotel, shared the same table – and the sun, the scent of orange blossom and the vistas of the Bay of Naples did the rest. Within a month Professor Schneider fell in love, married and brought back to his university this adorable, but quite useless from the point of adaptability, young woman called Clara.

As soon as she was confronted with the rigid discipline of a

177

prominent scholar, Clara dissolved into tears. Not for her the respectable, if dull, university get-togethers, where it seemed all the other wives of the faculty men vied with one another in dowdiness. The conversations Clara encountered were well above her head, the expected decorum and pecking order of the prescribed rank were a closed book to her. She threw in the towel after six months and left surreptitiously on an early train for an unknown destination.

Professor Schneider, although outwardly devastated, inwardly was rather relieved. He acknowledged that his marriage was a mistake, regretted the unnecessary turmoil Clara caused to himself and his well-tried, well-loved routine. It was then that he uttered the often-quoted words, 'never again'. He sent Clara's clothes to Oxfam and resumed his normal lifestyle. On the whole, the termination of his matrimonial failure was painless. The divorce was speeded up, all loose threads tied up. The unfortunate, much regretted episode in Professor Schneider's life was over.

His colleagues were of the same opinion. Hardly anyone pursued the subject in public. Privately they even considered Professor Schneider a 'lucky dog', who did not have to pay for a temporary aberration with long years of an unsatisfactory relationship, as some of the other members of the faculty had found out, to their own cost.

Things fell into the old pattern. Or so it seemed.

When Professor Schneider retired, two years ago, the question arose as to his possible domicile. He did not want to lose all contact with the academic world, so his choice fell on a cottage in a charming village some 20 miles from his last place of employment. He had a daily help, catering for him and keeping the place tidy, but otherwise there was little change in the circumstances he had enjoyed when living in the quarters provided by the college, of which he had been dean for the last few years.

He made little effort to meet the other inhabitants of the village, and soon earned himself the name of a recluse. However, on the advice of his doctor, whom he saw once a year for a check-up, he started to take a constitutional every evening after supper to prevent an unseemly middle-age spread. He found it an excellent diversion, both physically and mentally. Many of those deep-founded assumptions which he perhaps felt, yet was unable to formulate and articulate, suddenly, while walking, seemed to clarify themselves and became attainable. At the same time, that extra glass of brandy after supper (which he really shouldn't have had) seemed to release the painful grip on his gut.

The outskirts of the village bordered on a copse which, though owned privately, provided the locals with a pleasant change in otherwise rather ordinary scenery. There were one or two turns into the copse, and sometimes one could glimpse a parked car just inside the narrow road. But it was generally thought better to avert one's gaze in such a situation, as one might see more than one bargained for.

Professor Schneider, however, was usually so deeply lost in thought on his evening strolls that the frantic cries and the burst of gunshot issuing from one of the parked cars that particular Wednesday hardly penetrated his consciousness. Then a man rushed past him, went a little way, staggering, and collapsed more or less at his feet. The professor stumbled on the body of the stranger, and put out his hands to steady himself. In doing so, he inadvertently touched the prone body and instantly felt that his hands were covered with some sticky substance, which, on closer inspection, proved to be blood.

This unnerved the poor professor enormously. He looked quite bewildered, and cast glances around as if expecting some help to materialise from the gathering dusk. Then, as if in answer, a figure emerged from the parked car and swiftly approached him. The professor was horrified to recognise it was his former wife, Clara.

'Is he dead?' were her first words. Then she looked at the professor and exclaimed, 'I don't believe it! It is you, Leon, isn't it?'

The professor did not answer. He was still contemplating his hands and, filled with distaste, started to clean them, first on a handkerchief, and when that wasn't enough, on his jacket and trousers.

179

'We must call for help.' He could hardly speak.

But Clara objected. 'What, and get embroiled in this mess? The bastard had it coming to him, he was blackmailing me. We must get away from here as soon as possible. Do you live nearby?'

'But, Clara, we can't leave him, he might be still alive.'

'Well, do as you please, but considering your state, all bloody, don't expect the police not to jump to conclusions. I am off – coming, or not?'

Poor Professor Schneider was in a dilemma. The last thing he wanted was to be implicated in a murder, because as things stood now, it seemed to be the most probable conclusion. All the unsavoury publicity – no, he could not take it. On the other hand, how could he leave this stranger to die in the middle of nowhere, without making some effort to rescue him?

But Clara had already started to walk away and, as if spellbound, he followed her. Soon, his front door appeared, and he made for it. Clara, as if by instinct, stopped there, and more or less forced her way in. She took command as soon as the door closed behind them. 'You must take off your clothes and burn them, right now. Then have a bath, and we will talk.' She helped him with his clothes, bundled them up and asked, 'Where can I burn these?'

'I suppose in the boiler in the kitchen.' He knew he had lost all the initiative. He felt sick and disorientated. He tried to figure out what was happening to him, but Clara was already running the bath and practically pushed him into it.

Over coffee, she tried to get some sense into him. 'Look, if the police find out that I was at the scene of the crime, they are bound to question you, as my ex-husband. You had better co-operate then. Do you expect anyone tomorrow?'

'Mrs Tripp, of course.'

'Well, put her off. Say you have a friend arriving unexpectedly and you are going to be out for the day.'

And so it happened. Clara took care of everything. She got rid of Mrs Tripp, and established herself as housekeeper. She had to lie low for a while, at least till the end of the

180

inconclusive investigation which followed the shooting of an unidentified victim.

When Professor Schneider asked her when she would be leaving, she at first asked for more time. Later on she simply explained that since he was an accessory after the crime, it would be better if they stayed together. She would see to it that he had every comfort, even in bed – should he require it – but the fact was, she had never burned his clothes, and could produce them at any time.

Looking quite justified, she stated: 'If we go down, we go down together.'

A COMPARABLE LOSS?

'... the record shows. I took the blows, and did it my way ...' – the few finishing chords of the background music slowly petered out. Then there was silence. Another session by the record deck was over. Jake switched the player off, drank the remainder of his whisky and, not bothering to take the glass back into the kitchen, walked slowly upstairs.

This sort of ending to the solitary evening now happened practically every day. Jake concentrated on the business of getting to the top of the stairs without stumbling. I must cut down on drink, he thought in passing, and then smiled bitterly. He knew he couldn't do it. Whisky was the only reprieve from the overwhelming gloom and despondency that filled him all the time.

Jake never really considered whether by choosing his present way of life – which he called 'my way' – he was not in fact aggravating his lot. But Jake was not a reflective man. Not for him the agony of soul-searching or analysing his actions. He decided that life, having singled him out, had delivered such a blow as was impossible to accept – or sustain.

He had been on his own close on two years now. The humiliation he had undergone when 'the balloon went up' changed him profoundly. It drew Marion away and made him a recluse with his business in tatters. Friends and relatives tried to break the stone wall behind which Jake hid. They eventually retreated for good, because of his insistence that everybody should leave him alone. These well-meaning people realised in the end that this was what Jake really wanted, and stopped pestering him. Marion, his wife, left him too, finding it impossible to live with an alienated, bitter, companion. She suffered in her own way but relied on her family for consolation.

Jake had just reached the age of 50. A man of many virtues and some vices but, unfortunately, a proud man. In the past, this quality had stood him in good stead; it had added the necessary feature in establishing his business, in keeping up the standards of workmanship and delivery dates. The small building enterprise which he had started well back in his twenties had acquired respectability, and was highly recommended by the architects he worked for. What Jake had missed in formal education he supplemented with evening classes, and he picked up experience while being apprenticed. His detailed knowledge of the intricacies of the building trade, a receptive, keen mind, as much as the dedication to hard work, were the main reasons why, at 50, Jake could boast of a thriving firm, and a prosperous one too.

Jake could also boast and feel a sense of pride about his son Tony, a strapping, healthy lad, with brains, who was quite ready to fall in with his father's plans and join him in the firm when the time was ripe. Tony spent many a holiday working on the building site, acquiring practical skills and learning how to avoid pitfalls. Later on, he went to college to study architecture – and here lay the main reason for Jake's pride. Tony, as a graduate architect, would add another dimension to Jake's firm. They would now be able to undertake some projects which, till now, were impossible to enter into, because of the lack of an architect's qualifications.

Tony's graduation was the happiest day in Jake's life. Marion looked really smart in her expensive dress and hat. Jake, though not quite used to formal clothes, expanded his chest when Tony's name was called. At the party which followed the graduation, Tony's professors spoke highly of his achievements, and Jake, when saying goodbye to Tony that very evening, handed him the key to a brand new car, and a folder containing stationery bearing the new name of the firm: Jake Brisslow and Son.

Soon after Tony joined the firm an opportunity arose to

erect a dozen houses in the vicinity. Tony prepared designs and plans, and together they costed the project and submitted their quotation to the client. Most surprisingly, they were awarded the contract; the name of Jake Brisslow was probably a dominant factor.

The work started six months later and was completed on time. The houses were sold. Jake pocketed quite a substantial profit and made sure that all the building fraternity knew about it. He pointed his finger at Tony, the designer and the mainspring behind the project. Quite a few of the less well-wishing rival establishments, who felt considerably put out, were inclined to find fault with the design, if not with the execution of the work.

And then, out of the blue, one of the houses partially collapsed, followed in quick succession by two others. The outcry was terrific. There was a thorough investigation, a court case, publicity. The buildings were pronounced unsafe, due to faulty design. The sky fell in. The architect was blamed and Jake found himself handing over vast sums of money in compensation. The firm went into liquidation and Tony, in despair, shot himself.

Jake stayed long in bed most mornings. There was no need to get up. His head was aching, as it did every day, after the amount of alcohol he had downed the night before. He did not expect any news from the post. The house looked seedy and dirty – it revealed its desolation, especially in the daylight, with the sun streaming in through the unwashed windows. Jake, so as not to see it, sometimes stayed all day in bed but, on this particular morning, he had to get up to replenish his supply of drink from the supermarket. That meant shaving and looking for a fairly clean shirt. He had a long drink of water to quench the alcohol-induced thirst, and was about to put the kettle on for some tea, when the bell rang.

Let them ring – they will soon go away. Jake did this continually, ignoring the would-be callers. But this one was persistent. More to stop the noise, which aggravated his headache, than to find out who was bothering him, Jake went to the front door and opened it halfway.

184

A woman, holding a girl's hand, and looking rather annoyed, exploded: 'What in the name of goodness is the matter with you? Don't you open the door to anybody? I have been ringing and ringing.' Jake looked out and was about to shut the door in the face of the stranger, but he was too late. She had already put her foot in the doorway. 'Oh, no you don't,' she shouted. She practically threw the small suitcase she was carrying into the hall and, turning to the little girl, said: 'Here is your grandad. He's going to look after you now!' With that, she pushed the child towards Jake and walked away.

Jake was too stupefied to object. He glanced at the child, who didn't seem all that much put out. To tell the truth, she looked rather relieved. Then he heard the car start. He was speechless. But he let the girl in, where she sat on her suitcase and regarded Jake expectantly.

At last Jake spoke. 'What is your name?'

'Tonia,' she replied, and smiled. Then she added: 'Are you my grandad? Really?'

Jake considered her gravely. She looked like Tony when he was that age. 'Who was that lady who brought you?' he asked, after a while.

'Oh, that was Auntie Doris.'

'Where is your mummy?' he said, bewildered.

'She is dead. In heaven.' And she started to cry.

'And your daddy?' Jake put the question, but he already guessed the answer.

'He is dead, too.' Tonia stopped crying. 'He shot himself.' Apparently she considered the circumstances of her father's death rather exciting.

There was an impasse. Jake stood there, casting glances at the girl, at the shabby hall, at his own reflection in the mirror. He felt humble when he considered his own loss and the loss of this child.

Then he picked up the phone and dialled Marion's mother's number. When he heard Marion's voice on the line, he mumbled, 'Marion, come home, our granddaughter has arrived.'

BUT FOR A DETAIL . . .

Let me tell you about the first burglary I ever committed. It was unsuccessful. I got caught through my own stupidity. I was at that time an inexperienced burglar, not much over 20 and not used to taking necessary precautions. But I have learned since. My greatest mistake was not paying enough attention to details. And it is the details that matter. I also was not callous enough when dealing with people, particularly children. I was green.

In a way, as it turned out, it helped me in that particular instance. The lawyer who defended me at the trial made a big show of it, insisting that I, being so young, was not really a tough, hardened criminal. So I got away again with two years on probation. Fair enough. I have learned my lesson.

But first, a few words about myself. My family was poor, but not quite on the breadline. My father was strict. Mother left all the discipline to him. I think she was rather afraid of him because, even when not provoked, he would give her a black eye or two, just for the asking. But I was a clever little boy who could get away with lots of things, simply by outwitting him. He was a long-distance driver, probably not a hundred per cent straight himself either, come to think of it. (Once or twice his lorry had been nicked and it was never clear whether he was in any way involved.) He was not at home much of the time, except when he was on the dole. When he was home I had to mind my ways. But from the earliest times, if I set my heart on getting something, I had to have it – by hook or by crook. Yes, I was determined.

When I was at school, which I did not like because of the

discipline, I bullied the little ones and they had to hand over their pocket money to have some peace. But a teacher soon put two and two together and called in my father. I got a terrific hiding from him to 'teach me a lesson' and, yes, it did make me realise that I was foolish.

I had to find another way of supplementing my pocket money, so I switched to pinching things from the sweetshops or bookshops, mainly comics. Then I met this girl, Rita, and for a few years we did some silly stuff in bigger department stores, helping ourselves to clothing and some toiletry items. We got caught, the police were called, and both of us were put on probation. For a couple of years I went straight, because I did not fancy being sent to Borstal. But as soon as my probation was over, having by then left school and gone on the dole, I began stealing again. Most often pickpocketing from middle-aged ladies who came to the sales, and suchlike. In most cases it was peanuts. I never really went for cars, because I had no knowledge of how to get rid of the nicked stuff.

Then I thought, why not try going over some of the posh houses? I noticed people were very careless about locking doors and windows. I decided to have a go.

There was this nice big house at the corner of the road where I lived at that time. Some rich people must have moved in, judging by the two expensive cars parked in the driveway. The new people did it up something smashing, had it all painted, and put in a lovely iron gate. I knew the house quite well from the past because, as a youngster, I had been friendly with a bloke who, some years ago, had lived there in the top flat. I knew that the back of the house was well screened from the road. I even had the key to the back door, which my mate had lent me in the good old days, and which I had never returned. So I figured the chances were the new lot had not changed the lock at the back. Why not try my luck?

I watched the goings-on in the house for several weeks, and found that the couple who lived there went out every Saturday evening, coming back well after midnight. So one Saturday evening I set myself at a conveniently placed bus stop on the other side of the road, watching for the people from the big house to leave. They got into their car right on time, a little after half past eight. I gave them a quarter of an hour, in case they had forgotten something and came back, and then started walking towards the house. Not too quickly, yet fast enough, as if I was paying a visit to someone. I kept my hands in my coat pockets because I had already put on thin rubber gloves and I did not want anyone I might meet to notice that, by some stupid chance.

I closed the gate behind me. There was a light on in the hall and in one of the upstairs rooms, but that did not fool me. I knew this was what some people did when they went out, to give the impression there was someone at home.

I inserted the key in the lock and it went in, nice and easy. In a few seconds I was inside and made for the largest room, which I was pretty sure was the lounge. I was right. I drew the curtains as quietly as possible and switched on my torch. Then I made for the writing desk, which I picked out with the torch's beam.

One of the drawers was locked, so I did the lock with a penknife. I saw a wad of paper money, and stuffed it into my inside pocket, quick like. I was wondering whether I should go into the kitchen – ladies have been known to keep their housekeeping money there in some tin or other – when a noise caught my ear. I quickly turned and saw, lit up by the light in the hall, a figure of a child in pyjamas. It might have been five or six years old, and by the cut of its hair I guessed it was a boy.

I was speechless for a minute, then decided to play it softly, or the kid might start yelling. 'Your daddy sent me to collect some papers,' I said, not moving an inch. 'But I must go now.' And then added, 'And you should be in bed.'

'I was,' came the answer, 'But I couldn't sleep, and then I heard the back door, so I thought that the lady who usually looks after me when mummy and daddy go out had come after all. She phoned before to say she couldn't come tonight, and I agreed to stay on my own. But now I'm frightened. Will you stay with me?'

'Only for a little while,' I found myself replying. I was sorry for the little chap, but even more afraid that he would create if I went and left him now, and so bring in the neighbours.

We went upstairs, the boy holding my hand, commenting on my rubber gloves. I explained that I had to protect my sore hands from dirt and suchlike. He got into bed and demanded that I tuck him in and give him a big hug. I was furious with myself, but even more with the boy's parents for leaving him on his own.

Then all hell broke loose. I heard the car door slam, some quick steps up the stairs, then a woman started screaming, while I stood like a fool, panic-striken. Then I was hit on the head several times, and when I came to, the police were in the house and I was handcuffed.

Apparently the parents had become unhappy about leaving the boy on his own and returned early. The issue now was not so much that I had broken into the house, but whether I had meant to hurt the boy. But the boy said later that I was nice to him, and had tucked him in and given him a hug. So the police dropped that charge. There was also the matter of the boy's father striking me, which, to get a better deal, I agreed to overlook.

As I said before, I paid no attention to details. When I got into the house and saw a few toys scattered in the hall, I should have run for my life. I do now.

189

THE REUNION

My name is Tessa. The other day I attended a college reunion, organised to commemorate the centenary of the founding of our Alma Mater. It was extremely well attended.

We had not clapped eyes on one another for nearly 25 years, except in some rare cases, and so we had some difficulty with mutual recognition, despite the prevailing reassurances that 'you have hardly changed' bandied to all and sundry. It did not matter greatly that these exclamations had little to do with reality. They were uttered as an expression of goodwill and probably received by the majority of the old girls (except for the few who still clung to their former looks) with a pinch of salt.

After the preliminary sherry, we sat down to lunch, during which more drinks were served, so that when the time came for intimate exchanges, we were probably becoming more honest with each other.

I was flanked at the table on one side by Helen, a good friend of mine in college days, with whom I was reasonably close; we had lost contact over the years only due to her decision to settle in Canada. On the other side I was partnered by Rosie, who in the old days, was considered to be a beauty and an exceptionally promising academic (first-class degree on graduation). She always gave the impression that the world owed her a living and was never too keen on close, cloistered relationships with her sister students. She preferred the company of the male undergraduates, and not without success. Shortly after graduation she married a former student, another specimen of the human race endowed by nature with all possible assets.

I asked Rosie about Frank, but apparently that was the wrong question. They had parted company a long time ago, with mutual recriminations as to who was to blame. There was one offspring from their marriage, a son, now grown up but, from what I gathered, not quite fulfilling the hopes his parents had entertained for him. His mother did not have his photograph in her purse, from which I concluded that she did not hold him in great esteem or unbounded motherly affection. However, there were photos of the children of her second marriage, twins, if you please, just turned 12 and full of promise.

My other neighbour, Helen, had fared a bit better, if only because her unsatisfactory husband had removed himself from the scene by falling off a horse and breaking his neck, leaving Helen well provided for, with money in the bank and an extensive portfolio of blue-chip shares.

And there was I who, sandwiched between these two successful women, could in no way compete on their terms. Unmarried, of limited resources, even the dress I was wearing was second-hand from a charity shop. Not a bad dress, by any means, and since my figure is still very much what it used to be all those years ago, it gave me a certain confidence.

The widow with the blue chips suggested that we repair after lunch to her house for tea and reminiscences. It seemed a good idea, as the volume of noise after lunch, brought about by women's voices excited and loosened by alcohol, was exceedingly powerful.

We went to the car park, where a silver Mercedes was awaiting us. Rosie got into the driving seat and off we went, on that sunny afternoon, to explore our past, to bring back memories and generally improve our acquaintance.

Helen and I reclined on the luxurious, comfortable back seat, which lavishly enveloped us and seemed, somewhat, to diminish us in stature. The smell of leather pervading the car indicated that it was a recent acquisition.

I still don't know what got into me – perhaps some unacknowledged perversity, or an inability to leave things well alone – but on the spur of the moment I attracted Rosie's

191

attention and, out of the blue, confronted her, half humorously.

'You know, Rosie, you should have left Frank alone, he was really half engaged to Helen. They would have made a good team. You were too high-powered yourself to suit Frank. I am sure you were competing with him all the time, and so had little time for loving.'

'You are quite wrong, Tess,' answered Rosie hotly. 'It was not our ambition that proved to be our downfall. It was his constant carrying-on with other women. Anyway, Helen was not the only one to imagine that Frank meant business. You yourself, if I remember rightly, were head-over-heels in love with Frank. Now, admit it.'

Helen objected to being discussed in such a way. 'I was not that much in love with Frank. It was he who sought me out, and he probably would have married me if you had not pulled that dirty trick on him.'

'What do you mean, Helen?'

'You implied you were pregnant, and Frank fell for it.'

'Nothing of the kind,' protested Rosie. 'It was a lie. That was what the bastard told you, to get you off his back.'

Rosie took a corner much too fast, and I intervened. 'Listen, girls, don't get excited. And you, Rosie, remember you are driving a new car.'

'Who's talking?' Rosie turned momentarily from the steering wheel, giving me a nasty fright. 'You started all this. And let me tell you – and Helen will agree with me – you were in love with Frank. I wouldn't be entirely surprised if that wasn't the reason you never married.'

I found myself attacked on an issue which was too close for comfort. I kicked myself for having started this conversation. I should have known that my infatuation with Frank would not have passed unnoticed.

I gave a brief laugh, 'Don't be silly, Rosie! I hardly knew Frank. The two of you wouldn't leave him alone. You watched over him like a pair of hawks. As I remember it, it was strictly a two-horse race.'

Helen and Rosie joined forces then, and exclaimed,

192

'Come on, Tessa, don't play the fool. We both read the notes you sent to Frank. He used to show them to us. And we would giggle about them. You called him "Sunny Boy", didn't you – didn't you?'

I felt crucified. Yes, I called him that, and other fond names. I still had a packet of his letters, tied with a blue ribbon.

I felt myself getting red in the face – the chances were that those letters he wrote to me might have been written in the presence of one or other of these horrid creatures. Silly, sentimental me. But they were the only love letters I had ever received, so I treasured them.

Rosie must have noticed something, because she suddenly turned to me. 'I am sorry, Tessa, we shouldn't have said the things we did. I wish I knew where Frank is at the moment, or I would give you his address. He might have changed, settled down, turned over a new leaf.'

I don't know where I got the temerity to face them in what was, for me, a highly embarrassing situation. But I felt I must be vindicated.

'Don't worry, Rosie,' I replied calmly, 'I have got Frank's address, and his telephone number, too. You see, we have been lovers for the last five years.'

Rosie stopped the car in a convenient place. I got out of the Mercedes, and cheerfully waved them on.

MOTHERS' LOT

It stopped raining just as Joanna left the office. She put her umbrella away in her capacious shopping bag and hurried to the bus stop. There were large puddles everywhere, on the pavement and in the road, and, of course, in no time she got generously splashed by a passing car. That certainly did not improve her temper. She wanted to look smart on her weekly visit to her married son, Robin. His wife, Linda, always put Joanna to shame, so spruce and dainty were her clothes and general appearance, even while preparing the evening meal at the end of a tiring day spent in the company of two young children.

But, on the whole, Joanna approved of Linda. She was an efficient housewife. The children looked well-nourished and happy. As for Robin – he was extremely proud of Linda and never missed an opportunity to demonstrate his whole-hearted support.

Joanna purchased some sweets for the little ones during her lunchbreak, and a bunch of anemones for Linda. They still looked fresh, having been kept in water in a small vase in the ladies' room at the office.

In a way, Joanna wished it was not Thursday, the usual day for her visit to her children. All day long she was conscious of a dull headache, and the tablet she took at lunchtime did nothing to relieve it. And now the bus was overdue, and if Joanna arrived late at Robin's there was little chance of having some time with her grandchildren. They were whisked upstairs promptly at seven to the bathroom, and then to bed.

194

Still, she was in luck. She rang the bell at twenty to seven, and was greeted by the whole family as soon as the bell pealed. They must have been expecting her, perhaps even watching for her at the window. She distributed the sweets and was thanked for them. Linda added her own thanks for the flowers, disappearing to put them in water while Joanna, with the two toddlers on her lap, answered innumerable questions, to their delight. Robin, sitting across from her, looked on proudly, smiling and approving.

So it was with a certain consternation that his glance at the clock suddenly registered the time. It was a quarter past seven! No sight of Linda, the children's bedtime overdue, and no discernible signs of activity from the kitchen.

Without saying anything, Robin left the room and soon found himself in the kitchen. The anemones were lying on the table. Next to them stood a vase filled with water. But no Linda! He quickly mounted the stairs, poked his head into the children's room, then their own bedroom, but still there was no Linda to be seen. He tried the bathroom, even the toilet, with no result. He stood on the upstairs landing, and thought hard. Thank heaven Mother's here – she can stay with the children while I search outside, Robin quickly decided. A little anxious, he swiftly negotiated the stairs, let himself out of the back door, and then searched the garden thoroughly – in vain.

Stepping back indoors he faced the happy scene in the lounge. 'Mummy's been called away,' he announced lightly, 'so as a treat, Granny will put you to bed. As it's getting late, we will skip the bath. Just a good wash, and then straight to bed.'

'What about the bedtime story?' asked Robbie, the older child.

'A very short one,' Robin replied. He met his mother's eyes and shrugged imperceptibly. First they had to get the children off to sleep. Then there would be time for explanations.

He turned down the gas in the oven, as well as under the vegetables, and helped Joanna with the established routine prior to settling the children for the night. After a prolonged session of saying goodnight, he ushered Joanna into the kitchen, shut the door and, hardly trusting his voice, confessed: 'Linda has disappeared. Something must have happened, but I have no idea what.'

Neither had Joanna. Her headache increased considerably, but she told herself she must stay calm. 'Did you have a row with her? Was she upset about my coming?'

'No,' Robin replied, 'she was her usual self. She likes you coming. She often says so. Where is she, for heaven's sake?'

'Robin, dear, perhaps she's stepped out for a short walk or, on the spur of the moment, dropped in on a neighbour and got delayed. Give her another hour or so before you start worrying.'

They ate their supper in silence. Joanna washed up and considered the situation. Normally she would be taking her leave at about this time. But she couldn't do so now. There might be a telephone call, asking Robin to go and fetch Linda – that is, if she'd been taken ill somewhere, or involved in an accident. Then someone would have to stay with the children.

Robin appeared in his coat, the car keys in his hand. 'I'm going to look for her,' he announced. 'You will stay the night, won't you?'

Joanna nodded, and in a while could hear Robin starting his car. She looked in at the children, thankfully asleep, and then crept down the stairs, drew the curtains and sat down in the hall near the telephone, so that she could answer it immediately if it should ring.

When Linda rang, it was well after midnight. 'Where are you, Linda? What happened? We are practically out of our minds,' cried Joanna.

'I'm in hospital, but I'm all right. Is Robin there?' Linda sounded very upset, on the verge of tears.

'No,' replied Joanna, 'he is out looking for you.'

'Good! I mean, I'm not glad he is somewhere there in the dark, searching for me, perhaps getting desperate. I mean,' – she stopped, trying not to cry – 'I mean, it is easier for me to explain to you what has happened than it would be to him . . . After all, you are a mother yourself.'

Joanna could not quite follow. There was a pause, and then Linda said, more calmly: 'My niece was run over, and when my brother-in-law appeared at the door on his way to hospital, I had to go straight away. They did not think she would live.'

'But surely you could have told us where you were going?' Joanna sounded a bit nonplussed.

'You don't understand, Joanna. My niece is really mine.' Linda took a long breath. 'She is my . . . my daughter. I had her when I was only sixteen and my sister, already married, adopted her. But when I learned that her life was in danger, I lost my head. All I could do was to run to her.' She hesitated. 'Robin doesn't know anything about Alison; there was no need for him to know, and my sister made me promise never to divulge any of it to anyone. You are a good woman, Joanna, please, please explain my actions to Robin, so that they won't seem so strange. I mean, my going off like that. At that moment I had only one thought – to be with Alison.' Then Linda asked, in a voice bordering on panic. 'Are the children all right?'

Joanna reassured her. 'Yes, yes, they are fine, in bed, asleep. I'll look after them till you come home. And I will keep your secret. Leave Robin to me.' Then she added, 'Will Alison be all right?'

'They think she will pull through. I'm taking a taxi home this very minute. Thank you, Joanna. Bless you!'

DANGEROUS ASSOCIATION

It is difficult to explain why, on that specific occasion, Steven completely lost control of himself. Of all the people I know, he always struck me as the most even-tempered man, if anything inclined to conceal his emotions – more, unable to express them. I have known him for ages, from the time when we shared the same floor in a converted house in one of the less fashionable districts of London. Many of the Victorian houses in that area, once one-family dwellings, had changed their purpose and now housed half a dozen or so different tenants. My one-bedroom flat directly faced Steven's flat, and we often met on the landing, where we would exchange a few words. But, on the whole, I would be the one who first began our conversations.

When I moved out, I lost contact with him and then, surprisingly, met him again in a club for divorced people, both of us having succumbed to the institution of marriage, and failed.

I was already an established member when Steven joined, and one of my duties was to welcome new members and make them feel at home. I enjoyed this function quite a lot, and was fairly successful, because I have an outgoing personality and am always on the lookout for new opportunities to meet people.

I welcomed Steven warmly, and our old association provided a necessary topic to talk about. It helped, in a way, to break the ice for a rather diffident person already made vulnerable by the recent trauma of divorce, and now subjecting himself to the scrutiny of a roomful of strangers.

198

Steven soon settled down in a rather passive way, found a few cronies to have a glass of beer with, and blended well with the rest of the company. He took part in most of our organised outings, not contributing much as far as conversation was concerned, but being helpful and efficient in dealing with practical arrangements. He proved particularly useful when the means of transportation for our outings were being settled, be it a hired coach or a fleet of the members' own cars each carrying a few people. There he showed a special aptitude, resolving who went with whom, and so avoiding all unnecessary tensions. Since it was a chore nobody really relished, Steven found himself in charge of this function in general, and eveybody agreed this was an excellent choice.

That is, till Donna joined the club. It happened just after Christmas – a tricky time for most of the club members. They probably had spent the holiday on their own, or perhaps had spent at least part of it in the company of their estranged spouses for the sake of the children, while others, invited by their well-meaning friends and relatives in happier circumstances, had had the fact of their disrupted family ties well and truly rubbed in.

Donna had been divorced twice, and was inclined to have a very low opinion of the opposite sex. She was not really suitable material for a mixed-sex club, but one couldn't tell her that. After all, it takes all sorts of people to populate this world.

From the start, she was a disruptive element in the hitherto well-integrated group, and the results were soon visible. Donna had ideas about most things, including the running of the club, and didn't keep them to herself. She was bossy, but because of her extremely pleasant exterior, she got away with a lot of things. It even seemed strange, but her extrovert qualities attracted most male members of the club, except for Steven. And, of course, Donna decided to push herself on him. In no time she became his assistant, not noticing his unwillingness, querying his decisions, offering unwanted suggestions, while Steven remained unimpressed, mulish even.

To revive the spirits after Christmas, the club decided to take a skiing holiday in February and left it to Steven to choose a location and the transport arrangements. Donna, apparently an experienced skier, proved to be the proverbial pain in the neck, contradicting Steven where possible. But she did not take into account Steven's popularity. When it came to the vote, members approved Steven's plan, and that was that.

We all thought that, in the circumstances, Donna would withdraw her participation in the venture, but we should have known better. She joined the group of 20 or so on the flight to Austria, not inhibited by the decision of the club to disregard her suggestions. She limited herself to voicing criticisms of anything that could possibly be questioned. And so it went on.

Halfway through the holiday, the weather broke. It rained for a day or so, and the lower runs became slushy. To get any worthwhile skiing one had to use lifts to the higher ranges, with more taxing runs, and the inexperienced skiers in our group were not up to it. Donna had a lot to complain about, and so did some of the others. It was all done in the presence of Steven, and one could see that at last the criticism was getting through to him.

However, on the third day, the temperature dropped. There was a substantial fall of snow, and it looked as if the rest of the holiday would be all that one could wish for.

After lunch that day it was decided to attempt one of the shorter runs, without recourse to the lifts. Steven and I were practically the last to venture on the piste. Donna, surrounded by several of the male members of the party, took her time to commence her downhill run. Then, with a light-hearted shout, she was on her way, followed by her companions, who soon outraced her. Steven was next. He accelerated immediately and zoomed straight at Donna. They half-collided (some said he pushed her); he steadied himself and increased speed, disappearing into the distance. Donna, on the other hand, fell over. One of her skis broke off, and she started to roll downhill, her hands still clutching the ski sticks.

Then, one by one, they became detached and, with increasing speed, sometimes head over heels, she slithered down, then whirled to the left into a small outcrop of rocks, and came to rest there, against a solitary tree trunk.

I watched it all with increasing alarm, quite unable to react in any way, as several people (the rescue squad, I presumed – one carried a folded stretcher) sped swiftly by me to where she lay. They eased her on to the stretcher and went down the slope; I could see, on a connecting road, an approaching ambulance. We learned later that she was dead on arrival at the local hospital.

I immediately took off my skis, turned back and, after finding out which hospital Donna had been taken to, rushed there in a taxi. As there was no next of kin who could be contacted, I presented myself as her friend and was informed of Donna's death.

The rest of the party, who had started downhill first, learned about the accident only after returning to the hotel where we were staying. Shaken, I too returned to the hotel, where our group was just beginning to congregate. We were absolutely stunned. They asked me what had happened, but I was not to be drawn before I had had a chance to speak to Steven. He shortly joined the company. I asked him to follow me outside and practically screamed at him: 'Why did you do it, Steven?'

'She was the spitting image of my ex-wife,' he replied, turning on his heels and walking away.

During the investigation that followed, he absolutely denied having pushed Donna. The evidence of the onlookers was conflicting. Steven maintained that it was pure accident. He also denied any knowledge of what had taken place after their collision. He said he'd thought that Donna was all right, and had come to no harm, as in his own case. There was really no cut-and-dried evidence to justify criminal proceedings. Except, perhaps, for my short encounter with Steven. And I didn't say anything to anybody.

We returned home subdued, unwilling to discuss the subject. Steven never again showed up at the club.

A QUESTION OF SEMANTICS

The fax simply stated '. . . take care of Mrs Simpkins, she is arriving on the 10.30 ferry from Ostend'.

Inspector Gallan looked at his watch. That ferry should be docking in half an hour. The fax did not say much, but he had full confidence in his colleague on the other side of the Channel. There must have been some reason for the brevity of the message. He might still have time to phone old Lavall to find out what he was driving at. But, first, he had to hurry to the customs hall to be on hand when the ferry docked.

He reached his destination in ten minutes flat and dialled Lavall's number, but was too late. Lavall had just gone off duty. Thus, left to use his own judgement, Inspector Gallan announced to the customs officers on duty that he would supervise the next batch of arrivals, then quickly instructed the passport people to give him a hint as soon as they had dealt with Mrs Simpkins's passport.

She was nearly the last to leave the boat. At one time it looked as if she was not on it at all. Then, as the last cluster of stragglers had their passports scrutinised, came the pre-arranged nod, and a half-disguised lift of the hand, pointing at a slim, youngish woman carrying two suitcases.

She approached the Nothing to Declare bench and Inspector Gallan, who had positioned himself halfway between the two possible checkouts, was soon beside her.

'Would you mind opening your suitcases, madam?' he inquired politely, to be met by a surprised look. She started to say something, but checked herself. She put the suitcases on the bench and opened her oversized handbag to look for the keys. Having located them, she shut her handbag and, in what looked like a surreptitious way, drew it towards her person. 'Your handbag as well, please,' added Inspector Gallan, and started to empty its contents on to the bench. The handbag contained a surprising assortment of items. Apart from the usual ones, there was quite a number of diminutive screwdrivers, pliers, two miniature wrenches and a pocket-sized battery-powered blowlamp. But no money.

'What is your profession, madam?' asked Inspector Gallan.

'I am a mechanic, a precision engineer, that is.'

Inspector Gallan was nonplussed. 'How do you expect to reach your destination if you have no money?'

Mrs Simpkins replied hastily, 'My husband is meeting me.' Again, she was on the point of saying something more, but desisted. 'What is all this about?' The woman was getting impatient. The customs hall was now devoid of people. 'What are you looking for, Inspector?'

'This is just a formality, nothing to worry about.' And he led Mrs Simpkins to a room at the side of the hall and asked her to wait.

'Please inform my husband that I am being detained for some reason, or he will worry about whether I've arrived at all,' were her parting words, to which Inspector Gallan replied vaguely, 'Indeed,' and left.

Mrs Simpkins sat on the chair provided, and took stock of the situation. There must be some mistake. Monsieur Lavall had promised that she would have preferential treatment on arrival. He had said that he would send a message to that effect. She smiled, half amused, half irritated. She was certainly getting preferential treatment, left to brood in an empty customs hall; goodness knows when things would get sorted out.

A door opened and two women customs officers entered the room. One was carrying a cup of tea and, having put it in front of Mrs Simpkins, said, in a friendly yet quite official voice: 'Now do drink the tea, and then undress and put on this gown.' She indicated a green garment, similar to those handed to patients waiting for an X-ray.

'I will do nothing of the sort.' Mrs Simpkins put down the cup with such force that some of the tea spilled over. 'What right have you got to subject me to such an indignity? I shall complain!'

The officer's face had gone quite stern and it was obvious that she would not tolerate any fuss on the part of Mrs Simpkins. 'Look, we are only doing our duty. If you are clean, not carrying anything, this will take no more than ten minutes and then you will be free to leave. But we have to make sure you are not implicated in any contravention of customs rules. If you don't cooperate it will only make things worse for you.'

Mrs Simpkins got quite red in the face. Such humiliation! She was seething with anger, but was nonetheless certain that these two harridans would force her to undress if she refused. And that would only add further insult to the injury. She retired behind the screen, which she had only now noticed, and flung her clothes over as she removed them. Then she put on the hated gown and sat down on a chair, while a minute search of her clothes took place. When it was finished, she was asked to step in front of a screen similar to an X-ray machine, and a scan was made for internally concealed items.

The woman officer then said, 'Thank you for your cooperation,' and disappeared, leaving Mrs Simpkins' clothes neatly folded, ready to be put on.

Time dragged. It was already early morning. What is going on? thought Mrs Simpkins, and then suddenly she felt afraid. What if they arrested her? Accused her of some crime? One heard of such cases, but never expected to be involved. She had made up her mind to go to the door and bang on it till she achieved her aim of drawing attention to herself, and then demand to see her solicitor, when the door opened, and Inspector Gallan, smiling apologetically, entered the room.

'I am very sorry, Mrs Simpkins, for the inconvenience. There was a certain reason why we had to search you. We tried to be as quick as possible, but unfortunately these things take time.' He did not add that he had only just been able to locate

Lavall. 'Please accept my apologies. Your husband is waiting outside. You are free to go.'

Mrs Simpkins did not even look in his direction. She just gritted her teeth and said in a threatening voice, 'You just wait . . .'

But, of course, she never did anything about it. And so she never learned of the mistake Inspector Gallan had made when reading the fax from his opposite number in Belgium. The fax had actually asked for preferential treatment for Mrs Simpkins, who was a close friend of old Lavall's daughter. It was simply badly worded. After all, you can take care of someone in so many different ways.

A SHAGGY DOG STORY

The façade of the house was definitely handsome. It was double-fronted, the symmetry of the windows underlining its discreet dignity. The newly painted front door and window frames denoted prosperity and household pride. A brass knocker in the shape of a dolphin gleamed and proclaimed the inhabitants' attention to detail.

It was therefore most disappointing to discover, from the tasteful nameplates inserted at the side of the door, and accompanied by push buttons, the existence of three occupants. One would have preferred to imagine that this imposing building housed one happy family, instead of three different social units, with on the whole three distinct and probably wildly dissimilar life styles.

The bottom name slot carried the names of Dr and Mrs Ratzky, which made one momentarily wonder about the origins of the ground-floor tenants. Suggesting perhaps survivors of the Second World War trying to rebuild their lives. The middle name slot was more reassuring: Mr and Mrs Dickens. It had a respectable ring about it, a good, traditional English name, perhaps even some association with the celebrated writer of the last century. The top-floor slot had a rather long name, and an unusual owner, Ms Patricia Partridge, making one almost involuntarily abbreviate it mentally to a rather flippant form of Ms P.P.

Now, let's open the door and step inside, listen at the keyholes, find out the secrets, if any, of this dignified abode, because there must be a story behind each of the families living here, if only one could discover it.

Dr and Mrs Ratzky were a childless couple. That is, they had been on their own since the sad death of their only son, Patrick, who had been killed on holiday in Italy some 20 years ago, run over by a car. Mrs Ratzky blamed herself for this tragedy. It had happened in Rome, where they had arrived rather exhausted by the journey and quite uncertain as to the location of their hotel. Patrick was travelling in the back of the car and, to give him more room, the space between the seats on the left side of the car was completely blocked with the luggage. That way Patrick had the whole length of the back seat to himself, and could while away the tediousness of the journey by lying down and taking a nap. Consequently, the only door he could use, if for any reason he wanted to get out, was on the left side of the car.

The Ratzkys had just stopped to consult the map to get their bearings when Patrick spotted a place, on the other side of the street, that sold ices, and demanded one. Ordinarily, his parents would have insisted that Patrick should wait for one of them to let him out of the car and accompany him, but on this occasion they did not pay attention to their son's pleas. Impatient, he opened the door and stepped out right in front of a car approaching at speed. His parents were so engrossed in their perusal of the map that only the screech of the tyres alerted them to what was happening. But, too late for Patrick. He was dead.

Mrs Ratzky never recovered from this disaster. For the first six months she stayed in bed, with her head turned to the wall, refusing to eat unless forced and not saying a word to anyone. She was seen by countless psychiatrists, who each recommended a different approach to her condition – all in vain. Then, one day she got up, dressed, and resumed her duties in an automatic manner. But emotionally she was dead, burnt out, spent.

In the ensuing years she developed various habits which could not be described as anything but highly eccentric. She spoke to no one, yet held long conversations with Patrick, always asking for forgiveness. She never ventured out in the daytime, only after dark. She would suddenly put on her

207

outdoor clothes and announce to her long-suffering husband that she was going to the cemetery to look for Patrick's grave – which was a futile exercise, since Patrick was buried in Italy.

Dr Ratzky put up with his wife's quirks magnificently. He had, of course, his work as a GP to help him keep sane and, over the years, he developed a friendship with his secretary, Hazel. He visited her once a week, made love to her and then recounted to her all the ongoing problems of his tragic marriage. He poured out all his disappointments and worries about what would happen to his wife should he pass on first, and relived many, many times the terrible shock and anguish of that awful moment when he had picked up Patrick's body and realised he could do nothing to revive him. Hazel, a placid, rotund figure of a middle-aged woman, would pat his hands and mutter, 'I understand.'

Mr and Mrs Dickens were quite a different kettle of fish. They were what is nowadays known as 'upwardly mobile'. He, an inspector of taxes, had great hopes for the future, because of his special gift in hounding down recalcitrant taxpayers in the upper-income bracket. (He must have been cursed on many occasions while his uncooperative clients, found guilty, wrote out cheques, sometimes for four- or five-figure numbers, to pay back outstanding tax.) As matters stood at the moment, Mr Dickens could expect rapid promotion which would put him in the executive class, and deliver all the perks that that implied. At home he exuded confidence, and a quite remarkable sense of discipline towards his offspring, Charles and Henry, both blessed with sturdy constitutions and a mathematical turn of mind, clearly inherited from their father.

Mrs Dickens was a valuable partner in shaping a better, more rewarding future, as much for her husband as for her children. She did not spare herself, and was always busy with her household chores, some of which really went beyond the call of duty. Although the hall and the stairs were cleaned once a week by a domestic, paid for by contributions from all the tenants, this did not always satisfy Mrs Dickens. Quite often she would take out her Hoover and give a thorough going-over to the afore-mentioned areas. Only her personal intervention assured her that the standards of cleanliness she expected to encounter would be maintained. It was the result of her efforts too, that the brass knocker on the front door shone so brightly, as if to reinforce the respectability of the neighbourhood. She also put a lot of work and considerable forethought into the planting of seasonal flowers in the front and back gardens. The spring was ushered in with a splendid show of daffodils, followed by multi-coloured azaleas and rhododendrons. Then the whole forecourt was smothered in abundantly flowering nasturtiums, leaving just enough space for three cars to be parked.

Now, Ms Patricia Partridge, being single, and the youngest of the lot, had a very different lifestyle. She was tall, slim and quite pretty, and spent a fortune on clothes. They seemed to represent for her more than just an acceptable covering of her body. One could risk the opinion that they were a fundamental ingredient to the image she had of herself at any particular stage of her life. Some years ago she had plumped for the Bohemian look, acquiring her clothes from the outlandish boutiques in the Kings Road, Chelsea, now, most of them, defunct. She went in for long, dark, loose-fitting garments, topped by leather-trimmed jerkins and suchlike. Next, she shifted her choice to the then fashionable 'twenties' look. Her dresses became slick, close-fitting, barely covering her knees. As for accessories, she wore small cloche-shaped hats, long strings of beads, plus a coloured feather boa flung nonchalantly over one shoulder. Lately, a gypsy-peasant look took Ms P.P.'s fancy. Full-sleeved, heavily-embroidered blouses, long skirts gathered at the waist and exotic-looking waistcoats, seemed to be called for. And long earrings – so long that when Ms P.P. stood still, their tips rested on her shoulders. But, for all this, she was a cheerful soul, always ready to give a smile when met on the stairs, and her boyfriends, if staying the night, departed quietly at the first chink of daylight.

And so life passed for all the inhabitants in an unobtrusive way. Seasons changed, new calendars were purchased at the end of each December. If anything was obvious about the people who shared this prestigious address, it was the fact that they had little use for one another – or much interest. Some spent time contemplating the tragic past, others pinned their hopes on future advancement, or lived for the present, in a purely hedonistic way. It was quite impossible to imagine a cause that might have brought them together, something of such importance as would make them close ranks and promote a more personal involvement.

It was Charles and Henry who, surprisingly, contributed to the upheaval which suddenly confronted the three households, each wrapped in their own private world. It was all quite unexpected, for the boys were trained to behave sensibly and with circumspection. But, as it happened, they fell under the spell of a stray dog, which they encountered one day on the way to school. Quite innocently, they offered him some of their packed lunch and, of course, made him their friend for life. They tried to stop him following them home after school, but this particular mongrel, probably rendered streetwise by its chequered past, was not to be fooled. On reaching the house, he stopped on the forecourt and looked hopefully at this pair of young humans as if expecting an invitation.

Charles and Henry realised what they had got themselves into. What had been an amusing incident so far could spell grave consequences. There was no chance at all that their mother would ever allow them to keep the dog. They knew that from experience. They would certainly be in serious trouble if she were to discover that they had encouraged the dog by giving him titbits. There was nothing for it, they must quickly let themselves into the house and pretend to know nothing about the animal.

Dr Ratzky was the next to arrive. He was tired and dispirited at the end of another day listening to human ailments and problems. The sight of a stray dog reclining comfortably on the front doormat did not, I am sorry to say, fill him with any friendly feelings towards it. He shooed it away, and had there been a stone handy he would have availed himself of it, to ensure that the point he was making was to be taken seriously. The dog disappeared amongst the prolific nasturtiums and lay low. Dr Ratzky gave up. It was his evening to visit Hazel, that is, if Mrs Ratzky was in a fit state to be left alone.

Next morning, the boys found the dog waiting for them just beyond the gate and, once round the corner, looking surreptitiously about them, they again parted with some of their lunch and, emboldened by the friendly response, added a cuddle or two.

And so it went on, except that the dog, who had now acquired the name Raisins on account of his round, brown eyes, became progressively more difficult to restrain in his demands for attention.

One Saturday, Mr Dickens took his sons for their customary walk in the park. They were followed by Raisins, who was not deterred by several attempts on their father's part to get rid of him. 'Have you been encouraging this mongrel?' he asked the boys, exasperated by the dog's persistent presence.

'No, of course not.' The boys were prepared to swear, if necessary. But their father knew them better than that.

'Dr Ratzky noticed it last week in front of the house. Are you sure that the dog was not following you from school?' The boys denied it.

On Sunday, the weather being particularly clement, Mrs Dickens did some gardening, while Charles and Henry played nearby. Later on, they were joined by Ms P.P., who thought she would do a spot of sunbathing. Shortly after, Mr Dickens, having finished his perusal of the Sunday papers, suddenly felt in the mood to join his family. Dr Ratzky opened the French door leading to the garden and stepped out for a breath of air, while his wife, feeling slightly better that morning, watched from within the safe enclosure of the drawing room. And then the dog appeared and made straight for Charles and Henry. They had been rumbled.

'What are we going to do about this dog?' The question was put by Dr Ratzky to the company at large, and was met, momentarily, with silence.

Mr Dickens, feeling implicated in this matter by the rash behaviour of his offspring, was the first to speak. 'He must be got rid of. Leave it to me. I shall phone the RSPCA first thing tomorrow morning to have it removed.'

'Quite right,' piped up Mrs Dickens.

'Must we?' intervened Ms P.P. 'It looks harmless enough.' And indeed, the dog looked rather attractive, its shagginess somehow enhancing its appearance.

'But none of us wants the responsibility of keeping a dog.' Dr Ratzky was being rational.

'That's true, that's true,' everyone agreed.

'But I want this dog,' Mrs Ratzky suddenly cried, and for the first time in many years appeared in the garden. 'I am quite sure he is the reincarnation of Patrick.' She put out her arms and started calling, 'Patrick, Patrick, come to Mummy.'

And the dog went up to her.

A VOYAGE IN RELATIONSHIPS

On the night Steven and Liza became lovers there was no seduction on either side. Come to think of it, there was not even vague premeditation in their thoughts. It was really circumstances and proximity that brought about the event and plunged both into a relationship which was to be protracted and unpredictable.

Steven and Liza worked for a design firm, and as a mark of progress in their profession they were given, for the first time, an independent assignment with a set timetable and a date for completion. On the day before the meeting of the whole department and the client, they had spent arduous hours going over the final layouts and presentation. They were turned out from the office at seven o'clock by the cleaners, and decided to repair to Liza's flat for the last thorough re-examination of the project. There were still some small details which seemed to require attention and when, at last, they put away their proposed layout and notes, it was well after the time of departure of Steven's last train to the suburbs, where he lived with his parents.

It was then that Liza suggested that Steven should spend the night in her flat, sleeping on the living room sofa, and take the first train home in the morning to shave and change. Liza made bedtime drinks and went to fetch bed-linen while Steven, obviously tired, stretched out on one of the two armchairs in Liza's living room. When Liza, wearing a miniskirt, bent down to smooth the sheets and blankets, Steven, having caught sight of her long, well-shaped legs, and part of her thighs, suddenly made a grab for her waist from the back, not giving her much chance of disentangling her body from his hold. To her surprise she suddenly found Steven's proximity very welcome, so she turned over and put her arms around his neck. They started kissing and exploring each other's bodies, and some time later they were making love on that narrow, uncomfortable sofa, with great intensity and candour.

In the end, Liza fell asleep and, on waking, could hardly believe what had happened, the only proof being her clothes strewn around disorderly. Steven was not with her any more. She was extremely angry with herself. After all, she had worked with Steven in the same firm for the last two years and never ever had the least remote thought about his attractiveness. Now things had got complicated. Goodness only knows what Steven's behaviour would be when they next met at that very important meeting, presenting their common effort. She took a bath, had some coffee and departed for the office, full of foreboding.

She would have been very surprised to discover that very similar thoughts occurred to Steven on his journey home, with just enough time to shave and change. He was extremely vexed with himself. He did not really find Liza so attractive as to necessitate a conquest; her reaction came to him as a complete surprise. There was no time for explanations and excuses, and yet in a couple of hours he would have to meet her as a co-author of his first independent assignment. Would it prevent them from being on their best behaviour, would this idiotic occurrence make them shy with each other, just when they should impress the rest of the company with their vision and originality?

It was every bit as bad as he anticipated. Somehow the flow of his explanatory lecture never got off the ground. It lacked conviction. Liza's support proved mediocre. On two occasions she handed him wrong displays, she mumbled some of the figures she was required to quote; the whole venture lacked the desired effect – that of credibility and enthusiasm.

The prospective client was not impressed, the rest of the

team looked on with rather glazed eyes, that in itself an indication that the project lacked force, conviction. The client stalled in making a decision, vaguely implying that he had second thoughts about the presentation; the meeting was adjourned.

The rest of the day passed in low-spirited discussions between Steven and his immediate superiors, who were frankly disappointed. He had scarcely a chance to talk to or even see Liza, who was soon reassigned to some other team. Thankfully Steven put on his coat at the end of the day and speedily repaired to the nearest pub, where he ordered two double whiskies in quick succession. He then changed to lager, took it to an empty table, and sat there brooding on his rotten luck.

Liza went home straight after work, made herself a sandwich and tried to watch television, but her thoughts would not leave last night and today's happenings. She was furious, both with Steven and even more with herself. What on earth had happened to her normal self-control? Had she gone crazy to allow a fellow for whom she hardly felt any liking to spoil her chances at work? This was unacceptable to her, and as the evening wore on she grew more and more upset.

When the bell rang she answered the door rather unwillingly – thinking it was probably one of the girls from the office coming to commiserate with her. But it was Steven who presented himself at the door and without a word put his arms around her. And again Liza let him have his way, except that this time they did not use the narrow sofa but drifted into the bedroom.

'Why have you come tonight?' asked Liza, when she regained some composure after the breath-taking interlude of lovemaking.

'It was the only place I could think of,' came the reply. 'In some way you were the only person I wanted to be with after the mess I got myself in this morning. I knew I wouldn't have to explain anything to you as I would to anyone else. I thought I could talk the whole thing through with you, and then when I saw you, all I wanted was to make love.'

215

'But we are not in love with one another, are we?'

'How can you tell? We could easily be, but haven't had time to realise it.'

'Do you think so?'

Steven stayed the night. It was the beginning of a strange relationship which seemed at times to grow into an important commitment, and then suddenly wane and represent only a superficial casual affair. Liza thought that the fault lay at the very commencement of her involvement. It was so prosaic, so devoid of romance, almost incidental. How can a beginning of that sort grow into true love, a lasting relationship? Yet at times, she thought, she loved Steven, understood the way he functioned, easily responded to his moods and enjoyed his company. The way he thought, the animation he showed towards most subjects, reflected her own attitudes to life and beauty. The more she discovered his qualities (and faults) the more she became fond of him, except for this funny uneasy feeling that they had started their affair on the wrong footing and because of that they could not quite trust each other. Surely a woman should love a man before she allowed him the intimacy of her body?

In a peculiar way Steven viewed the situation similarly, if from a different angle. At first he thought that once the hurt of his professional failure healed he would not need, nor even want, the company of someone who had witnessed the humiliation he endured. But surprisingly it did not happen. He really fell in love with Liza. His feelings increased with time, except that he couldn't make out why Liza had adopted that rather compliant attitude at the very beginning; in some way he would have wanted to woo her, pursue her, and not be taken into her life without any reserve. Was she an easy girl, used to casual encounters?

Some months passed. It became common knowledge in the office that Liza and Steven were 'an item'. One or two people made comments, asked if they were going to name the day. Liza would give a short laugh in reply and try to answer in a noncommittal way. 'Not yet,' she would say. 'We must be sure we get along,' or 'There is no need to rush into a marriage

216

before you are sure it has a chance' and left it at that. She was in fact telling the truth, for the decision to come together permanently, formally or informally, was far beyond Liza's state of mind. Steven once or twice mentioned his willingness to move into Liza's flat, but she was not too enthusiastic about it. She somehow felt that allowing Steven to move in would acknowledge the fact that their relationship had reached a new phase, a new dimension. She was not quite sure how to express her reservations with a more defined assessment of her feelings towards Steven, but somehow she was not wholly convinced that the expectations of happiness to which she felt entitled were totally met in her present circumstances. There was something lacking, some important ingredient, though her common sense quite often tried to persuade her that she might be searching for a relationship which had very little chance of materialising. Is this all I am going to get from life? she would ask herself, and then reject the idea. Sharing life with Steven, no matter on what basis, would be a tacit admission that yes, that was all she would get from life. And so Liza put off any serious discussion about the future, much to the annoyance of Steven, who did not really share her reservations.

For him, it was an open and shut case – they loved one another, got on well, felt comfortable in bed – both were free and reasonably established in their work, why not join forces and move together with a view to getting married in the not too distant future? It is debatable how much deep commitment lay at the bottom of his rather simplified reasoning. Steven had been under some pressure from his parents to settle down and, as the years passed by, he became more and more convinced that the old-fashioned way – by which he meant his parents' way – of ordering one's life had a lot to recommend it. It added a certain weight to one's position in society, especially at work, when promotion was at stake. It also made life more accountable and orderly. If he had any doubts as far as Liza's past was concerned, he was prepared to overlook them. At the moment he felt himself to be in love with her as sincerely and deeply as he considered himself capable of. And so it annoyed him greatly that Liza prevaricated, neither sending him away nor accepting him entirely.

Therefore it was not surprising that, after a period of reasonable tranquillity, doubts set in on both sides. They started to argue about small, unimportant details which not so long ago they would have been able to laugh at. Steven started to get jealous if Liza so much as looked at another man. Liza implied that she was quite free to look at whoever she chose. Soon there was no more talk about moving in together; a certain coolness crept in, even into their lovemaking, which became more an act of habit than ecstasy.

With holidays approaching, Liza decided to break away and announced that she was going to Spain on her own, to see what it felt like to be apart from Steven, and in a way to test her feelings towards him.

'Are you going with another man?' asked Steven.

'Of course not,' Liza replied. 'It is just that a break like this would do us good – both of us. We have arrived at a point of decision, and to see things more clearly a separation will enable us to take a good, honest look at what has been happening to us since we started this affair. Instead of breaking our arrangement for good, it is really much more sensible to take holidays separately and then come to a conclusion. We can't go on for ever the way we are now.'

Steven shrugged his shoulders. Evidently Liza had made up her mind – nothing he could say would sway her. Let her go, he mused to himself, perhaps it is time for some action either way.

And so, on a cloudy but humid day in August, Liza embarked on the journey to the airport. She took the tube. She didn't want Steven to accompany her, afraid that there might be some emotional appeals, last-minute regrets, and she was not prepared to submit herself to such an ordeal. She had made up her mind to put away her present entanglement and enjoy the break in her routine to the full, on her own, not having to reflect on Steven's or her own feelings. She was glad to be amongst the crowds in the prevailing holiday atmosphere, being part of the great summer upheaval that seems to take over a vast number of people in August.

She boarded the plane, made herself comfortable and opened the magazine she had purchased at the news-stand. She felt relaxed and unencumbered. She didn't have to take notice of anyone or anything. She was being on her own, single.

Next to her sat a young couple, obviously not long married, judging from the solicitude they showed for each other, each constantly inquiring as to the comfort and well-being of the other. Rather overdoing it, reflected Liza and, as if to balance this obvious show of affection, as soon as it was allowed, she tilted her seat backwards, shut her eyes and relaxed.

Halfway through the flight, the stewardess appeared in the aisle, smiled reassuringly, took up the microphone and asked the passengers to return to their seats, extinguish cigarettes and put on their safety belts. In a while the pilot's voice explained that unfortunately the aircraft had developed a technical fault and would be returning to Heathrow, or might even ask for an emergency landing closer at hand. There was no need to worry. There was no imminent danger, but would the passengers comply with the emergency rules now in operation.

The reaction of the passengers was predictable. A moment of silence, and then questions from several sources, fastening of belts, putting out cigarettes, hardly discernible exclamations from a few nervous women, and silence again – but of a different kind. Silence pregnant with tension. Ever increasing. The stewardesses sat down on folding seats in the aisle, after having checked that their directions had been obeyed. And so the return journey began.

Liza's first thoughts were of dismay at having her holiday spoiled in such an irritating fashion. She was even quite angry, and only later on she acknowledged the possible implications of the announcement. Could we crash? Surely not – I must put this unhelpful thought right out of my mind. She suddenly felt very alone.

The couple next to her had their hands entwined, their

219

heads as close together as the safety belts allowed. Liza stole several looks in their direction, but they were entirely preoccupied.

Next, a voice sounded in the cabin. It belonged to the captain. He explained that in the circumstances he had asked for an emergency landing in France at the nearest airport, Bordeaux, and felt quite confident that they would touch down in about half an hour. In case of crash landing, he reminded the passengers that they should put their heads down on their laps and then, once the aircraft was on the ground, proceed in an orderly fashion to the emergency exits. The flight attendants would supervise the operation. 'Please do not panic,' he added. 'An orderly exodus gives everybody a chance to disembark while a stampede only results in hold-ups or injury.'

Liza, sitting by the window, knew she would be disadvantaged. She was beginning to lose her composure. Some terrifying vistas penetrated her head. She had to exercise all her self-control not to shake. The passengers started to shift in their seats – there were several half-concealed outbursts. Mothers were trying to distract their children from crying and not doing a very good job of it. The couple next to Liza whispered. He tried to convince his companion that, stastically speaking, they had a good chance of a reasonable landing. The percentage of air disasters was minimal compared to the amount of aborted journeys. These happened quite often, except that they were not much publicised. Liza could not help overhearing, and relaxed just that little bit, which allowed her to stay put, strapped to her seat, which for the last few minutes had seemed untenable. She looked at her watch. Ten minutes had passed. Impossible – it felt more like an hour. In a peculiar way, up till now she had kept any thoughts about Steven far from her mind. Suddenly they flooded her brain and grew in force.

Her relationship with Steven now acquired a different aspect. It seemed safe, normal and highly desirable. She was even persuaded to consider her behaviour in setting out on her own as rather selfish. She would have liked to have him

220

next to her at this very moment, without even defining the nature of their relationship. It was not important any longer what held them together. It was the word 'together' that mattered. She suddenly wanted very badly to be with him, to be cherished, perhaps not in a perfect way but in a way only he was able to express.

The plane droned on. It was becoming hot in the cabin – presumably the air-conditioning had been switched off for some overriding reason. People started to complain, the tension grew alarmingly. There were some dark red faces and curiously enough some very pale ones. One or two people undid their safety belts, only to be reprimanded by the stewardesses who, from time to time, patrolled the aisles.

Then came the captain's voice: 'We are landing in five minutes. Please do not panic. There is no imminent danger of explosion.' They descended, lower and lower. From the window Liza could see fire engines and ambulances racing to the landing strip. Then came a whole series of bumps, staggers, the screech of tyres tested to the limit. The plane lurched to one side – and stopped.

The exit chutes were in operation within seconds. There was no discernible panic, though some shoving and bumping occurred. Liza followed the young couple, who still held hands. In fact he was dragging her as if she had lost the power of movement. 'No stopping, no stopping,' cried the stewardesses, and the next moment Liza was sliding down the chute. At the bottom someone caught her and with a powerful movement cast her aside, reaching for the next person. They were all herded away from the plane to a point where they stood passively, as if unable to take control back into their hands now that they had been deprived of it by authority. Some families were embracing, mothers clung to their children, there were tears all round. Someone was screaming, 'Never again, never again.'

Liza stood alone. She looked around, but she was no more part of the crowd; she was so very alone, so desolate, so diminished, as if she had left her 'self' on the plane.

They were taken to the airport lounge and given some

221

drinks. People were talking together, exchanging remarks on the skill of the pilot, congratulating one another on the lucky escape – not so Liza. Several people approached her but she was absolutely dumb; couldn't put two words together. Someone remarked, 'It's the shock, it takes different people in different ways.' A nurse took her arm and led her to a cubicle, asked her to lie down and relax. She did as she was told, glad to take the weight off her feet. Her legs were buckling under her.

Soon an official from the airline was announcing that in a couple of hours a substitute plane would be available to take them to their destination. But Liza didn't want to continue her journey. All she wanted was to go home. She wasn't the only one. The next flight to Heathrow took the faint-hearts back. Liza couldn't get to her flat quickly enough, and treated herself to a taxi all the way from the airport. She fumbled in her bag for the fare and her keys. Then she stumbled into the familiar surroundings, tired beyond belief. Is it only twelve hours since I left? she asked herself.

Evening was approaching fast. It was dark in her living room and she reached for the switch. It was only then that she noticed Steven lying full length on the sofa.

'What are you doing here?' she asked.

'Waiting for you,' came the answer.